R0200705689

11

PALM BEACH COUNTY
LIBRARY SYSTEM
3650 Summit Boulevard
West Palm Beach, FL 33406-4198

SCARLET
FEVER

SCARLET FEVER

A NOVEL

RITA MAE BROWN

ILLUSTRATED BY LEE GILDEA, JR.

BALLANTINE BOOKS

NEW YORK

Scarlet Fever is a work of fiction. Names, characters, places, and incidents
are the products of the author's imagination or are used fictitiously.
Any resemblance to actual events, locales, or persons, living
or dead, is entirely coincidental.

Copyright © 2019 by American Artists, Inc.
Illustrations copyright © 2019 by Lee Gildea, Jr.

All rights reserved.

Published in the United States by Ballantine Books, an imprint of
Random House, a division of Penguin Random House LLC, New York.

BALLANTINE and the HOUSE colophon are registered trademarks
of Penguin Random House LLC.

LIBRARY OF CONGRESS CATALOGING-IN-PUBLICATION DATA
Names: Brown, Rita Mae, author.
Title: Scarlet fever: a novel / Rita Mae Brown.
Description: First edition. | New York: Ballantine Books, [2019] | Series: Sister Jane; 12
Identifiers: LCCN 2019034600 (print) | LCCN 2019034601 (ebook) | ISBN 9780593130001
(hardcover: acid-free paper) | ISBN 9780593130018 (ebook)
Subjects: LCSH: Arnold, Jane (Fictitious character)—Fiction. |
Murder—Investigation—Fiction. | Fox hunting—Fiction. | GSAFD: Mystery fiction.
Classification: LCC PS3552.R698 S33 2019 (print) |
LCC PS3552.R698 (ebook) | DDC 813/.54—dc23

Printed in the United States of America on acid-free paper

randomhousebooks.com

2 4 6 8 9 7 5 3 1

First Edition

With admiration,
dedicated to:
John Harrison, professional huntsman,
who saved the Deep Run hounds after lightning
struck the kennel, burning it to the ground.

CAST OF CHARACTERS

THE HUMANS

Jane Arnold, MFH, "Sister," runs the Jefferson Hunt. *MFH* stands for "Master of Foxhounds," the individual who runs the hunt, deals with every crisis both on and off the field. She is strong, bold, loves her horses and her hounds. In 1974, her fourteen-year-old son was killed in a tractor accident. That loss deepened her, taught her to cherish every minute. She's had lots of minutes, as she's in her early seventies, but she has no concept of age.

Shaker Crown hunts the hounds. He tries to live up to the traditions of this ancient sport, which goes back to the pharaohs. He and Sister work well together, truly enjoy each other. He is in his early fifties. Divorced for many years and a bit gun-shy. He has been injured.

Gray Lorillard isn't cautious in the hunt field, but he is cautious off it, as he was a partner in one of the most prestigious accounting firms in D.C. He knows how the world really works and, although retired, is often asked to solve problems at his former firm. He is smart, handsome, in his mid-sixties, and is African American.

Crawford Howard is best described by Aunt Daniella, who commented, "There's a great deal to be said about new money and Crawford means to say it all." He started an outlaw pack of hounds when Sister did not ask him to be her joint master. Slowly, he is realizing you can't push people around in this part of the world. Fundamentally, he is a decent and generous man.

Sam Lorillard is Gray's younger brother. He works at Crawford's stables. Crawford hired Sam when no one else would, so Sam is loyal. He blew a full scholarship to Harvard thanks to the bottle. He's good with horses. His brother saved him and he's clean, but so many people feel bad about what might have been. He focuses on the future.

Daniella Laprade is Gray and Sam's aunt. She is an extremely healthy nonagenarian who isn't above shaving a year or two off her age. She may even be older than her stated ninety-four. Her past is dotted with three husbands and numerous affairs, all carried out with discretion.

Anne Harris, "Tootie," left Princeton in her freshman year, as she missed foxhunting in Virginia so very much. Her father had a cow, cut her out of his will. She takes classes at the University of Virginia and is now twenty-two and shockingly beautiful. She is African American.

Yvonne Harris, Tootie's mother, is a former model who has fled Chicago and her marriage. She's filed for divorce from Victor Harris, a hard-driving businessman who built an African American media empire. She built it with him. She is trying to understand Tootie, feels she was not so much a bad mother as an absent one. Her experience has been different from her daughter's and Tootie's freedoms were won by Yvonne's generation and those prior. Yvonne doesn't understand that Tootie doesn't get this.

Walter Lungrun, M.D., JT-MFH, is a cardiologist who has hunted with Sister since his boyhood. He is the late Raymond Arnold's son, which Sister knows. No one talks about it and Walter's father always acted as though he were Walter's father. It's the way things are done around here. Let sleeping dogs lie.

Betty Franklin is an honorary whipper-in, which means she doesn't get paid. Whippers-in emit a glamorous sheen to other foxhunters and it is a daring task. One must know a great deal and be able to ride hard, jump high, think in a split second. She is Sister's best friend and in her mid-fifties. Everyone loves Betty.

Bobby Franklin especially loves Betty, as he is her husband. He leads Second Flight, those riders who may take modest jumps but not the big ones. He and Betty own a small printing press and nearly lost their shirts when computers started printing out stuff. But people have returned to true printing, fine papers, etc. They're doing okay.

Wesley Blackford, "Weevil," stands in for Shaker in hunt season. He is in his early thirties, andsome and kind, and the hounds love him and vice versa.

Kasmir Barbhaiya made his money in India in pharmaceuticals. Educated in an English public school, thence on to Oxford, he is highly intelligent and tremendously wealthy. Widowed, he moved to Virginia to be close to an old Oxford classmate and his wife. He owns marvelous horses and rides them well. He thought he would forever be alone but the Fates thought otherwise. Love has found him in the form of Alida Dalzell.

Edward and Tedi Bancroft, in their eighties, are stalwarts of the Jefferson Hunt and dear friends of Sister's. The Bancrofts have had their share of joys and sorrows.

Ben Sidell is the county sheriff, who is learning to hunt and loves it. Nonni, his horse, takes good care of him. He learns far more about the county by hunting than if he just stayed in his squad car. He dates Margaret DuCharme, M.D., an unlikely pairing that works. The DuCharmes are an old family. Margaret could care less.

Cynthia Skiff Cane hunts Crawford's outlaw pack. Crawford has gone through three other huntsmen but Cynthia can handle him. Sam Lorillard helps, too.

Cindy Chandler owns Foxglove Farm, one of the Jefferson Hunt's fixtures. She's not much in evidence in this volume but, like all landowners, she is important.

Drew Taylor is president of the Taylor Insurance Agency, which he inherited. Drew is a good rider and reliable foxhunter. He spends on whatever he wants: new trucks, trailers, cars, lots of exotic travel destinations. He divorced long ago.

Morris Taylor is Drew's younger brother and has all the drive his brother lacks. He has done quite well as a nuclear specialist building reactors. Unfortunately, he now suffers from senile dementia.

Bainbridge Taylor is the son of Morris and a deep disappointment to his father. In his early thirties, he never really found his way but always managed to find good drugs and liquor. He's trying to clean up.

Harry Dunbar owns an antiques shop, high-end English eighteenth-century furniture being his specialty. Possessing a sharp sense of humor and a discerning eye, he hunts with the Jefferson Hunt. He could have a second career as an escort to hunt balls.

Kathleen Sixt Dunbar is wife to Harry, although neither speaks of the other. She lives in Oklahoma City. They remain on friendly terms. No one knows they are married.

THE AMERICAN FOXHOUNDS

Lighter than the English foxhound, with a somewhat slimmer head, they have formidable powers of endurance and remarkable noses.

Cora is the head female. What she says goes.

Asa is the oldest hunting male hound, and he is wise.

Diana is steady, in the prime of her life, and brilliant. There's no other word for her but *brilliant.*

Dasher, Diana's littermate, is often overshadowed by his sister, but he sticks to business and is coming into his own.

Dragon is also a littermate of the above D hounds. He is arrogant, can lose his concentration, and tries to lord it over other hounds.

Dreamboat is of the same breeding as Diana, Dasher, and Dragon, but a few years younger.

Hounds take the first initial of their mother's name. Following are hounds ordered from older to younger. No unentered hounds are included in this list. An unentered hound is not yet on the Master of Foxhounds stud books and not yet hunting with the pack. They are in essence kindergartners. **Trinity, Tinsel, Trident, Ardent,**

Thimble, Twist, Tootsie, Trooper, Taz, Tattoo, Parker, Pickens, Zane, Zorro, Zandy, Giorgio, Pookah, Pansy, Audrey, Aero, Angle, Aces.

THE HORSES

Keepsake, TB/QH, Bay; **Lafayette,** TB, Gray; **Rickyroo,** TB, Bay; **Aztec,** TB, Chestnut; **Matador,** TB, Flea-bitten Gray. All are Sister's geldings. **Showboat, Hojo, Gunpowder,** and **Kilowatt,** all TBs, are Shaker's horses.

Outlaw, QH, Buckskin, and **Magellan,** TB, Dark Bay (which is really black), are Betty's horses.

Wolsey, TB, Flaming Chestnut, is Gray's horse. His red coat gave him his name, for Cardinal Wolsey.

Iota, TB, Bay, is Tootie's horse.

Matchplay and **Midshipman** are young Thoroughbreds of Sister's that are being brought along. It takes good time to make a solid foxhunter. Sister never hurries a horse or a hound in its schooling.

Trocadero is young, smart; being trained by Sam Lorillard.

Old Buster has become a babysitter. Like Trocadero, he is owned by Crawford Howard. Sam uses him for Yvonne Harris.

THE FOXES

Reds

Aunt Netty, older, lives at Pattypan Forge. She is overly tidy and likes to give orders.

Uncle Yancy is Aunt Netty's husband but he can't stand her anymore. He lives at the Lorillard farm, has all manner of dens and cubbyholes.

Charlene lives at After All Farm. She comes and goes.

Target is Charlene's mate but he stays at After All. The food supply is steady and he likes the other animals.

Earl has the restored stone stables at Old Paradise all to himself. He has a den in a stall but also makes use of the tack room. He likes the smell of the leather.

Sarge is half-grown. He found a den in big boulders at Old Paradise thanks to help from a doe. It's cozy with straw, old clothing bits, and even a few toys.

James lives behind the mill at Mill Ruins. He is not very social but from time to time will give the hounds a good run.

Ewald is a youngster who was directed to a den in an outbuilding during a hunt. Poor fellow didn't know where he was. The outbuilding at Mill Ruins will be a wonderful home as long as he steers clear of James.

Mr. Nash, young, lives at Close Shave, a farm about six miles from Chapel Cross. Given the housing possibilities and the good food, he is drawn to Old Paradise, which is being restored by Crawford Howard.

Grays

Comet knows everybody and everything. He lives in the old stone foundation part of the rebuilt log-and-frame cottage at Roughneck Farm.

Inky is so dark she's black and she lives in the apple orchard across from the above cottage. She knows the hunt schedule and rarely gives hounds a run. They can just chase someone else.

Georgia moved to the old schoolhouse at Foxglove Farm.

Grenville lives at Mill Ruins, in the back in a big storage shed. This part of the estate is called Shootrough.

Gris lives at Tollbooth Farm in the Chapel Cross area. He's very clever and can slip hounds in the batting of an eye.

Hortensia also lives at Mill Ruins. She's in another outbuilding. All are well constructed and all but the big hay sheds have doors that close, which is wonderful in bad weather.

Vi, young, is the mate of Gris, also young. They live at Tollbooth Farm in pleasant circumstances.

THE BIRDS

Athena, the great horned owl, is two and a half feet tall with a four-foot wingspan. She has many places where she will hole up but her true nest is in Pattypan Forge. It really beats being in a tree hollow. She's gotten spoiled.

Bitsy is eight and a half inches tall with a twenty-inch wingspan. Her considerable lungs make up for her tiny size as she is a screech owl, aptly named. Like Athena, she'll never live in a tree again, because she's living in the rafters of Sister's stable. Mice come in to eat the fallen grain. Bitsy feels like she's living in a supermarket.

St. Just, a foot and a half in height with a surprising wingspan of three feet, is a jet-black crow. He hates foxes but is usually sociable with other birds.

SISTER'S HOUSE PETS

Raleigh, a sleek, highly intelligent Doberman, likes to be with Sister. He gets along with the hounds, walks out with them. He tries to get along with the cat, but she's such a snob.

Rooster is a harrier bequeathed to Sister by a dear friend. He likes riding in the car, walking out with hounds, watching everybody and everything. The cat drives him crazy.

Golliwog, or "Golly," is a long-haired calico. All other creatures are lower life-forms. She knows Sister does her best, but still. Golly is Queen of All She Surveys.

SOME USEFUL TERMS

Away. A fox has gone away when he has left the covert. Hounds are away when they have left the covert on the line of the fox.

Brush. The fox's tail.

Burning scent. Scent so strong or hot that hounds pursue the line without hesitation.

Bye day. A day not regularly on the fixture card.

Cap. The fee nonmembers pay to hunt for that day's sport.

Carry a good head. When hounds run well together to a good scent, a scent spread wide enough for the whole pack to feel it.

Carry a line. When hounds follow the scent. This is also called working a line.

Cast. Hounds spread out in search of scent. They may cast themselves or be cast by the huntsman.

Charlie. A term for a fox. A fox may also be called **Reynard.**

Check. When hounds lose the scent and stop. The field must wait quietly while the hounds search for the scent.

Colors. A distinguishing color, usually worn on the collar but sometimes on the facings of a coat, that identifies a hunt. Colors can be awarded only by the Master and can be worn only in the field.

Coop. A jump resembling a chicken coop.

Couple straps. Two-strap hound collars connected by a swivel link. Some members of staff will carry these on the right rear of the saddle. Since the days of the pharaohs in ancient Egypt, hounds have been brought to the meets coupled. Hounds are always spoken of and counted in couples. Today, hounds walk or are driven to the meets. Rarely, if ever, are they coupled, but a whipper-in still carries couple straps should a hound need assistance.

Covert. A patch of woods or bushes where a fox might hide. Pronounced "cover."

Cry. How one hound tells another what is happening. The sound will differ according to the various stages of the chase. It's also called giving tongue and should occur when a hound is working a line.

Cub hunting. The informal hunting of young foxes in the late summer and early fall, before formal hunting. The main purpose is to enter young hounds into the pack. Until recently only the most knowledgeable members were invited to cub hunt, since they would not interfere with young hounds.

Dog fox. The male fox.

Dog hound. The male hound.

Double. A series of short, sharp notes blown on the horn to alert all that a fox is afoot. The gone away series of notes is a form of doubling the horn.

Draft. To acquire hounds from another hunt is to accept a draft.

Draw. The plan by which a fox is hunted or searched for in a certain area, such as a covert.

Draw over the fox. Hounds go through a covert where the fox is but cannot pick up its scent. The only creature that understands how this is possible is the fox.

Drive. The desire to push the fox, to get up with the line. It's a very desirable trait in hounds, so long as they remain obedient.

Dually. A one-ton pickup truck with double wheels in back.

Dwell. To hunt without getting forward. A hound that dwells is a bit of a putterer.

Enter. Hounds are entered into the pack when they first hunt, usually during cubbing season.

Field. The group of people riding to hounds, exclusive of the Master and hunt staff.

Field Master. The person appointed by the Master to control the field. Often it is the Master him- or herself.

Fixture. A card sent to all dues-paying members, stating when and where the hounds will meet. A fixture card properly received is an invitation to hunt. This means the card would be mailed or handed to a member by the Master.

Flea-bitten. A gray horse with spots or ticking that can be black or chestnut.

Gone away. The call on the horn when the fox leaves the covert.

Gone to ground. A fox that has ducked into its den, or some other refuge, has gone to ground.

Good night. The traditional farewell to the Master after the hunt, regardless of the time of day.

Gyp. The female hound.

Hilltopper. A rider who follows the hunt but does not jump. Hill-toppers are also called the Second Flight. The jumpers are called the First Flight.

Hoick. The huntsman's cheer to the hounds. It is derived from the Latin *hic haec hoc,* which means "here."

Hold hard. To stop immediately.

Huntsman. The person in charge of the hounds, in the field and in the kennel.

Kennelman. A hunt staff member who feeds the hounds and cleans the kennels. In wealthy hunts there may be a number of ken-nelmen. In hunts with a modest budget, the huntsman or even the Master cleans the kennels and feeds the hounds.

Lark. To jump fences unnecessarily when hounds aren't running. Masters frown on this, since it is often an invitation to an accident.

Lieu in. Norman term for "go in."

Lift. To take the hounds from a lost scent in the hopes of finding a better scent farther on.

Line. The scent trail of the fox.

Livery. The uniform worn by the professional members of the hunt staff. Usually it is scarlet, but blue, yellow, brown, and gray are also used. The recent dominance of scarlet has to do with people buying coats off the rack as opposed to having tailors cut them. (When anything is mass-produced, the choices usually dwindle, and such is the case with livery.)

Mask. The fox's head.

Meet. The site where the day's hunting begins.

MFH. The Master of Foxhounds; the individual in charge of the hunt: hiring, firing, landowner relations, opening territory (in large hunts this is the job of the hunt secretary), developing the pack of hounds, and determining the first cast of each meet. As in any leadership position, the Master is also the lightning rod for criticism. The Master may hunt the hounds, although this is usually done by a professional huntsman, who is also responsible for the hounds in the field and at the kennels. A long relationship between a Master and a huntsman allows the hunt to develop and grow.

Nose. The scenting ability of a hound.

Override. To press hounds too closely.

Overrun. When hounds shoot past the line of a scent. Often the scent has been diverted or foiled by a clever fox.

Ratcatcher. Informal dress worn during cubbing season and bye days.

Stern. A hound's tail.

Stiff-necked fox. One that runs in a straight line.

Strike hounds. Those hounds that, through keenness, nose, and often higher intelligence, find the scent first and press it.

Tail hounds. Those hounds running at the rear of the pack. This is not necessarily because they aren't keen; they may be older hounds.

Tally-ho. The cheer when the fox is viewed. Derived from the Norman *ty a hillaut,* thus coming into the English language in 1066.

Tongue. To vocally pursue a fox.

View halloo (halloa). The cry given by a staff member who sees a fox. Staff may also say tally-ho or, should the fox turn back, tally-back. One reason a different cry may be used by staff, especially in territory where the huntsman can't see the staff, is that the field in their enthusiasm may cheer something other than a fox.

Vixen. The female fox.

Walk. Puppies are walked out in the summer and fall of their first year. It's part of their education and a delight for both puppies and staff.

Whippers-in. Also called whips, these are the staff members who assist the huntsman, who makes sure the hounds "do right."

SCARLET
FEVER

CHAPTER 1

February 21, 2019   Thursday

A flash of scarlet caught Sister Jane's eye then disappeared as a gust of wind blew snow off the trees below. The day, cold, tormented those who thought spring should be around the corner. The calendar cited spring as starting March 20 with the equinox, but the weather gods did not seem to be planning warmth anytime soon.

The winter of 2018-2019 burst pipes, ran up electric bills, sent country people to dwindling firewood piles. Jane Arnold, Sister, master of the Jefferson Hunt, could deal with most of the troubles. It was cold hands and icy feet that she hated.

Another gust of wind sent swirls of snow as trees bent low. Far ahead she again saw Wesley Blackford's scarlet coat as he rode alongside the glittering hard-running creek, ice clinging to the bank sides.

She couldn't see her hounds. Nor could she see the whippers-in, those outriders assisting the huntsman. Sitting on a rise above the creek she peered into the forest, much of it conifers. Behind her stood a small field of riders desperately wishing to drop down out of the wind. Hearing Wesley, nicknamed Weevil, horn to lips, blow hounds forward she turned Lafayette toward the path down. He, too, was eager to move off the rise in the land. As the two carefully picked their way over the frozen ground covered with three inches of snow, more snow slid down Sister's neck from bending tree limbs. Lafayette reached level ground then stopped, snorted. His ears swept forward.

Those behind the master also stopped, wishing she'd move on because some of them still battled the wind. Right in front of Lafayette and his human cargo sauntered Target, a red fox, dazzling in his luxurious winter coat. Looking neither to the left nor the right, he crossed in front of the master, walked to a downed tree trunk secure across the creek, roots upended at the near end. Hopping up, he picked his way over, alighting on the other side.

Now what? No point bellowing "Tally-ho." One should normally count to twenty to give the fox a sporting chance. This arrogant fellow didn't need a sporting chance. Target had them all beat and he knew it. He kept a den on Sister's farm, under the log cabin dependency. Also, chances were that with the wind a "tally-ho" would be swept away. Still, Sister had to do something so she walked into the blue spruces, firs, and high pines. The space between the trees meant everyone, about fifteen people on this inhospitable day, could fit in. Turning Lafayette's head toward the creek, she waited and counted. If she didn't hear hounds after reaching one hundred she'd move on in the direction she saw Weevil.

"One, two." More snow down her neck.

On she counted as the small field huddled, shoulders up to

their ears. A few people wore earmuffs but she couldn't do that. She wouldn't hear her hounds and would most likely mislead everyone.

"Fifty-one, fifty-two." She grasped a heat pack in her coat pocket while keeping her left hand outside, freezing, because she held her crop in that hand.

As she was right-handed, she mused to herself, perhaps she could afford to lose her left.

"Seventy-two."

Trident shot in front of her without speaking. A young hound, a bit of a kleptomaniac, fast, he stopped suddenly and put his nose to the ground as his sister, Tinsel, caught up. Now the entire pack, twelve couples today, twenty-four hounds, for hounds are always counted in couples, milled around the tree roots.

Diana, a hound of remarkable intelligence, a true leader, opened while the others puzzled. *"It's him."*

Asa, an older hound, amended this. *"Him, but fading."*

Pickens leapt up onto the large trunk but hopped off, as he couldn't keep his balance.

Parker carefully stood on the trunk, succeeding where his brother failed. *"He's crossed. Here are his tracks. There's a bit of scent left."*

"We've got to go with what we have." Diana, not fooling around with the tree trunk, jumped into the icy creek, not deep, crossed to the other side, where the scent was a little better. *"Come on, move your asses!"*

The entire pack quickly assembled on the other side of the creek bank, moving with determination.

Sister marveled at their logical powers as well as that fantastic determination so typical of the American foxhound, a hound bred for Mid-Atlantic conditions, conditions designed to make even a saint cuss.

She heard hoofbeats; Weevil came up behind his hounds. She stepped out of the woods, took off her cap, and pointed in the direction the fox had moved in. No need to speak. All it would do would bring up the hounds' heads.

The handsome young man nodded to his master, asked his horse to step into the water, which the fine animal did without a minute's hesitation, crossed, and reached the other side just as the entire pack opened, a sound of exquisite beauty and excitement even to people who didn't hunt. Perhaps it is the sound of our history calling to us.

Sister followed her huntsman and made it across as Betty Franklin, her best friend and a whipper-in, blasted across the creek. The master stood still, for the whipper-in had right-of-way. Betty hadn't gotten out of position so much as she couldn't find a decent creek crossing. While they all knew this territory, the rains made some crossings treacherous, the silt piling up below. She touched her hat with her crop, a thank-you to the master's quick thinking, and charged off.

The field, well trained, now followed.

Sister, up ahead, negotiated a small drift then shot out of it back onto what she hoped was the old farm road. One couldn't see what was underneath the snow and it was easy to slide off the road. Her hope was to look where it was the flattest.

Hounds roared, sang, shook the treetops, bending low as they were.

The riders in the field, most of them experienced foxhunters, for novices often forsook hunting when the weather turned ugly, felt their pulse pounding. The old hands knew the scent had to be red hot.

Scent sticks in a frost or disappears in very cold conditions. The mercury needs to nudge a few degrees above freezing for it to lift and then scent can turn favorable. But today was not a favorable day so hounds had closed with their fox and the scent was hot, fresh for a brief time before the cold ruined it.

Hounds, with their tremendous olfactory powers, could pick up what a human could not, no matter what the conditions. Hounds followed scent but they didn't understand it. In truth no one did. Xenophon, born in 430 BC, the great Athenian major general, observed it but no one from that time until today truly understood it. Perhaps Artemis did but she wasn't telling.

Lafayette lived for these runs. He and Sister had been a team for eleven years. Both were advanced in years. Didn't mean a thing. He had his Absorbine Jr. rubdowns after a hunt and she had her Motrin. That was their only concession to the years.

Clever, in his teens, Lafayette had an uncanny instinct for negotiating deceptive ground. His hind end slipped a little, he quickly brought up his back legs. Sister stayed in the tack. On they ran. She burst into a meadow, saw the pack at the other end of it, Weevil right behind and Betty to the right. She had no idea where Tootie, the other whipper-in, was but she didn't worry. Staff work was excellent, plus they liked one another.

Diana and Dasher, her littermate, hung a few steps behind two youngsters, Audrey and Aero, who exhibited blinding speed with the recklessness of youth. Of course, they overran the line.

"Stop, you idiots! Get back here." Diana turned in midair, heading west where the sun had not hit the hills, which meant it was going to be even colder.

Betty, in her mid-fifties, an old hand, saw the youngsters overrun the line, not because she could smell scent but she trusted Diana. If Diana or Dasher or any of the older hounds turned, then it meant the fox had.

No doubt about it. Riding Outlaw, a solid fellow, Betty reached the outside of the two overexcited youngsters, urging them to turn but not really rating them. No point in scolding. They had figured out something was amiss and were hurrying back to the pack.

Like humans, hounds learn by doing and observing.

Steam rose off horses' hindquarters. People were actually sweating in their heavy coats and winter undershirts. Sister, her eye never leaving her huntsman, reached the other side of the meadow, plunged onto a narrow path, more snow down her neck, and soared over a large tree trunk. High winds had scoured central Virginia last week. Neither she nor her staff knew what lay across paths or how much destruction had been done. Jefferson Hunt covered two large counties. They'd find out when they found out. Work parties, hopefully, would follow. Windy though it was at this moment, at least there were no thirty-mile-an-hour gusts. The wind, too, would blow scent, which is exactly why Target crossed an open meadow. However, a bit to the left of the fox tracks, hounds stuck with it, opening loudly again once in the woods.

Another five minutes of hard running and Sister pulled up at the ruins of a modest house, the chimney standing like an upturned finger, alone, the fireplace visible. The chimney had not fallen down but the rest of the place lay strewn about. Hounds dug at the side of the stone fireplace.

Weevil dismounted, blew "Gone to Ground," praised his hounds.

The fox, deep in his snug den, heard the commotion outside. He knew all the hiding places in a five-mile range.

"I know you're in there," Parker baited him.

Tinsel added her two cents. *"You're afraid to come out. We're ferocious, you know,"* said a hound who was anything but, although she was puffed up from the run.

He said nothing, waiting for them to leave. Target was wise and in his prime.

Weevil called them together and mounted up as Tootie, a young woman, the other whipper-in, arrived at the site. She had also had a devil of a time finding a crossing from her left side of the pack. She took the left, Betty had the right.

"Come along," Weevil sang to them.

Hounds packed in behind him, the whippers-in on each side. They walked back to the trailers perhaps two miles away at Foxglove Farm. Foxglove was a cherished fixture, being in their territory since the beginning of the hunt in 1887.

Coming up to Sister, Harry Dunbar, mid-fifties, trim and tidy with a salt-and-pepper beard and moustache, complimented the pack. "What terrific work on a dicey day. You must be proud."

"I am." She smiled. "It pleases me when people in the field actually pay attention to the pack and know what's happening." She paused. "You've ripped your coat again. Harry, a few more of those and you'll turn into an icicle. The cold has to be stabbing you."

"I'm parading my manly toughness," he joked. "You will, however, be pleased to know I ordered a heavy scarlet Melton from Horse Country. I'll retire this and thankfully be warmer."

"You've worn this coat ever since I've known you and that's, what, since 1990?"

"No, 1989," he said. "I'd opened my shop and you paid me a call, inviting me to hunt. Well, I took you up on it. On the subject of coats, my weazlebelly is as old as this Melton, used when bought, but I save that for the High Holy Days or joint meets. Scarlet is expensive."

He spoke of his tails, which for men are often called weazlebelly, shadbelly for the ladies. Worn with a top hat the tails reek of elegance as well as dash. Flying over fences in top hat and tails never fails to impress itself upon the memory of those who see it.

"You're right about the expense, but the truly serviceable hunt attire, the stuff that lasts generations, which some does, costs both men and women. Those wonderful English fabrics." She turned to face him fully as they rode. "Could you get heavy English fabric? That dense twill?"

"Marion has worked her magic despite the uproar in England."

Marion Maggiolo, proprietress of Horse Country, made annual pilgrimages to England and Scotland in search of their fabrics, unmatched by any other nation no matter how hard they tried. Given that warmth was now hanging on until later November she also pioneered lighter hunt coats with fabrics from Italy, to keep a rider comfortable on fall days where the mercury might even nudge seventy degrees Fahrenheit. For the old hunters, these high temperatures were confusing. Might have been for the new ones, too.

"When will the coat be ready?"

"Next week, I hope. I waited too late, trying to squeeze one more year out of these tatters. I expect I won't be using the new one until next winter."

"You might be fooled."

He smiled. "You've got that right. I wake up and wonder what season I'm in. Sometimes I even wonder if I'm in America."

She nodded. "I think many of us feel that way. I'm older than you, of course, but I'm coming to the dismal conclusion that it's all smoke and mirrors. No one really knows what's going on."

"Sister, you are not old. You will never be old." He thought a moment. "About no one really knowing what's going on. Honest to Pete, I now think simple competence is revolutionary."

They both laughed, old buddies who had hunted together for decades. Hunting together is not as strong a bond as being in a combat unit under fire but it's strong, partly because hunting can be so unpredictable. One soon sees who has courage, who has brains, and who has both. Truthfully, the horses have more of both than the humans.

Harry reached over, touching Sister's elbow with his crop's stag handle and wrapped in thin strips of leather. "Drop by the store, will you? I've found a Louis XV desk much like the one you and Ray inherited from his uncle. The one that was stolen all those years ago."

"Oh, what a siren song. You are trying to seduce me. Trying to sing that money right out of my pocket."

"What man isn't?" he teased back. "But do drop by. It would be restorative to see you when we both aren't freezing."

She smiled at him, agreeing, then looked ahead, riding forward to Cindy Chandler, an old dear friend.

"What the hell?" Sister blurted out.

Reaching the trailers, Cindy Chandler stood in her stirrups. Booper, her horse, gingerly stepped forward. Sister also stood in her stirrups.

An expensive maroon Range Rover had driven through Cindy's fence by the cow barn. Clytemnestra, huge, and her equally huge son, Orestes, charged about, which set Booper off. No one wanted to tangle with the evil-tempered heifer and her dismally stupid son.

Cindy slid off, handing her reins to Sister. While no one expects a master to perform a groom's duty these two had been friends for over forty years. Each was always happy to help the other, status be damned. Sister knew Cindy was the only person who could sweet-talk Clytemnestra, who actually followed Cindy, her son in tow, into her special cow barn, quite tidy and warmish considering the day.

Morris Taylor, sixty-two, in a T-shirt and jeans, sobbed next to the Range Rover, its nose in a drainage ditch, steam hissing from under the hood.

"I didn't mean to do it."

Sister, now dismounted, motioned for Tootie to come over, handed the gorgeous young woman the reins to both horses, and walked over slowly to Morris, as Weevil, who didn't know the man, approached from the opposite direction.

"Morris, it's Janie."

"Sister, Sister. I didn't mean to do it." He shivered.

As Weevil removed his coat to put over Morris's shoulders, Morris shrank away. "Who are you? Don't touch me."

"It's all right, Morris. He is a friend."

"Who is he? Why does he want to touch me?"

"He wants to put a coat on you," she told the shivering man, who now held on to her for dear life, a life preserver, which in a way she was.

Betty motioned for Weevil to give her the coat, touched her temple. He understood.

"Morris, it's Betty Franklin, your old dancing partner."

"Betty? Betty?" He struggled to place her but didn't shrink away.

"Come on. Let's get you into the house." Sister gently guided him, holding on to his right arm while Betty had his left, toward Cindy's house.

People threw blankets on their horses. Weevil, having pulled his work coat out of the hound truck, and Gray, Sister's partner in life, were already fixing up a temporary fence to keep in Clytemnestra and Orestes for tomorrow, when they would be put out to pasture.

Weevil asked no questions as they worked.

Gray volunteered, "A former hunt club member. Morris Taylor."

"Drew Taylor's family?"

"Brother. Senile dementia. He must have found or stolen the car keys. He's pretty far gone."

Weevil, hammer in hand, drove a nail into the makeshift board. "Hope this holds."

"Let's get another one plus one of her old barrels for a barrier. You never know about that damned cow," Gray grumbled.

As Sister and Betty walked the crying man to the welcoming house, Sister thought to herself, "There but for the grace of God."

Perhaps.

In the house, having endured the cold for two and a half hours, Sister wrapped her hands around a cup of hot chocolate, glad for the warmth. Today the cold seeped into her bones. Seemed to affect the others the same way. The members sipped tea, coffee, and hot chocolate and a few braced themselves with strong spirits.

A knock on the door sent Cindy to open it.

"I am so sorry to keep you waiting," Drew Taylor apologized.

"No matter, come on. Morris is over there with Betty and Weevil, whom he met today. Chattering away."

Having completed the temporary fence repairs, Weevil and Gray were now inside.

"Had a devil of a time getting a client out the door." Drew blew air out of his nostrils, looked at his brother, sighed. "How much damage is there?"

Cindy released a deep throaty laugh, one that sent men into a transport. "A few fence panels. Don't worry about it. I fear, however, your Range Rover will need to be towed. All the way to Richmond, unfortunately."

He smiled, as he'd always liked Cindy, had done so for decades. "I should never have kept that car."

"You look important driving it."

"Why Rover doesn't open a dealership in Charlottesville I will never know. It's a pain in the ass."

She placed her hand on his forearm. "Morris cried quite a bit. He's afraid you'll be angry at him."

Now noticing his brother, Morris became fearful. "I didn't mean to do it."

Betty stood up but Drew motioned for her to stay seated. Morris now clung to her hand so she was pulled down.

"It's all right, buddy, but where did you find the keys?" Drew lifted an eyebrow.

Defiantly, his younger brother said, "I'm not telling. You can't make me tell."

People looked then looked away, except for Harry Dunbar, who stared for a minute, shook his head, then averted his eyes.

"Lower your voice, Morris," Drew ordered.

Again a fearful look crossed the not-unattractive suffering man's face.

Sister walked over. "Drew, glad you got here. Missed you during the hunt, which had some good moments."

"And some cold ones." He smiled. "I'll be out Saturday." He looked down at Morris. "Maybe I can find someone to drive him in our old truck. You know, so he can be part of things."

"That's a good idea," Sister agreed. "Morris has always been social and it's not too different now. He seems to remember some of us but not our names. If I say my name he nods."

"There are days and then there are days." He put his hand under his brother's armpit. "Come on. I'm taking you home."

Morris shrugged him off. "I don't want to go home. There are no women at home."

Betty couldn't help it. She burst out laughing.

"Come on."

"I'm not going," Morris refused.

"You know, Morris, you have a point. No women. Men need women." Betty smiled at him. "How about if I walk you with Drew and we figure out how to get some girls to the house."

Morris brightened. "I like to talk to women. I like to look at them. I like breasts."

"Oh God." Drew moaned.

Sister shrugged. "It's all right. He says what everyone else is thinking."

Drew looked around at the small group, noticing Harry Dunbar. A slight sneer appeared on his lips then he refocused on his brother, dismissing the man he loathed, a man he had accused of cheating him and seducing his late mother. Neither charge had ever been proven.

Harry, seeing Drew, turned his back, a maneuver he also used in the hunt field.

To the credit of both men, once the initial uproar had passed, and that was years ago, they did not drag club members into their dislike. The members carefully sidestepped it as well.

What had happened was Mrs. Waycross Taylor, Missy to her friends, had died, leaving behind exquisite eighteenth-century furniture as well as a few lovely small sculptures from the late eighteenth century, early nineteenth, all English. Neither Drew nor Morris wanted any of it. Neither man had an aesthetic bone in their bodies and their wives were all for the modern, at that time, as well as brighter colors. No silk moire for them.

So Drew and Morris called Harry, told him to pick up the stuff after he gave them a price. He did. Twenty thousand dollars, which sounded reasonable. One small graceful Hepplewhite incidental table alone was worth that, but they neither knew nor seemed to care. So Harry wrote the check, brought a moving van, and took the entire lot, rooms full of fabulous furniture.

A pair of George III gilt-wood armchairs, circa 1770, sold for nine thousand dollars. The gilt candelabra held by two fetching female figures, breasts exposed and perfect . . . well, they were bronze-gilded, how could they sag after all those centuries? Anyway, the candelabra had adorned Missy's formal dining room table. The two ravishing ladies stood about forty-six inches high. That included the base and the candelabra, which they held a bit sideways so their bosoms met the eye. Harry sold the pair for eighty-five thousand dollars. That's what did it. The sons might have absorbed the sale of the gilt chairs but this, this sent them into orbit.

A few hunt club members at the time felt that the Taylors may have been carried a little fast, to use the old Virginia expression. However, most believed the brothers had been stupid. They could have asked for bids.

Missy Taylor spent lavishly and she could afford to, for her husband, Waycross, a born salesman, expanded the Taylor Insurance business, started by his father. Before there were multiple listings, Taylor got all the big estates, partly due to his prowess in the hunt field. He hunted many of the estates he later sold. Socializing came naturally to him, as did easily clearing a stout four-foot fence. Well respected, he increased his fortune. Multiple listings became the norm. It certainly made it easier for buyers and sellers but not necessarily the listing agent. Waycross adjusted, worked well with other firms. The business expanded.

Drew stepped into the business. Morris hated selling, loved science, went to MIT. He wound up working as a nuclear physicist for a private company that built nuclear reactors. He inherited the moneymaking gene, for certain, along with old Waycross's brains. Drew, not so much. He coasted. Taylor Insurance was kept afloat by his agents.

Morris's hopes for his own son were dashed because Bainbridge, now an adult, harbored little ambition and indeterminate brainpower.

Before his accelerating decline, Morris, too, hunted and rode well when he retired, moving back to Charlottesville. Building reactors had taken him all over the country in his prime but when he could he had joined the local hunt. He was well liked and certainly respected, making his decline all the more painful.

Behind their hands many a person whispered, "Why couldn't it have been Drew?"

Weevil, seated next to Betty, rose, walked to where the Shaker pegs were lined up by the front door, grabbed Betty's heavy hunt coat and his own. He returned.

"Thank you, Weevil."

He helped her put it on.

"I could do that," Morris offered.

"Thank you for thinking of it." Betty beamed at him.

Betty, Weevil, and Drew propelled Morris to the front door. Drew lifted his own lamb fleece coat off a peg.

Weevil filled him in. "No coat. Took almost a half hour for him to stop shivering."

"You know, I've an extra in the car. I'll run out and get it." He opened the door and a wedge of frigid air pushed in.

"I don't want to go." Morris's eyes glazed over. "I hate him."

"He's your brother," Betty said soothingly.

"So what? He talks to me like I'm an idiot. I forget things, Betty. I do, but I'm not an idiot. I built nuclear reactors. I know things."

Weevil's eyebrows raised and Betty nodded in agreement.

"You built Three Mile Island. You worked on big projects."

"I remember all that," he said as his brother came back through the door, handing Morris a down jacket.

Betty moved to Morris's right side while Weevil took his left. Both intuited that if Drew touched his brother, resistance would accelerate.

They walked him to Drew's brand-new BMW X5. Had to have cost at least seventy-two thousand, with every gadget known to the Germans.

Drew paused for a minute. "Damn, he really did plow through that fence. I'll pay for it, obviously."

"The good news is, Cindy coaxed Clytemnestra and Orestes into their barn and closed the door," Betty noted.

"Thank God the cow didn't attack the Range Rover." Drew exhaled.

Weevil noticed the enormous cow giving them the evil eye from her barn window. "Don't count her out. Best to get the wrecker here before she gets out tomorrow morning."

"Good point." Drew smiled at him then opened the door and slid behind the wheel, while Morris would not close his door.

Betty kissed him on the cheek, closing the door, and Drew quickly locked it.

The two staff members walked back to the house, the snow and ice crunching underfoot.

"When did his dementia start?" Weevil asked.

"I don't truly know. I noticed a change four years ago. Little things. He'd forget a name, lose a reference. The lapses became more pronounced until finally he drove to Roger's Corner." She mentioned a convenience store out in the country. "Didn't know where he was. Roger called Drew. Ultimately he took his brother in and now has a part-time housekeeper. I guess you'd call him that, he's a nurse, really, I don't know, but it's a young man who watches him. Morris has a son, but he's not a success story. So far he's not done much for his father. They fight then Morris fights with Drew."

"The nurse must have been off duty today," Weevil noted.

"Maybe. Sad. The whole process is so sad."

They gladly stepped inside, peeled off their coats.

"I didn't think I'd be here so long." Weevil walked over to Sister. "Let me get the hounds back."

"Fortunately, their trailer is closed up and full of straw, but yes, it's a good idea. None of us could have predicted the accident. Better he took out Cindy's fence than one of us."

Weevil motioned for Tootie, and they left together.

The breakfast—hunt tailgates or food at a member's house are called breakfasts, no matter what time the hunt is over—was breaking up.

Cindy said to Sister, "Hope we hunt at Mud Fence Saturday. The weather report is not promising."

"There's time between today and Saturday. I'll worry about it the night before," the tall, silver-haired master replied.

"You're good at that."

"Worrying?"

Cindy laughed. "Not worrying."

"I have Gray to do that for me." She lifted her eyebrows as her partner walked over.

"What?" the handsome man, mid-sixties, said.

"Worry. I told Cindy I don't worry because you do it for me."

"I don't worry. I think ahead."

She looked at him, light brown skin, a thin military moustache gray over his upper lip. "Whatever you say, darling."

He smiled back. "You're up to something."

"Me? Never."

She was, but she would wait to see that desk first.

CHAPTER 2

February 22, 2019 Friday

"Take it out now," Aunt Daniella instructed Yvonne Harris, Tootie's mother.

Pulling down the oven door, heavy hotpads on her hands, Yvonne withdrew the square pan, placing it atop the stove. "Got it."

"Now put a towel over it until it cools."

She opened a drawer, pulled out a red-striped kitchen towel, carefully draping it over the pan.

"The secret to spoon bread is getting it out of the oven in time. That and a tablespoon of Duke's mayonnaise when you stir the batter. Don't tell about the mayonnaise."

"Won't. Smells good." The former model inhaled the enticing fragrance, as did Ribbon, her half-grown Norfolk terrier, spoiled rotten.

The ninety-four-year-old woman, in fabulous shape, one of the great beauties of her generation, leaned back in the kitchen chair, watching Ribbon clean the plate. "What a good idea."

Yvonne smiled. "Makes washing dishes easier. I hate a dishwasher."

Ribbon licked the empty batter bowl Yvonne placed on the floor.

"How's your fox?"

"Comes and goes. Ribbon pays him no mind. Sometimes I look out the back and there he is, curled up in the special doghouse filled with old towels and rags. I've grown quite fond of him."

"I was so obsessed with making spoon bread I forgot to ask you if you'd like a drink. I have your favorite bourbon." Yvonne had both Blanton's and Woodford Reserve.

"Too early but I'll have a cup of tea. I see your shiny teapot over there."

"Sister gave me that." Yvonne filled the pot, turned on the flame. "Heard the cold was numbing yesterday. Tootie, tough nut, actually admitted she was glad to go in. She also told me about Morris Taylor driving a Range Rover through Cindy Chandler's fence."

Aunt Daniella nodded while the water came to a boil. "Gray called to tell me the same thing."

Gray and his brother, Sam, were Aunt Daniella's nephews, the sons of her departed sister, Graziella, herself a beauty but not wild like Aunt Daniella. Free-spirited as she was and remained, the lady excelled at covering her tracks.

"Shouldn't he be in a home? Some kind of structured living?"

"According to Drew, Morris's mind is like a house. The upstairs lights go on and off. A few are now definitely off and some downstairs are flickering. He says he can take care of him, plus he has a part-time male nurse."

"But driving? How did Morris get the keys?"

"I don't know. And there's so much attention paid to dementia now. When I was young I remember a few older people becoming forgetful but I can't say that they completely lost it. Then again, diseases carried us off earlier. Perhaps in time they would have become a blank."

Yvonne poured the tea. "Can't say as I saw anyone when I was a kid. Then again, other things can hide it, I suppose. Drinking, drugs. People assumed that was the problem. How's your tea?"

"Hot. What kind is it?"

"Assam. Tootie, who is beginning to pay attention to such things, said the Range Rover and Drew's BMW X5 were new, or almost new."

"The Taylors are not on food stamps. They inherited the insurance company. I suppose Drew will get by but it will fritter away when he dies. Morris has a useless son. Really, Drew should sell it now while Taylor Insurance still has a good reputation. I read about your ex-husband building an auto manufacturing plant in Zimbabwe. The government . . . well, the dictator, really . . . gave him all manner of enticements."

"I'm sure he did, and some of them walked on two legs." Yvonne rose to fetch a plate, putting cookies on it.

"Oh well, Yvonne, half of marriage or looking desirable is theater. You are well out of it."

"I am." Yvonne sat down. "Are there car manufacturers in Africa? Then again, are there roads in Africa?"

"Not like here. Having never visited Africa I can only imagine there must be a great disparity between the countries. A pan-Africa highway, one north and south and one east and west, for starters, would seem to me to be a great boost to businesses and outside investors. But how to get all these nations to cooperate, especially when many of the citizens are being robbed blind?"

"You know, Aunt Dan, whenever I am fed up to here," she drew her hand up to her neck, "I remind myself of situations like that or of Syria. I've visited Egypt, South Africa, Botswana, Zimbabwe, and Namibia. Glad I did. Cape Town is one of the most beautiful cities in the world. The natural beauty alone is thrilling, and I admit, seeing the pyramids and the Sphinx was overwhelming. But I was always glad to get home."

"I can imagine. Time to take the towel off, wrap the pan in aluminum, and put it in the refrigerator."

"Don't you want to test it?"

"Good idea."

Yvonne walked over to the stovetop, brought out a knife, cut a sizable square for each of them, brought out the creamery butter, two spreading knives, two small plates. "Here goes."

"Spoons. We need spoons."

"Oh, Aunt Daniella, of course. That's why it's called spoon bread."

The two carefully poked their spoons into the heart of the golden corn bread.

"Well?"

"Aunt Dan, your recipe did the trick. I can't wait to spring this on Gray and Sam."

The phone rang. "Excuse me. I told Tootie to call me this afternoon. I'm taking her and Weevil to dinner." She pulled out her cellphone. "Hello."

"Mom. Remember the accident I told you about? It's on the news."

"A car going through a fence?"

"Yes, because his son who was supposed to watch over Morris was found by the side of the road in his car with all the Taylors' silver."

"Dead?"

"No, on drugs or something."

After Yvonne hung up the phone she relayed the news to Aunt Daniella then laughed. "It's funny living here. Barely a day went by in Chicago without a murder, a big robbery, a protest. Here it's silver in a car by the side of the road."

"Too compromised to keep driving. I mean, if you've stolen silver you should keep going."

Yvonne looked at the older woman. "You'd think he'd have the sense not to get loaded."

"Yes, you would."

CHAPTER 3

February 23, 2019   Saturday

"*B**other,*" Mr. Nash thought to himself as the many rigs pulled into Close Shave, the farm where he lived. Mud Fence's footing had proved so dreadful Sister switched the hunt, with both landowners' permission. The Mud Fence owners suggested the switch.

The red fox, a large fellow, somewhat new to the area, had learned about Jefferson Hunt during cubbing season, which started right after Labor Day. If those crazy people wanted to run around behind hounds, fine. He felt no obligation to entertain them, especially today, for the low clouds and light drizzle, so fine you could barely see it, meant he'd stay inside his spacious den. Years ago the den had been inhabited by reds but as is the nature of such things the girls married, moving not terribly far away, and the boys sought dens elsewhere. Nature favors the female.

Mr. Nash accepted this. He and three younger males in the area did not yet have mates but he felt confident in time he would find the right vixen. As it was mating season, and late this year due to the insufferable weather, he searched every day, but not today.

As the red fox curled up in his straw-filled den, a few old shredded towels in there as well, the trailers parked nose out toward the farm road. Close Shave maintained excellent farm roads, crusher run on them as well as all around the six-stall barn, which the new owners of this old place were restoring. Crusher run, small crushed stones, gray or tan, often provided a better road surface than slightly larger stones. The horses would come later but there the owners were, bundled up, offering stirrup cups. Good people.

"God, why do they have to take a drink? Let's go!" Rickyroo, one of Sister's Thoroughbreds, danced a bit under her.

"Calm down, Ricky." She patted his sleek neck.

"You're the master. Why do you tolerate this? The sooner we're off the sooner we find a fox," he sassed as she continued to pat him, which he liked.

"No thank you." Sister smiled at Della Vosburgh, the owner. "I can't drink, as I'm staff. And I look forward to you and your husband cubbing with us next year. The stable is coming along."

"I can't wait." Della smiled, her dimples adding to her friendly demeanor.

"Gather round," Sister called to the field, thirty-five strong on this iffy day. "We'll head south toward Chapel Cross." She glanced skyward. "The worst should hold off for a bit." She looked at Weevil, as did most of the women in the field, although she had a purpose in doing so, for he was her huntsman. "Hounds, please."

"Madam." He smiled, leaned over a bit, and said in a low voice, "Let's boogie, babies."

"I love it when he does that." Tinsel giggled.

Sterns up, they pranced, packed in front of their huntsman, walking down to the fence line separating the stable paddock from a large pasture.

First Flight burst with the diehards; no threat of bad weather could keep away Kasmir Barbhiya, Alida Dalzell, Dr. Walter Lungren, Jt-MFH, Gray and Sam Lorillard, Freddie Thomas, everyone wearing heavy gloves, too.

Tedi and Edward Bancroft, Sister's dear friends and neighbors, her oldest members, in their mid-eighties, no longer rode out in bone-chilling weather or rain. Sensible though it was, she missed them, for they always rode in her pocket, which was their right as the oldest members of the club. They had earned their colors back before most of the current members had been born.

First Flight filled out with only fourteen people today. Everyone else was jammed up in Second Flight, led by Bobby Franklin, Betty's husband. Ben Sidell, the sheriff of the county, rode with Bobby, who had noticed over these last few years that the sheriff, fortyish, missed little. Ben was a good man to have around. Drew Taylor, smartly turned out in his scarlet Melton, rode in Second Flight today.

Following slowly in his truck was Shaker Crown, now in his early fifties. Sister's longtime huntsman had cracked vertebrae in his neck from a strange riding accident. He was on medical leave, so to speak. He hated it. A rival hunt's huntsman, the very attractive Skiff Kane, hunting Crawford Howard's outlaw pack, drove, for Shaker was not to drive. She tended to him and as fortune smiled on them, they spoke the same language.

"Goddammit!" he cursed. "I hate not riding. Hate it!"

Perhaps she didn't speak the same language at that moment.

"Honey, keep your pants on."

He tried to turn his head toward her but the neck brace limited his motion. "Later."

"Ha," she rejoined as the First Flight easily popped over a jump built to resemble a chicken coop, and therefore was called a coop.

Sister quietly sat while Ricky smoothly took the coop. Rarely did she ever need to squeeze this glossy bay. He knew all the horn calls, knew the various hound voices, and could smell the fox a lot better than she could. Ricky believed he was assisting a limited creature. After all, she only had two legs, and a weak nose, but he gave Sister credit, she had sharp eyes and quite good hearing for a human. Then again, he loved her and she loved him. However, he felt it imperative that she let him make the decisions, such as where to take off for a jump. Mostly she did, for she trusted this horse.

Sister's attitude was if you don't trust your horse, don't ride him. If you don't trust your hounds, don't hunt them. The problems were always with the people, for some evidenced not one grain of sense. No way you could trust them in the hunt field or elsewhere. But those tried and true over the years, like Betty or the young Tootie, you'd go to the wall for such people and they for you.

Twenty minutes passed as they trotted along. *"Faint."* Angle, a young fellow, inhaled.

"Yeah." Zandy concurred. *"The fellow who lives here won't be bolted. Sticks in that den."*

"He doesn't know the territory but so much." Asa, the oldest hound hunting, spoke. *"In time he'll give us some runs once he knows all the hideaways."*

"I thought this was breeding season. Why isn't he out?" Pookah asked.

"Good question." Taz wanted to find scent.

"Lots of competition around here and too much rain. Nonstop rain or snow," Parker, a hound now in his prime, offered. *"Foxes at Crawford's barn and outbuildings. Foxes at Mud Fence Farm and Tollbooth Farm and tons at Tattenhall Station. If we push past Tattenhall, due south, there are all those foxes around Beveridge Hundred and the farms farther south. He needs to settle in."*

Diana stopped, nose down, slowly following a teasing trail that was warming up. *"Somebody. Don't know who."*

Hounds opened, moved forward at a trot, for the scent wasn't heavy. If they ran too fast they might lose or overrun it. On a day like today, better to be prudent.

"Push your fox," Weevil sang out to them as he watched Tootie glide over a stone wall on her beloved Iota, a horse she'd had since private school.

Bobby led his charges to a gate. Ben dismounted, unhitched the gate, opened it. Everyone rode through. Freddie Thomas, a strong rider in her fifties, on a new horse today, stayed. No one should be left alone at a gate because most horses when they see other horses move off will move off, too. One shouldn't be left holding the gate, only to be dragged along holding on to reins. That promised a surefire bad outcome.

"Thanks, Freddie." Ben tapped his crop to his cap. "How do you like the horse?"

"So far, so good. Alida found him for me."

"You can go to the bank on Alida."

Freddie laughed. "Believe I will."

That fast the hounds opened, the humans shut up and squeezed on. They needed to catch up to Second Flight, which had broken into a gallop. People in Second Flight could ride but they did not take the big jumps. A log or something perhaps two feet they'd jump but other than that they kept all four feet on the ground.

"Jeez," Ben muttered, trying to catch his breath.

Up ahead the hounds charged through the last big field belonging to Close Shave, stepped into a woods that would eventually back up to the old Gulf station at the crossroads, but the fox had other ideas.

Pickens, Parker's littermate, crossed the asphalt road, barreled into a new estate being built from land cut off from the Gulf station, which had holdings on both sides of the road. Since the Gulf station's owner and his brother sat in jail, Millie DuCharme, wife of Binky DuCharme, had sold off the land. She said she couldn't take care of it. Well, she could, or her son could, but she was showing signs of greed in her old age despite her pleasant personality. She sold everything else to Crawford Howard.

A large sign, deep maroon background, gold letters in script, announced Crackenthorpe, the name for the estate that was not yet built. At least everyone knew the name, although it was not the name of the owners. That story would be told sooner or later. Every place in Virginia had to have a story. As the colony was founded in 1607, stories covered the Old Dominion. Some of them were even true.

Checking the road, Sister trotted across, slid down the small embankment onto Crackenthorpe land, then galloped on. The fox was turning toward the chapel that sat on the northeast corner of Chapel Cross.

The hounds pressed on then swerved east, then stopped.

"Unfair!" Audrey whined.

Was, too, for the fox had hurried to where a bulldozer sat, there to clear ground. He had run right through the oil slick.

Hounds milled about but the oil stink filled their nostrils.

Cora, moving away, circled the area, paused, then called out, *"Tollbooth. He's headed for Tollbooth."*

On they ran. Tollbooth and Mud Fence were east of the church, abutting each other beyond the church lands. By the time they reached Tollbooth, Gris, the hunted fox, was secure in his den with his partner, Vi. Their den utilized the old hay shed; doors closed, it was cozy. They enjoyed being in the shed itself, for there was old hay scattered about, half in the shed and half out. Tunnels had been dug underneath, too, just in case a human left the doors open.

"Blow 'Gone to Ground,' " Shaker fussed in the truck.

Weevil was dismounting to do that as Tootie rode up to hold Matchplay's reins.

Weevil blew the happy song then patted the hounds' heads. "Well done. Well done."

"Tricky." Cora stuck her nose back into the den entrance.

"Come on, girl." Weevil effortlessly swung back up.

He drew for another hour but the drizzle intensified into a light steady rain, footing worsened, so they trotted back to Close Shave. A cold rain seems colder than a falling snow. People were glad to dismount, their feet stinging when boots hit the ground. Sheets were tossed over horses. Many people loaded their horses, feed bags hanging inside, to keep the animals out of the rain.

As most sheets, called rugs if they are heavy, are waterproofed, the horses would have been okay in the rain but it was thoughtful.

The people then walked to an outbuilding that had a gas fireplace at one end, for it was formerly a repair shop for farm equipment. Della and Lamar set out tables, chairs, and the bar. Everyone pulled up chairs, the warmth felt wonderful, for the rain chill seeped into their bones.

Sister, thirsty, gulped a tonic water with lime.

"Refill?" Ben Sidell asked.

"Sheriff, thank you, no. How are you?"

"Sit with me for a moment. I need your insights." He pulled up a chair for her.

"Now, what woman could resist flattery like that. Insights. Shoot."

"You've known generations of people here. I'm learning. You probably heard that we picked up Bainbridge Taylor with a bagful of silver. His name was not made public. The officer who found the car thought he was drunk, and the officer didn't know who he was. Turns out he was on Oxycontin plus booze. He's in the hospital."

"Lucky to be alive, I would guess."

"And lucky to be apprehended by a young officer who doesn't know the family. The doctors used Naloxone. They're getting accustomed to this, I'm sorry to say. I expect Bainbridge will be identified in this afternoon's paper. The reporter will certainly know the Taylors, I think."

She nodded. "I'm sure someone must have told you his father, Morris, ran through a fence at Cindy Chandler's."

"They did. Thinking of either father or son driving is unnerving. But here's the thing, the son swears he did not steal the silver and he did not take a drink. He admits to the pills. And, of course, his uncle paid off the media. So is this a young man who has not had to suffer for his misdeeds?"

"To a point." She drew in a breath. "Bainbridge is a failure in his father's eyes. Drew says Morris still knows his son. They don't speak. Bainbridge discovered drugs instead of education at private school. It's a well-worn path."

"Yes, it is. Bainbridge has no arrest record but he did say he spent time in rehab. One of those expensive ones."

"I suppose it worked. He's switched from cocaine to legal drugs. Maybe that's progress. He's doing business with a better class of dealer."

Ben, crossing one leg over the other, shrugged. "Says he's not hooked but he found the pills and why not?"

"I don't believe it. You know neither Drew nor Morris ever showed signs of addictive behavior. Morris had a very good mind, which we all figured is why he was so hard on his son. Bainbridge wasn't a stupid kid but he wasn't brilliant. Morris couldn't understand that."

Gray came up, smiling. "Do you need to be saved?"

"From Ben? Never." She smiled back then looked at the group around the stove. "But I think Weevil does."

Gray nodded, headed toward Weevil, Tootie, Shaker, Betty, and Skiff.

"Those staff discussions can go on forever. How is Shaker, by the way?"

"Oh, Ben, he's healing, but the vertebrae remain a little

crooked. The doctors want to straighten them out, perhaps even place a small pad there, but Shaker says no one is going to cut into his neck."

Ben pressed his lips together. "I can understand that." He noticed Drew in deep conversation with Freddie.

"The other thing, Drew came to the hospital then called on me to ask if we were going to press charges. Because of the silver and the drugs."

"And?"

"I looked at him and said, 'It's your silver.' "

"Ah," she murmured.

"He won't press charges. He said he would pay any bills and he also promised he would send Bainbridge back to rehab. Morris originally sent the kid . . . well, he's not a kid anymore . . . years back but Drew said he would do it now. Said sometimes a person has to repeat these things and he's right about that. It's not one size fits all."

"Do you impound the silver?"

"I suppose I should, but no, I gave it back to him. Had the Taylor crest on it. But you know, it does seem odd that a thirty-two-year-old man would steal his own family's silver, drive off the road, and stay put. Yes, he was loopy but he could have run."

"Does. It's the curse of our time, drugs. Well, if I hear anything, I'll tell you. As I said, father and son about hate each other and I can attest to the fact that Drew is not impressed by his nephew. However, he's trying to help." She, too, noticed him chatting up Freddie. "Never misses a pretty girl."

"Are you sure I can't get you another drink?" Ben asked.

"No, thank you."

They both rose and walked closer to the stove.

"I'm telling you the pink slips will fly, or fall like those raindrops outside," Freddie Thomas, an accountant, predicted to Drew.

"The banks will be clever," Gray, who had joined the conversation, offered. "They'll promise no one will lose their job then start the contraction process maybe a year later," he added.

Drew nodded. "Never fails."

The group knew that Gray had been a partner at one of the most prestigious accounting firms in Washington, D.C. A firm that was often called in to examine government department records, so their name spread fear as well as confidence.

Kasmir, a good businessman, having made great sums in India with his pharmaceutical business, also agreed. "It's the way business is done now but I thought the merger would be with a Southern regional bank and, say, Chase Manhattan. That would give both banks in the merger a wider geographical presence."

"This is what I don't understand." Sister held her hands toward the stove. "The Dodd Frank Act was to clean up banking, right? And banks are now bigger than ever. The community banks paid the price. Or so it seems to me. Big, big, big."

"And accountable to whom?" Freddie held her hands palms upward. "I am not anti-bank. I believe banks are a pillar of the economy, but not as they are today. On the one hand, they're hogtied thanks to the mortgage crisis of their own making. On the other hand they keep merging and are now so big, Congress fears them despite blabbing to the contrary."

Everyone started talking at once then Sister said, "We should all move our money to Chase Manhattan in New York."

"Why?" they asked.

"Well, the late Mrs. Jeffords owned Count Fleet, a very great horse. Foxhunters should always support horsemen. Even if Chase is no longer guided by equine wisdom, let's give them a chance."

They laughed, ate more, talked more. Turned a rainy day into a happy day.

Mr. Nash could smell the food. He wasn't all that far from the old hay shed. Why didn't they go home? Humans always left food. A Virginia ham biscuit and a moist pound cake would be perfect on this wet day.

Humans were slow, insensitive to the vulpine palate, and noisy, so noisy. However, they could cook. That was worth something.

C H A P T E R 4

February 25, 2019 Monday

"Lascivious." Harry ran his hand over the burgundy leather surface of the Louis XV tulipwood desk.

"Yes, it is." Sister took a step back to admire the desk, a minor work of art, really. "I will never know what happened to Uncle Arnold's desk."

"Which is why I wanted you to come and see this one." He guided her to the desk, pulled open the center drawer using the gilded ornate handle, a key slot above it.

Sister inhaled the odor of the wood and leather. "You are tormenting me. So you know, I purposely did not mention anything to Gray. Why weren't you at the hunt Saturday, by the way? He and others asked about you."

"Annapolis. Allaire Ritter wanted me to give a ballpark figure for some of the family pieces. You know Allaire, hunts with Fair Hills in Maryland. I don't know as she has any intention of selling but I gave her my estimates as well as dealers in New York City. She wanted to make sure she connected to the upmarket best."

"Well, in a city where a tiny flat rents for about fifteen hundred a month, that would be the upmarket."

"Sister, that rental would only get you an apartment in a so-so neighborhood." He shrugged. "Insane."

"Is there a way out of these exorbitant rents in our big cities? People need to live there for the jobs, or they're drawn by ambition. While I think rent control a possible answer, how can that work if those civic worthies whether city or state keep raising taxes? You have to be able to raise rents to cover costs. Heating alone will kill you."

"I know. I also know we have it pretty good here in Virginia. Richmond, Norfolk, Virginia Beach are very affordable." He smiled. "Not Northern Virginia."

"Occupied Virginia." She laughed. "How is Allaire? I haven't seen her in a year or two. I'd run into her when hunting at Green Spring Valley. She always had good horses."

"Fat as a tick." Harry laughed. "Naturally, she has no wrinkles."

"You are wicked."

"I suppose it beats a face-lift. Aren't you surprised by how many men now undergo face-lifts?" He raised a steel gray eyebrow.

"No. Getting old is a sin." She laughed. "Dying is un-American. What can we do?"

He laughed with her. "Say the hell with it and go on. Now, Madam, what do you think of this desk?"

"Sensuous. I think the marquetry so graceful. You know, well, of course you do, I love Louis XV."

"Because you are a woman of exquisite taste." His eyes sparkled. "Actually I love it, too, although my area is really eighteenth-century English furniture, with a smattering of French. But what draws me to this period is their innocence. No one saw the clouds building on the horizon."

She thought about that. "They were too busy indulging themselves. But speaking of those clouds, that's one of the things about Louis XVI. That furniture, the black and the gold, very dramatic and the straight lines. It almost prefigures Art Deco in the structure, I mean the basic structure. I admire it but I truly love Louis XV. Oh, why am I babbling on about this?"

"Because it is fascinating. We look back with knowledge. They lived in the middle of it and poor Louis XVI, following Louis XV, handsome but not the smartest; even had he been, a powerful man couldn't have stopped the madness. Something about the Bourbons. Even the brightest ones couldn't see the noses on the front of their faces."

"Who can? When it gets that irrational, that rigid, who can?" She looked again at the desk. "Then again, people can't seem to leave one another alone."

"Mmm. When I'm alone in the shop, I look around at the paintings on the wall, the fabrics, the colors, and I imagine they lived in simpler times, but of course our ancestors did not." He motioned to her. "Come sit with me a bit. We'll both repose in beauty."

She sat on the dark green Chesterfield sofa, a safe choice for anyone interested in comfort. "When did you open the shop? Remind me?"

"In 1989. I think sometimes about painting the year on the door but 1989 on a building constructed in 1780 seems out of place." He grinned.

"You have a point there." She smiled at him.

"I had no idea what I was doing. I put a down payment on the house, opened the shop, and prayed."

"Your prayers were answered. Wouldn't you do it all over again? Just take a chance. I wonder about people living their gray little lives hagridden by the need for security, and of course there is no security. And we think it all comes from money." She inclined toward him. "Americans put their faith in external things, but then again the French Revolution, the times of poor Louis XVI, the cover was Liberty! Equality! Fraternity! But don't you think it was really Envy! Spite! Greed!"

"Sister, you should teach history."

"I'd be drummed out of the academy in no time." She laughed.

"Do I think envy and greed drove those thousands forward? I do. No different in Russia or Spain or you name it. The cover is always something noble-sounding, perhaps that way no one will hear the guillotine."

She grimaced then looked back at the desk aglow in the soft light. "Fortunately, that Louis had no idea."

"No, but he certainly had beautiful mistresses." Harry laughed.

Sister laughed with him. "I'd think one woman would be bad enough."

He lowered his voice. "Ah, no female equivalent. Are there some kept men? Well, yes, but it's not the same. Powerful men want beautiful women. Think of them as flesh and blood Ferraris."

"That's awful," she said with feeling.

"I don't doubt that it is but it's real. It's a form of parading your power, as was some of this furniture. You could afford it so you did and showed it off."

"Well," she thought about it, "yes."

"People don't change, Sister. We've known what we are for thousands of years but we can't admit it. How did we get off on this? I'm trying to sell you the Louis XV desk."

"Oh, we can and do wander."

"Speaking of wandering, how about Morris Taylor driving through Cindy Chandler's fence? His deterioration was upsetting, even though I can't stand him or his brother. It was shocking to see him."

"It was. There's such a strong resemblance among the Taylors. Morris and Drew look a lot like their father. Morris's son looks like the family. You see that often in horses and hounds, as well."

"Karma."

"What?"

"Morris. It's karma." He spoke with conviction.

"I don't know." She did think the Taylors had been foolish, but best to stay neutral.

"I believe in karma. I also hope I do not suffer a protracted decline."

"I hope so for both of us. There's a lot to be said for a quick exit."

He folded his hands over his chest, leaning back. "Did you notice the *bois de bout* marquetry, stylized, floral design?"

"I did. Beautiful."

"I will sell you that desk for twenty thousand dollars." He reached for her hand. "Were it original, the price would be over one hundred thousand but this is a reproduction made in the eighteenth century."

"Harry, I don't have twenty thousand in my back pocket."

"How about stuffed in your bra?"

"You're incorrigible." She laughed at him.

"True, so true, but you need that desk. Think of Uncle Arnold."

"I'm thinking of Gray."

"Oh poof." He waved his hand. "A little kiss here and there, plus it is your money."

"Oh, I know but he is so careful. If I overspend he gets the vapors."

"Accountant." Harry waved his hand again. "But have you ever noticed neither he nor any other accountant suffers the vapors when it's something they want?"

"I have seen him agonize over a new pair of Dehner boots. Ultimately he did get measured for them. His feet demanded it. But he does suffer. Mercer, his cousin, shrewd about profit, could get him to spend money. It was hard to believe they were related."

"Oh, how I miss Mercer. You know Aunt Daniella comes into the shop, she brings Yvonne Harris with her. Aunt Daniella can be so naughty. Mercer was like his mother." A pause followed this with a wistful postscript. "I do so wish Yvonne would be naughty."

"Ha." Sister giggled, a beguiling trait.

"I have the answer. Ask Gray for half for the desk. Make him part of it. Tell him to meet you halfway and rip his clothes off. That will work."

She flopped back on the sofa, holding a pillow to her lap. "You are the worst man I know."

"Oh, I hope so." He grinned.

She responded, "I do want the desk. You knew I would. Can

you give me time to try and figure this out? I have mourned Uncle Arnold's desk ever since it was stolen years ago."

"Take your time. Think it through. There are other Louis XV desks out there but none as beautiful as this one. I mean it."

"I will."

"And I promise I will not sell it to anyone but my respected and beloved master."

"You forgot to add foolish."

"Oh, Sister, what good does it do to be sensible all the time? You only live once."

CHAPTER 5

February 26, 2019 Tuesday

The entrance to Horse Country in Warrenton, Virginia, bespoke established grace. The floor beckoned with a checkerboard black-and-white pattern, a pattern beloved for centuries in Northern Europe, especially in the estates of the powerful. The wall immediately to one's right glowed with mahogany bookshelves, the top shelf a half moon, and above that a line of boots, and whatever Marion Maggiolo, the proprietress, wished to put up there. The shelves themselves yielded treasures, be they old signs from long-ago times or more boots, nineteenth-century books bound in red Morocco with gilt edges. Sometimes a two-seater carriage sat before all this, other times, a comfortable chair covered in the store's signature zebra print, although not a true skin, of course.

The store also reflected a quiet version of success. So if you walked in there, you felt successful.

The rear of the store housed the library full of more leather-bound books, some rare and expensive, others from the 1920s–1950s and well within reach of a modest budget. Jenny Young oversaw the library.

Wherever one looked beautiful items sang a siren song, the old silver in the north cases, the clothes along the south side of the wall or in the smaller room off and behind the northern cases, clothing designed to make people look good, perhaps too good. Scarlet then as now made men bedazzling. To say scarlet led women to their ruin might be an overstatement. If the lady had discipline perhaps she could resist. Then again, why resist?

Such ideas were not swirling in Jean Roberts's mind, for closing time neared. She began to put items away for the night. Business had been booming since cubbing, which starts after Labor Day, and the Christmas season had proved intense and profitable, thank you, Jesus.

"Your scarlet isn't in yet," Jean called out to Harry, who was meandering down an aisle.

"I know. I know. I came up to see you."

"Then why are you walking away?" she fired back.

"These goods are irresistible."

"I thought I was irresistible," Jean replied.

He stopped and smiled. "Indeed, but an irresistible woman can get you in more trouble than silverware."

"Both can melt your credit card. Why didn't you call? I could have saved you the trip. Your scarlet should come in next week."

"I really came up to see you. Take you to dinner. I have a proposition and we are old hunting buddies. I can trust you."

Jean, hands poised over the jewelry case, blinked. "Harry, you've never said anything like that to me before."

"I should have. I should have told many people how I value them but here I am telling you."

"Thank you. I have an Ashland Basset meeting. It should be over at seven-thirty."

"How about I meet you back here at eight? Lower parking lot. We can switch to my car."

"Sounds good."

He peered into the case where Jean was removing jewelry to a special drawer for safekeeping. "That is stunning!"

"Erté. Pavé diamonds and emeralds. Obviously."

"Let me see it."

Jean pulled the ring out of the case. She was going to put it in the drawer anyway. Slid it toward him.

Harry carefully picked it up, inspecting the workmanship. "You know, Jean, there are people today who don't know who this designer was."

"There are people today who don't know a lot of things and don't care. Like history, for one." Pointing to the ring she inclined her head. "Design is of no consequence to them."

Bedazzled by the ring, fox's tail over his nose, Harry shrugged. "I think it's always been that way. Doesn't matter the century or the country. Few people care about aesthetics in any form."

"You're right."

He slipped the ring, a woman's ring, on his pinkie then wiggled his fingers. "Perfect. Jean, let me wear this, I'll give it back when I pick you up for dinner. But just for two hours let me commune with Erté."

"Well, okay."

"You girls get the best stuff. You know that." He grinned at her.

"Depends on the stuff," Jean shot back.

Harry nodded in agreement, stuck his hand in his pocket, waving to Jean with his other hand.

He picked up a dish on a counter, fox in the middle, placed it back, then disappeared downstairs.

Roni Ellis glanced up. "Harry, are you in the market for a new saddle?"

He smiled. "No. Just looking. Can't help myself."

He then climbed back upstairs.

Six on the dot, Jean walked through the aisles, called down to Roni, "I'm on my way to my meeting. See you tomorrow."

"Have a good one." Roni came to the foot of the stairs. "Tell Diana Dutton hello." She mentioned one of the members of Ashland Bassets.

"Will do." Jean slipped on her coat, tied a necessary soft wool scarf around her neck, left by the front door, locking it behind her, for it was closing time. Harry walked out with her, kissed her on the cheek as he opened her car door for her. "Eight o'clock."

By six-twenty Roni had double-checked the main office. Everything seemed in order. She looked behind the main counter. The jewelry had been removed from the glass case, put into a shelf, the shelf Jean locked. Roni did not unlock it. No need. Jean never failed to secure valuables.

"Well, good." Turning off the lights, Roni opened the front door and was greeted by a blast of February night air. She closed it, locked it, and sprinted to her car parked in the top lot.

The next morning, February 27, Wednesday, as the sun was

rising a bit after quarter to seven, the light provided a soft glow, given the lay of Alexandria Pike. Few cars rolled on the paved road. That would pick up in a short time.

One early riser, Shirley Resnick, coffee cup in her right hand, slowly drove down Alexandria Pike toward the imposing cream-colored courthouse at the top of the hill.

She blinked. Stopped in the middle of the road. There was no traffic. She turned right into the bottom parking lot of Horse Country. Placed her coffee cup in the cup holder of her Accord. She sat for a minute, put the car in park, let the motor run, and stepped outside to the crumpled man sprawled at the bottom of the steep side stairs rising to the front door.

Kneeling, she slightly shook him. He was stiff. She recoiled, hurrying to her car, picked up her cellphone, and dialed 911.

CHAPTER 6

February 27, 2019 Wednesday

Noon

Sister, across from Walter Lungren, waited for Betty to join them for lunch at Keswick Club, where Sister was a founding member. Not much for country clubs, she remained fascinated by the history of this one. The golf pro was murdered in 1977. Killer never found.

Betty swept in the door, took her seat facing the Pete Dye golf course.

"Even in February it looks good, doesn't it?"

"Soon as spring comes I am challenging Pat Butterfield to a match here. Then he'll challenge me at Farmington Country Club," Walter predicted.

Pat Butterfield was the senior master at Farmington Hunt Club, which back in the twenties hunted at the newish country club, Farmington Country Club, under the leadership of the intrepid Berta Jones. Farmington, built as a working plantation by Jefferson, one of his few private architectural commissions, fell upon hard times in 1927.

Keswick had also fallen upon hard times. Bought in 1990 by Sir Bernard Ashley, it was now restored far beyond its former glory.

"He's pretty good. Good tennis player, too." Sister smiled, for she adored Pat.

"We've all endured a rough season." Walter folded the menu, knowing what he wanted.

"Rough. Yes. But how about what's happened at Horse Country? On the morning news." Betty's blue eyes opened wider.

Sister noticed a stiff wind crossing the practice green. "What happened?"

"Harry Dunbar was found dead at the bottom of the side steps," Betty answered.

"What?" Sister was aghast.

Walter nodded. "No signs of foul play, I suppose that's the proper term, but the back of his head was cracked. No one knows but the simplest explanation is he slipped going down to his car, fell backwards."

"Hmm." Betty sighed. "The steps are steep but not that steep and there is a handrail."

"I was in his shop Monday. He was full of the devil, as always. Oh, I am so sorry." Sister reached for her napkin to dab her eyes.

"I'm not forecasting a murder," Betty said. "No rain, a light frost, yes. He could well have slipped, but wouldn't it have to be a ferocious one? You know, head over heels, or in this case heels over head, and then crack." She said this almost with relish.

"Hard to say. He was in great shape, most of us foxhunters are.

I assume an autopsy will be requested." Walter handed Sister his napkin. "Sister, I am sorry. I didn't know you all were that close."

"You hunt with someone for years. You do become close even if unaware of it. He had such energy, such a playful sense of humor."

"It is a shock." Walter tried to sound comforting. "It was a most unlikely fate."

"Here's what I don't understand," Betty said. "Why was Harry Dunbar at the stairs? The interview with Jean Roberts and Roni on the news, both said the shop was locked. Roni was the last one out. Not a sound inside. It's quite odd." Betty liked Harry well enough but she did not feel close to him.

"Not so odd," Sister posited. "What if he forgot the time, needed something, say ShowSheen?" She mentioned a special shampoo for horses. "He ran up the steps, realized the shop was closed, and then ran down. Slipped."

"Maybe he was lurking in the store." Betty was not giving up.

"Betty, for God's sake, what would Harry Dunbar be doing hiding in Horse Country while Roni locks up? What's he going to do? He's rich enough. He doesn't have to steal a thing." Sister wanted to get their lunch meeting going, and try to forget this terrible news if only for a short time.

The meeting, short, hunt club odds and ends, followed lunch, which Sister couldn't eat. Betty realized her friend was truly upset about Harry's death.

After a half hour of discussing the budget, a shortfall thanks to the terrible weather, they adjourned, promising to think of ways to raise money.

Once home Sister sat next to Gray on the sofa in the library. He put his arm around her.

"You never know, do you?"

She wiped her tears with a Kleenex. "No. Honey, I believe a swift death is a blessing to whom it befalls. For the rest of us the shock is fierce. He was so full of life."

"That's the wisdom that comes with age."

"I qualify." She weakly smiled.

"Never." He kissed her cheek. "These last years the hunt club has lost many older members. It was their time. I've lost a few of my old college buddies. Again, it was their time." He pulled her a little closer. "Do you ever find yourself looking for old friends in the hunt field?"

"Often. There are times when I think I'll see my son, and he's been gone since 1974. A movement out of the corner of my eye, a nicker. I don't know what it is but it startles me. It doesn't really depress me."

"I have no idea how you recovered from such a loss. How does anyone?"

"You just do. Look at Aunt Daniella. You know she misses Mercer. The two of them were inseparable, but you go on."

She mentioned Aunt Daniella's late son, a bloodstock agent who died in his late fifties. Unfortunately, in his death he had help.

Gray shook his head. "Those two fought morning, noon, and night and loved every minute of it. Every evening the two of them sitting in her living room with huge glasses of bourbon in their hands. No one knew bloodlines like Mercer. When you think about it, that's what killed him. He knew too much."

"That's one murderer who will never get out of jail."

"Idiot," Gray said. "Why do people think they can lie, cheat, steal, murder, and get away with it?"

"The delusion of the criminal mind. I won't get caught. Even the crime bosses, worth multimillions, either get caught or killed. Maybe this comes down to people never learn."

He rested his head against hers. "Sometimes I wonder how it would be if Mother had lived. She was beautiful like Aunt Dan, but reserved. Mom was devoted to me and Sam."

"Mothers and sons. It's an ancient dialogue." Sister smiled. "Fathers and daughters. Incredible bonds for the most part. I mean, I love Tootie like a daughter. She's been with me since seventh grade when she boarded at Custis Hall. I love her but it's quite different with a girl."

"Seems to be. I love my son, I see him maybe once a year, but I relish his success. And I can understand why he wanted a veterinary practice in Colorado once he finished up his residency in Nebraska. If I had a daughter I think she could wrap me around her little finger." He laughed. "Even Aunt Dan can do that."

"What about me?"

"I'm putty in your hands."

"I'm glad to know that," she truthfully confessed.

He changed the subject. "Would you want to know when you would die?"

"No. Never. Would you?"

"If it would give me time to tell people I love them. I'm not so good at that. I try. I tell Aunt Dan. I sometimes tell my brother. Not often."

"You tell me."

"That's different. You're the woman I love. I can say things to you I'd never say to anyone else, even Sam."

"What about Mercer? He was gay. Didn't that make it easier?"

He shook his head. "No. Loved him. He was my cousin but his being gay didn't mean I'd tell him more than another man. God, when we were kids we would beat the crap out of each other. Sam, too. Mercer had such an eye. Like his mother. He and Aunt Dan can pick the perfect colors for people, fabrics. I can't."

"You always look good," she complimented him.

"Mercer taught me a few things but I have to work at it."

"Mercer and Harry were friends."

"A lot in common. Funny, because Harry had a sort of artistic streak, I don't know what else to call it, people thought he was gay, especially because he was friends with Mercer. He wasn't. Harry was a gentleman but he used women."

"What do you mean?"

"Oh, he'd pay attention to those with means, with fabulous houses."

"Gray, I never heard of him behaving in a low fashion." She turned to look up at him, he was slightly taller than she was.

"He didn't, but I think many of those women, older and widowed, fostered hopes. But I can't say as I ever saw him, um, make promises. I do think Harry Dunbar escorted more widows and single ladies to hunt balls than any man living. I often wonder how many sets of scarlet tails he wore out."

"Which reminds me. Men love evening scarlet and so do women. Would you ever wear evening scarlet to a white-tie affair?"

Gray replied quickly. "Of course not. Honey, you know the invitation cards have to have *evening scarlet* on it. If it is white tie only then you wear regular tails. Granted, evening scarlet is expensive but . . ." He paused. "We all want to show up in our evening scarlet with our girl on our arm."

"How would you feel about a woman in evening scarlet?"

"Hmm, if a master I'd get used to it but that's as far as I would go."

"I agree. Half the fun of a hunt ball is to see the men who have earned their colors in scarlet and the women in black or white evening gowns. Nothing looks like that."

A silence followed this as they snuggled into each other.

"Honey, I am sorry about Harry. You two could make each other laugh and he was good in the hunt field."

"Bold." She inhaled deeply. "I'll miss him." She wiped her eyes with another Kleenex. "I realize what wonderful people are in my life and Harry was one of them. But these are tears of joy. I know how lucky I am. I hate to think of anyone leaving life but my life really began the first time you kissed me. The sun came into it. I couldn't live without you."

His eyes glistened then he laughed. "Don't make me cry."

Then they both laughed.

CHAPTER 7

February 28, 2019   Thursday

A long wide pasture alongside a wide hard-running creek set off the house at Heron's Plume. As it was, this southernmost fixture proved rich in scent, soil, architecture, and owners. Over the last two hundred and thirty years the bottom land made a fortune for Robert Pickett, the first owner of what was then two thousand acres. Growing hemp, corn, wheat, and pumpkins, Pickett made enough money in those early years to throw up good brick barns and a two-story brick house flanked by brick outbuildings. Brick, easy to come by with all the clay in central Virginia, stood the test of time. So did the Picketts, the last male perishing in 1932. However, Madelenine Pickett had married a railroad baron by the name of Ingram. As the male Pickett line died out, the female surged ever onward. The family gave generously to nonprofits, especially those of a medical nature, the county rejoiced in the longevity of the blood. Proto-feminists, subsequent female Ingrams took the Pickett surname.

The brick gates into the estate, white topped with a flat pediment, had a large brass square on the right gate with script saying "Heron's Plume." The left gate, another polished brass square, simply announced "1789."

The curiosity of it was that the gorgeous place never hosted foxhunts. No one really knew why. Sister always viewed it with lust but was far too well-bred to ask for permission to hunt.

Fate stepped in. Walter Lungren, in a fit of upgrading his wardrobe, happened to be shopping in the upscale men's store in Barracks Road Shopping Center. Chalmers Perez, a pile of fine cotton shirts on the counter, stood in front of him. They chatted amiably, knowing each other superficially. Chalmers grabbed his chest, gasped, and dropped. Walter, a cardiologist, knew exactly what to do, literally saving Chalmers's life. He also visited him every day in the hospital, for the fifty-two-year-old man needed a new heart valve. As the heavyset Chalmers recovered, the two men talked about his diet, his need for exercise, and more, his need for discipline. Without prompting, the owner of Heron's Plume, married to a Pickett, Dulcie, invited Walter and Jefferson Hunt to ride at the old estate, which he promised overflowed with foxes.

He was right. As this was Jefferson's first year on the grounds, a learning year, lots of hunt and peck, they discovered Mr. Perez told the truth. Foxes ran Heron's Plume.

The day, overcast and cold, was at least relatively dry. Weevil, as soon as the small field mounted up, cast east along the creek, hitting in two skinny minutes. The red never showed himself but he wove in and out of brick buildings that had once housed cattle, horses, hay, plus a sumptuous chicken coop. Humans could live in that chicken coop, for Chalmers's chickens were his pride. If the chicken was rare and a good layer, he had it.

The fox doesn't live that can resist a henhouse but no fox could dig under, climb over, or even try to lure one of these prized birds into his jaws. However, this fox was smart enough to circle the glamorous pile then shoot straight up to a low ridge, maybe one hundred feet high, total lift above sea level maybe six hundred feet, enough for the wind to slice you if it was blowing, because once up there you were exposed.

The hounds felt it. The wind was really only about twelve miles per hour. Enough.

Trees, mostly evergreens, for the deciduous trees were denuded, swayed in the wind.

"Where'd he go?" Tattoo cried in frustration.

"He either dipped on the other side or he has a den up here." Dreamboat, nose down, kept trying.

As the ridge ran from the southwest to the northeast, the other side was on the northeast from where the pack and the field climbed up. Wind usually hits from the west, northwest in this part of Virginia and it was hitting now. The pack dropped over the path on the ridge but scent had been blown to bits.

Weevil wisely clucked to his hounds, "Come away."

They did, following him down. Once down in the lovely valley again they hit another line and damned if this fox didn't run to the buildings, as well. Each time the pack encountered a building it slowed them, for they followed the scent around the building.

The fox literally ran rings around them.

"Woodpile." Dasher flew over the hard ground, as the line had warmed a bit when the sun hit it.

Screaming, they flew behind the big hay barn, behind the

grain silo, and hooked a right turn, winding up at the woodpile, where the fox scurried into a perfect den. So many creatures frequented the woodpile that the fox could chat up most everyone and even pretend to hunt mice. Given that the owners left so much grain on the floor of the silo, this fellow and most of the other foxes could eat leftover oats all winter. The corn had filled a smaller silo. That brought everyone in, too.

The wind picked up, Sister felt her face tingle plus the cold made her eyes tear.

Riding up to Weevil, she wiped her eyes. "Cast crosswind. That should get you all the way down to the farm gate. Then you can turn into the wind, which will be a bitch, I know. Hunt back to here. If we don't get anything, call it a day."

"Yes, Madam."

Sister watched as he turned Showboat, Shaker's handy Thoroughbred, crosswind, the pack obediently following their huntsman, who gave a little toodle.

Cindy Chandler, riding with the Bancrofts up front, liked being on this new fixture despite the trying conditions. The field, small, reflected her curiosity and her pleasure. The idea that after two hundred and thirty years Heron's Plume finally was open to them seemed like magic.

Betty Franklin mirrored the pack, riding on the other side of the creek branch, which at this point was wide, roaring.

Tootie, on the left, followed outside the fence line, for the club had not yet had time to build jumps. After a half hour trying, Weevil lifted the pack, heading back to the trailers.

Everyone was glad to reach them, including the hounds. Chalmers and Dulcie hosted a breakfast.

"You look great," Walter praised Chalmers once inside the house.

"Thirty pounds." He patted his ever-shrinking stomach. "Dulcie's support; well, everyone I know has really helped me. After that heart attack, I knew I had to change my life."

Dulcie, his wife, had taken up walking with him, preparing meals low in fat, and watching his portions. She'd lost weight as well, not that she really needed it but most women feel they do so she was happy.

"Funny how we ignore ourselves until Mother Nature smacks us in the face. Here I am, a doctor, and I can be as pigheaded about my health as the next guy," Walter confessed.

"You look in good shape."

"Oh, I'm okay but my wind isn't what it should be, and I use the excuse that I don't need to run because riding takes care of it but it doesn't. Need to use all those muscles."

"What are you two talking about?" Sister joined them. "This is a lovely breakfast. Thank you."

"Dulcie loves to entertain. But we are glad to have you. You know, it's a beautiful sport, although I don't envy you on the cold, cold days."

"I'm not sure I do either." She smiled. "Ah, here comes Gray."

Now the four of them talked about an uproar in the county schools over T-shirts and ball caps with slogans, which upset some kids or at least their parents.

"I'm for school uniforms," Sister posited.

"Saves money. Everyone looks alike and no one will be wearing naked ladies or whatever the offense du jour is."

"Naked ladies are a lot more fun than the more political stuff," Chalmers mused.

"Maybe not if you're a young woman." Gray smiled. "Don't know. As far as I know, images of naked men haven't lured women into wearing them."

"Of course not. All a young lady has to do is stand there. You all would take off your clothing in a heartbeat," Sister teased.

They laughed, chatted more, then Chalmers asked Walter, "How about Harry Dunbar? What a loss. You know he was often called to museums as an expert. I think the number of those is dwindling."

"Maybe it depends on the period," Gray spoke up.

"Chalmers, we all knew Harry for years. Good rider. Slowing down a bit but he said business had picked up. Cut into time," Sister said.

"Sure does." Walter nodded.

"But didn't Harry and Drew Taylor get crossways years back?" Chalmers wrinkled his brow. "Honey, come here." He turned to Sister, Gray, and Walter. "She remembers everything."

Dulcie recapped the distant uproar concerning Mrs. Taylor's furniture legacy. "Well . . ." Chalmers paused. "Drew was precipitous."

"Because he didn't get other opinions?" Walter had just been out of school when all this happened.

Betty, joining them, piped up. "The Taylors feel they are old Albemarle County and should be treated as such. Harry, for his own cover, should have suggested they get other opinions."

"Betty, why? The brothers told him to clean out the junk; their words, according to Harry. If that's what they thought, how can they come back later weeping and wailing? His exact word, *junk*."

"That may be so but no one likes their ignorance made plain, do they?" Betty touched on human vanity. "And then again, Harry was in a business where a four hundred percent markup isn't unusual. I'm not saying antiques dealers are crooks but they can slap on whatever price the market will bear." She paused. "I guess that applies to anyone."

"Art galleries are worse. Dulcie and I tread carefully."

"You have such extraordinary work, but you and your wife specialized."

Dulcie beamed. "We love sporting art, most especially of dogs. When we started collecting it was such a tiny group of people and the work was pooh-poohed by the modern art set. We got hooked. There's a world of talent in those paintings, as well as emotion."

As if on cue, a magnificent Gordon setter padded into the room to stand by Dulcie.

Her hand dropped to its well-proportioned head. "Living art."

Gray smiled. "Sister feels the same way about her hounds."

Sister inclined her head, saying to Dulcie, "Don't we all love our animals and think they are the best?"

Dulcie nodded then asked, "Did you buy that Louis XV desk? Oh, Sister, those inlaid flowers, that marquetry. Really divine."

"How did you know about that?" Sister noted Gray's slight intake of breath.

"Oh, you know Harry. He called me down to look on his big computer at the American Kennel Club gallery museum. He said if I ever or we ever wanted to sell any of our collection there was a growing market. He knows the AKC director; of course, Harry knows, or knew, everybody. I can't get used to putting him in the past tense."

"None of us can, honey." Chalmers put his arm around his wife's shoulders.

"Fate? His time? I don't know. But I do know as I grow older these goodbyes do not get easier. If anything they cut deeper," Sister replied.

"The human condition." Gray reached for her hand even as he wondered about the desk.

As the foxhunters left with thank-yous, Gray lingered to talk to Chalmers about a D.C. legal firm they both knew; Sister, outside, took Betty by the elbow, vigorously propelling her toward Betty's trailer. "What is the matter with you?"

"What do you mean?"

"Harry was not a cheat. The Taylors got what was coming to them."

"He was hardly a saint."

"Well, who the hell is?" Sister's eyebrows raised.

"I believe he did take advantage of people. And maybe the Taylors had it coming, given their social pretensions, but still. He could take advantage of people."

"Only if he disliked them."

Betty had to smile. "There is that. I always thought we should have bought Drew's mother a tiara, the queen of western Albemarle County."

They both laughed as they reached the truck cab. Gray had walked out of the house.

Sister, under her breath, "Do not say a word, one word, about the Louis XV desk."

"I didn't know anything about it. Why didn't you tell me?"

"Betty, I'm suffering the tortures of the damned over it. I was working up my nerve. I can't throw money around like that."

Hand on the door handle, Betty, voice low, "How much?"

"Starting at twenty thousand. I might have whittled it down. But still."

"A lot. Then again, you have never gotten over your uncle's desk being stolen. I don't know. I can't hardly pay the damn electric bill for the shop and then the house. Gets higher and higher every winter. But if I had the money, you know what, I'd buy whatever I damn well wanted." She opened the door, climbing into the cab. "I'll drop off Magellan. Outlaw had a fit this morning when I tacked up his pasture mate instead of him. Spoiled brat."

"He's a great horse."

Betty smiled, ear to ear. "He is. I'm spoiled, too. Hey, I'll clean tack tomorrow. I've got to run to the shop because clients are coming in for wedding invitations. Mother of the bride and bride are not in agreement. I can't stick Bobby with two warring women."

"Wise. I'm glad to hear true invitations are coming back. You said business was picking up."

"Thank God. Nothing looks as good as a beautiful piece of paper, exactly the right color with exactly the right font and ink color cut into the paper. None of this computer or thermographed stuff. It's cheap and it looks cheap. For the great moments in life you need correct invitations."

"That's why you and Bobby do the hunt ball invitations. Okay, see you tomorrow."

Sister opened the door to her dually, ten years old and in great condition because she fanatically took care of it.

Betty drove off in front as Gray fired up the engine. "Louis XV."

"Well, I didn't buy it so I saw no point in bringing it up." What a fibber she was right then.

"Janie."

She shifted her weight in the comfortable seat. "All right. I would have told you but I can't buy it."

"Is it as beautiful as Dulcie said?"

"Ravishing."

"Ah."

They rode in silence, the farm was at the most now twenty minutes away hauling horses, going the speed limit.

"Honey, it is your money."

"And you are an accountant." She smiled at him because she knew it took a lot for him not to make a judgment. "I often wonder why it is that the two men in my life were and are money men. My father was good with money, as well."

Gray, eyes on the road, thought about this. "Well, when you deal with money you see how easy it is to lose it. Ray," he named Sister's husband, who died in 1991, "could make money. He was a stockbroker. He had a kind of aggressiveness about money that I don't have. I'm not a risk taker, not with money, anyway. I'm not cheap, at least I don't think I am. But I'm careful. Sam is careful, since he cleaned up his life. Mercer was more than careful. Mercer was shrewd, but Aunt Daniella? Now, there's a gambler at heart."

They laughed, for Aunt Daniella proved fearless in all respects.

"What I think is funny is that both the men in my life were, are very masculine."

"Toxic?" He turned slightly toward her.

"I try to avoid those ever-evolving ideologies," Sister answered. "For whatever reason I am attracted to manly men. Broad shoulders. Little hips. Hard muscles. Strong faces. Big egos. Well, enough ego to succeed. I mean, Gray, does anyone get anything done without an ego? I have one. I'm better at hiding it."

"You're a woman. You're better at a lot of things. But are you smart to hide your ego? You are."

"Those heated replies from young women about how the qualities that make a man successful are derided in a woman, how a man can be called driven, while the woman is a bitch. That sort of thing. It's true but it's changing."

"It's changing, honey, because men can't get the job done anymore. In truth, I don't know if anyone can. But back to men and women. You do look good, sugar; oh, you do look good and you affect me. I'd be a liar if I said you would have the same impact if," he paused, "you had not been blessed by nature. We are animals, after all."

"You sweet thing." She smiled. "Yes, we are animals. In some ways that's as it should be. In other ways, a difficulty. But then again, we are of a certain age. For my generation a man needed a 'can do' attitude. He needed to carry the weight willingly in his way and we needed to carry it in ours. Of course, it is different now but I'm no different."

"For which I am grateful. We're supposed to change with the times but some changes . . ." He shook his head. "I don't know."

"Well, I do know I could never be with a drag queen." She stopped then laughed. "Sometimes in an evening gown I feel like a drag queen."

"You mean I can't raid your closet?"

"You'd never fit in my clothes."

"I don't have your beautiful breasts."

"The moustache wouldn't help."

They laughed, happy in each other's company. They really were the right two people for each other.

Gray pulled the trailer next to the stable so they could unload without fuss. Tootie and Weevil were in the kennel. Their horses were turned out, rugs in place. Betty's trailer, neatly parked in the parking lot, displayed how muddy the roads were.

Horses unloaded, cleaned up, given fresh water and a bit of warm mash, were then turned out to romp before nightfall. Those four-legged kids could have hunted hard and long but they needed their playtime, equine gossip, and kicking up hind legs. What a life.

Finally back in the house, showered, hunt kit neatly hanging on pegs in the mudroom to be brushed tomorrow, boots polished, the two sat down for a restorative drink.

Golly, Raleigh, and Rooster plopped on the floor of the kitchen. Sister boiled water for tea. Gray made himself a simple scotch, two ice cubes with a splash of water. He could never understand why one would buy good liquor then besmirch it with stuff. Maybe an orange peel or lemon but that was the limit.

"Sure you don't want a hot cup of tea to chase your drink? I still feel a bit of cold in my bones."

"I can take the cold. It's the rawness. Snow is easier than cold rain."

"Is." She brought her cup to the table.

"Baby," he rarely called her that, "take me to see the desk.

Now, I am not going to pay all of it, but if it's that special we can split it. You have talked about that desk ever since I returned from D.C."

"Thank you, honey." She took a sip. "Gray, it goes so fast, both life and money."

CHAPTER 8

March 1, 2019   Friday

Aturn-of-the-century low brick building that had once housed a large machine shop on Harris Street in Charlottesville had been turned into offices, including a high-tech gym. A long polished hallway ran through the center of the old rectangular edifice.

Sister Jane opened the door to the gym, stepping into the hall at either the wrong time or the right time. Exiting in front of her, Drew and Bainbridge Taylor were deep in an argument.

"I am not doing this," Bainbridge spat.

"It's your father." Drew glanced up, seeing Sister.

Bainbridge turned in the direction of his uncle's line of sight. "Don't listen to him. I know they've all said I stole the silver from Pitchfork Farm, was loaded on drugs. It's a lie. All a lie."

Sister calmly replied, "Bainbridge, gossip is part of life. First of all, why would you steal the family's silver? Makes no sense."

"Right." He stood straighter, feeling justified. "Mother left half the silver to me, half to my father, plus I am his heir. My ever-so-solicitous uncle took the silver into his house when my father began to lose it."

"I did. Dammit. I don't know who goes in and out of your place. A bunch of worthless assholes. They'd steal the silver."

"So I'm a worthless asshole, too?"

"Gentlemen, I think I should be going."

"No." Bainbridge implored her. "You're a straight shooter. I've known you all my life. I want you to hear my side of the story. I'm not as bad as Uncle Drew makes out."

"Bainbridge, I don't think you're bad but I do think you need a career that can focus your many talents. You always were a bright kid." She exaggerated, for Bainbridge was only average.

"Which is why he got into so much trouble." Drew unfortunately opened his mouth as Sister was soothing his nephew. "He was doing okay until his mother died three years ago. Fell apart, and of course that's when Morris began to really unravel."

"I did not fall apart."

"I'd say losing your job, drinking and drugging, hanging out with those worthless people count as falling apart." Drew sounded triumphant.

"Might I ask what you two are doing here?" Sister hoped to steer the conversation away from recrimination so she could get the hell out of there.

"An Alzheimer's support group. I asked Bainbridge to come."

"That was good of you, Bainbridge." She smiled at him. "I suppose there are stages one can recognize. I don't really know."

A silence followed this then the young man said, "He's crackers. Knows who we are but babbles. Sometimes I know what he's saying. Other times he's talking to Mom even though she's been gone three years. And sometimes, and this is really weird, Dad talks to his own mother. I can't stand it."

"He can't help it." Drew's anger was rising again. "And I want the silver back. It's not safe in your apartment."

"No. That's my half. What if you sell it behind my back?"

Sister folded her arms across her ample chest more to rest her shoulders than anything, for her one shoulder ached in the cold. She ignored Bainbridge's accusation, grateful that Drew did also. "Is it possible that you all could talk to the coordinator of the support group without other people there?"

As she said this others filed out from the room, which with the door open could be seen to have couches and comfortable chairs placed for people to relax and talk.

"I don't need therapy and I'm not a drug addict. Yes, I did have some Oxycontin in my system when I was picked up but I took that for pain. I'm not hooked." Bainbridge's lower lip stuck out.

"I certainly hope not," his former master rejoined. "I don't so much think of this as therapy, but you two have a lot on your hands. If you could cooperate it might be easier."

"The truth is, Bainbridge, your father will never get better, only worse."

"You don't know that. He has lucid moments. And maybe there are new drugs coming on the market that could help." The young man sounded both defiant and sorrowful.

"Amazing breakthroughs happen it seems every day. How wonderful it would be if one happened in time for your father. He was a brilliant man," Sister remarked with feeling, then looked at Drew. "Is he ready for structured living? I mean, do you think it's gone that far?"

"No." Bainbridge raised his voice.

Ignoring him, his uncle replied to Sister. "You saw him at Cindy Chandler's. He knows his old friends, he more or less knew where he was, even if he didn't remember how he got there. But change terrifies someone with dementia or Alzheimer's. Were I to move him into a home I think he'd lose it. At least with me he lives in familiar surroundings. He still knows who I am. He has his own room with those things Bainbridge and I took from his old home and we put up a lot of pictures of Sharon." He mentioned Morris's deceased wife.

"I see."

Bainbridge hopped in. "He chirps around at the house. My worry is he'll wander off. His nurse doesn't keep track of him plus he's expensive."

"We aren't at this point yet but when it comes I will have to put him away or lock him in his bedroom. I know it sounds awful but there will be items that he might still recognize. As for his nurse, what else can I do?"

She nodded. "Well, I don't envy either of you this decision."

"And the best home is in Gordonsville. Really the best and that's about eight thousand dollars a month. There's always a doctor on the premises."

"Drew, I had no idea." And she didn't either.

"There are quite a few worthy homes in the area but they begin to, well, diminish when the price falls under four thousand a month. With four thousand you usually get a doctor at least part-time and the staff has trained nurses as well as a locked ward for the most advanced cases. Then, too, if you don't have a physician, drugs can't be administered. The patient has to be driven to the hospital and that frightens them. Then you must restrain them. Sister, it's awful."

"You're not putting my father in a straitjacket."

"I hope not."

"Is there no way the two of you can formulate some kind of schedule? Bainbridge, maybe you can be closer. A care schedule. Hire nurses when the deterioration accelerates?" She wanted to be helpful.

"Up to a point." Drew sighed. "That's the goal. To keep him home. Now that Bainbridge has moved back from town I'm a bit more hopeful."

Bainbridge hated the loss of money for a nurse, as his father had done very well. His pension payment alone could keep a small family comfortable. "There's enough money to keep him home."

Drew hesitated. "With some prudence."

"How did Morris get the keys to the Range Rover?" Sister changed the subject.

"Oh." Drew sagged against the wall, his legs felt tired, he felt tired. "That was, as you know, Sharon's pride and joy. He bought it for her brand new even as she was failing fast. Still looked brand new. Her lung cancer progressed so rapidly. He bought it for her and she could only drive it maybe six weeks after that. But Morris parked it by her bedroom window when it came to that so she could see it. We thought we had all the keys. I use it sometimes. Well, a lightbulb must have gone on upstairs." He pointed to his head. "Because he found a second set of keys he must have put away when she died. Odd. I mean it is odd how information comes and goes."

"I should have the car," the tall young man grumbled. "You have everything."

"When I'm sure you aren't drinking or snorting whatever up your nose, maybe."

"I don't do cocaine."

"I guess you don't have to. Aren't opioids stronger?"

Without a word, Bainbridge turned on his heel and walked out of the building.

"Dammit," Drew cursed.

"I'm sorry, Drew."

A long sigh escaped his lips. "Half the silver does belong to him. He told the truth about that. But that silver originally belonged to his great-grandmother and he shouldn't break up the pattern. God knows, Sharon would turn over in her grave."

"She left too early," Sister wisely commented.

"Funny, Bainbridge is a grown man but he needed his mother. Father and son never did see eye to eye and now with this deterioration, it's worse. He needs to help care for Morris and I really need to find round-the-clock staff soon. I mean, if Bainbridge were to lose his temper I'm not so sure he wouldn't haul off and clock Morris."

Sister's hand flew to her chest. "Oh, I hope not, Drew. I truly hope not. Talk to Bainbridge. This might be an opportunity to make amends."

"Elder abuse is rampant and unreported. Ask Ben Sidell." He named the sheriff, and did not respond to Sister's suggestion.

"We only have a few hunts left. Seven, I think, Tuesdays, Thursdays, and Saturdays, then we hit St. Patrick's Day, and poof, end of the season. Come on out more. It will do you good."

"I'm so busy. Actually, business is picking up."

"You need to get your mind off this. You have a fixture card. Next Saturday after this, we'll be at Tattenhall Station. Give you time to adjust your schedule."

"You know, you're right. What if the fox crosses over to Old Paradise?" He named a fixture owned by Crawford Howard, who had had his fights with Sister and Jefferson Hunt.

"We've reached a rough accord." She beamed.

He smiled. "Now, that is an invitation."

CHAPTER 9

March 4, 2019   Monday

"You've had your hair lightened." Sister squinted at Jean Roberts.

"No I haven't. That's gray mixed in with the blond."

"I believe you. Thousands wouldn't," Sister fired back to laughter.

Marion, Roni, Martha Kelley, Suzann Strong, and Debbie Cutter crowded around the desk in the main office to eat a delivered lunch. Marion, overloaded with work, had wanted to see Sister but lacked time for one of those wonderful leisurely lunches. So the girls ordered in and sat around as Jenny Young manned the front desk, running back and forth to the back room. As it turned out, their timing was good. Only a few people straggled in on a cold rainy day during lunch hour. Courtney Nashwinter and Emily Kendrich remained downstairs, as they'd had an early lunch. Given the expensive tack downstairs, someone needed to be there.

"Is this rain ever going to stop?" Debbie wondered.

"Only if we build an ark," Suzann quipped.

"As the oldest person here I go on record to swear this is the wettest six months I have ever lived through. Started during cubbing. You all know I hate to cancel a hunt and I've canceled plenty, including Saturday's," Sister said.

"What a downpour." Jean nodded. "We didn't take the bassets out yesterday. Can you imagine trying to run with the mud up to your ankles?"

"Miserable," Roni agreed.

"You are the only person who has been in here since Harry Dunbar was found who hasn't asked about it." Jean wiped her fingers on a napkin. "I know you want to know."

Sister sighed. "A loss. I so liked him."

Roni was the first person on the scene after the cop showed up. "We all did. He was a good customer."

"Tell me everything." Sister leaned back in her chair, knowing "the girls" wanted to talk.

Marion interjected, "Here's the thing. I've heard this ad nauseum but I'm starting to think like a law enforcement officer. Listen carefully. Are any details changed or has a newer memory popped up? In crisis people do forget things."

"True," Sister agreed.

"I have no story to tell. That was my half day," Martha Kelley added.

"Aren't you glad?" Suzann asked.

"Of course I'm glad," Martha replied.

"All right. You first, Roni."

"Actually, Shirley Resnick found Harry at the foot of the stairs. You don't know her. She's the registrar at the courthouse and always goes to work early. Anyway, there he was. She called the police. They called Marion but I came in a half hour early that day so I actually got here first."

"And?" Sister inquired.

"And, who knows? The night before there was nothing unusual. Dark and cold outside. I locked up the store. If someone was hanging around I think I'd have known."

"Wait. Let's be orderly." Jean took over. "Roni and I, on Tuesday, February 26, were the last ones in the store. I left a bit after six as I had an Ashland Basset meeting. Roni was downstairs, I called that I was leaving and I did. Earlier, Harry had walked through the store, looking at the silver, then he went downstairs. We left together, going our separate ways."

To the sounds of paper plates hitting the metal wastebasket, Jean remembered. "That new Melton he ordered. The one tailored perfectly. He asked about it. I said it would probably be ready next week. As always he had energy, noticed everything."

Marion nodded. "Harry bought a heavy-weight Melton with satin lining. Waterproof. Lovely cut. Only needed a tiny nip along the sides to be sleeker. Even the length of the arms was fine. With the tailoring, almost nine hundred dollars. But those things last."

"The good stuff does. I still wear a vest of my grandfather's," Sister agreed. "What will you do?"

"Sell it in the store, I guess. What really costs is the top hat, those run five hundred and ninety-five dollars," Suzann said.

"His top hat was fine," Jean interposed.

"Because he took care of everything. The only reason he bought a new coat was that the seams finally gave way on his old coat, which was used when he bought it. I suspect the coat was about sixty years old, that heavy cavalry twill." Marion appreciated fabrics.

"Can't find heavy twill now. Have to buy it used. Coats. Breeches. Drives me crazy," Jean remarked. "We are out there in all kinds of weather, rain, snow, sleet. We do better than the Postal Service. Nothing is as good as the old stuff. That's why Harry wore his old coat until the threads gave way, I swear. There really is no such thing as improvement in hunt clothing."

Marion slightly shook her head. "Yes there is, Jean. The coats for hot weather are better. Well, they are new, really. We didn't used to have the heat we now have during cubbing. It's crazy, isn't it, the weather? Anyway, I found heavy twill."

They all nodded.

"Back to Harry. Did he appear sober? He could put the stuff away but he wasn't a drunk. Just wondering."

"He was fine," Jean said.

"He slipped and fell." Roni then added, "There was one oddity." She thought a moment. "He had in his pocket a fox ring designed by Erté."

"The one in your Christmas catalog?" Sister's eyes lit up, for she had truly wanted it. "The one where the tail is wrapped over his snout? How beautiful."

"That's the one," Jean said, offering no explanation about Harry and the ring.

"I told the detective who questioned me, all of us." Roni stood up to go back to work. "We hadn't sold the ring for Christmas. It wasn't in the case."

"You think he stole it?" Sister thought this odd. "He'd never do that."

"Then he would have had to be in the store after it was closed and he would have to have known where we keep jewelry after hours." Marion leaned forward. "The detective chose not to tell the media this and I don't quite know why. But it really makes no sense."

"Well," Sister drawled. "It does if they suspect this may not have been an accident."

"He was at the foot of the stairs with the back of his skull cracked." Jean's eyes opened wide.

"It's still possible that it wasn't an accident. Cracking some-one's skull can be done with a number of tools." Debbie looked at Jean.

"Oh, Debbie." Martha also stood up. "I've been rereading Agatha Christie lately. She'd be with you on this."

"And you?" Sister glanced up at the pretty woman.

"It does seem unlikely. More like bad luck."

CHAPTER 10

March 7, 2019   Thursday

The sound of water often brought relaxation to people. Not at Mill Ruins, an old Jefferson Hunt fixture formerly owned by the late Peter Wheeler, who had bequeathed it to the hunt club. Walter Lungrun lived there now on a ninety-nine-year lease. The waterwheel turned, water flying off the paddles. Usually the sound pleased Sister but today as she rode by, all she could hear was water. Water melted from snowbanks and overrunning streams. Water dripped off trees. Water, water everywhere. You could drink most of it, unlike the Ancient Mariner.

The temperature climbed to fifty-three degrees Fahrenheit. She had crawled into bed last night with a frost already on the ground and woke up to what felt like the tropics after the recent cold weather and the snows.

Good thing the drive into Mill Ruins had been paved years ago. Potholes here and there testified to the fact that it should be paved again, but what an expense. Better to fill in the holes once winter had truly passed, which according to the calendar was to be at 5:58 PM, March 20, the vernal equinox.

Much as Sister wanted to believe that day would herald spring she knew better. Central Virginia suffered some bitter April snowstorms. March was always tricky but you knew that. April really could break your heart. She thought of T. S. Eliot, of course. As she was quoting "April is the cruelest month" to herself, a deep voice broke the recall.

"Somebody I don't know," Asa sang out.

Noses down, hounds trotted. While they liked to know whom they were running, any scent was better than no scent, plus this was an opportunity to learn the ways of a new fox.

Mill Ruins, large in scope, hosted foxes. The senior fox, James, lived behind the mill itself. What a crab. The other foxes, most newer to the area except for Grenville, a gray, who lived in the back acres called Shootrough, gave the old red fox a wide berth.

James bitched and moaned about everything and everyone. Hated the hounds, naturally. Felt the other foxes were worthless unless they gave the hounds a run. Why should he trouble himself? They'd come sniffing around his den and those younger hounds had no respect. They would sass him in his own den. Nothing one could do about the young whether fox or hound. Useless, a useless younger generation. The world, of course, was coming to an end. He predicted this often and at high volume. Even Walter, sitting in his den after a long day at the hospital, could hear the furious barking as James would walk around the house, the barns, pick up anything edible, then retire to his den.

The pack walked straight to his den once Weevil mounted up. Shaker had given Weevil an overview of the various fixtures as well as the quarry. Weevil called hounds away. They were now trotting down the farm road curving behind the old mill, splitting two large wet pastures, fenced in.

Hortensia, a gray, had crossed the pastures perhaps twenty minutes ago after a night out, not so much from hunger as from boredom. Game of any variety, who had been staying warm and dry in their dens, were glad for a little sunshine and warmth. She'd crossed the pastures, the road, the old farm paths all over the place, to return to a sturdy outbuilding almost as old as the mill itself. Two stories high with a sharply sloped roof, this was the original hay shed, with hand-hewn beams. Walter still stored hay in the top story, some of it filtering down below, where he put up two hay wagons and a small tractor for pulling same. Hortensia heard the hounds so she didn't curl up in a hay wagon that she liked, as an old horse blanket had been tossed in the back. Instead she went to her den, warm enough although she was tired of being inside. At least on the hay wagon she could look about.

Hounds picked up her line, crossed the sodden first field, leapt over a stout jump in the fence flanking the road, moved across the soaked road to clear the matching jump opposite the one they had just taken.

All Sister could hear apart from her hounds was squish, squish, squish. Aztec, her chestnut Thoroughbred, slipped in a few places. A good athlete, he kept his balance, but slipping and sliding on horseback works your obliques. Sister knew her muscles were working overtime.

At the corner of this pasture a tidy three-log jump had been built in the fall by Walter from a downed tree. In a perfect world each side of fencing would have a jump in it but that takes energy and sometimes money if one had to purchase the materials. As a large gum tree had come down, he'd cut up the trunk, placing the jump in the corner, where it served double duty.

Weevil skidded a bit into it but Kilowatt easily sailed over without a rub. Seeing the bobble, Sister rated Aztec, trotting now. They, too, made it over, only to sink into mud on the other side.

She could hear the oomphs behind her but no cries or cussing. The field proved small on Thursday, which was normal. Given the terrible weather all season, most hunt fields were small throughout the Mid-Atlantic.

Hounds ran now. She kept up. They passed a small shed, tidy, for Walter loathed debris of any sort. Hounds reached the impressive hay barn, doors open a crack for ventilation.

"She's here," Little Tinsel yelled at the den opening.

All the hounds crowded around as Hortensia moved farther back in her den. Why did they have to make so much noise?

Weevil dismounted, squeezed through the slightly opened doors to go to the den. Hortensia's fragrance filled his nostrils. He praised the hounds, patting each one on the head, and blew "Gone to Ground," leading them out, where he closed the doors a bit more.

Mounted up he moved back to the pastures, intending to go all the way to the rear of the fixture if needs be.

Yvonne and Aunt Daniella drove slowly on the road.

"Sure glad this is four-wheel drive," Yvonne said.

Behind her, Bainbridge drove an older Tahoe that was one of his father's cars. Morris sat in the seat next to him. He knew what was going on.

On his horse, Drew, in a light twill scarlet frock, stood out. He had a coat in every weight, as well as a black frock. He looked wonderful and as he was the only man in the field apart from Walter and Sam Lorillard, Gray being up in Washington, Drew had the ladies all to himself, a pleasant event.

Freddie Thomas rode with him, an even more pleasant event.

On they struggled. One footing mess after another. Reaching the creek at the bottom of the road now crowded by two thick woods, Yvonne opened her window a crack.

"My God, it sounds like Niagara Falls," she exclaimed.

"Does." Aunt Daniella also ran down her window a bit. "Warm but the air's raw. Do you notice?"

"All that moisture." Yvonne closed the window. "I'm not going down there. I know this machine can go through that crossing but I'm not doing it. Let me pull over to the left. What's his name again . . . ?"

"Bainbridge."

"Another snotty Virginia name?" Yvonne raised her eyebrows.

"As a matter of fact, yes, but not as snotty as the Taylors would wish. Bradford beats them hands down."

"Bradford."

"From 1607. Came with Captain Smith."

"Ah." Yvonne smiled. "You know them all, too, don't you?"

"Well, not from 1607, but yes. Blood still matters here and strange to say, but do remember I am a Laprade and a Lorillard. And remember we were free blacks resented, I fear, by many. The old families all have tales of bad behavior, woe, sickness handed down from generation to generation, but in the main, they still contribute."

"Even the crazies?"

"Define crazy." Aunt Daniella folded her arms across her chest.

"You know, clinical depression, stuff like that."

"Well, of course, until recently we didn't have such terms, but take for instance many of the old families, even back to the seventeenth century. Most saved their family Bibles. What we now call manic depression runs in many families. If you read what happened to a few of them in each generation it's apparent, and yet every generation of the old families contributes. Just the way it is."

"Well, your family has."

"Thank you but we, too, have had our misfits. For us it usually involves someone speculating. Land stuff or stocks. A strain of gambling seems to run in the Laprades. Now, I do not bring this up in front of Gray. He is so upright. It is possible to be too good."

"He certainly made a name for himself in Washington."

"Of all the places to be too good." Aunt Daniella laughed. "Ah, there goes Bainbridge, passing you as slowly as a mother hen."

"Nice-looking."

"The Taylors are, and they greatly resemble one another through time. But the Taylor blood has watered down. Not stupid, mind you, but just enough money to make bums out of them."

"Ah, yes. Lots of that in Chicago."

"Do you ever miss Chicago?"

"I miss the symphony and the theater. Forgive me, Aunt Daniella, but Richmond is not a cultural powerhouse."

A long pause followed this. "No. Richmond will catch up. Personally, I like the Philadelphia Museum of Art, as well as their Natural Museum. Much as I appreciate the cultural resources of New York, I like Philadelphia better. Maybe it's because they were Quakers and opposed slavery early."

"They did, didn't they?"

"Before the war, New York had something like over thirty thousand slaves. I do tire of the posturing."

"The times in which we live."

"Yes, everyone is a pure little daisy in a field of bullshit." Aunt Daniella laughed.

"So unimaginative, isn't it?" Then Yvonne laughed, too. "I mean, I truly hate my ex-husband but that video of him on the sofa with the two women he was keeping, the further away I get from it the funnier it is. No pure daisies there."

"Better than a financial scandal, that's for sure."

"Do you hear anything?"

Aunt Daniella pushed the electric button and the window purred down. "Not a thing. Sister will need to call the hunt. They've been out over an hour. They did have a small run. The footing is only going to get worse. Stop while you're ahead."

As if hearing the older woman, Sister called Weevil to her. After a brief discussion he lifted hounds. They walked back to the trailers. No one was disappointed, for the footing worried everyone. There wasn't one rider who didn't have splashes of mud all the way up on their breeches. Coming in early reflected how bad the weather had been for this hunt season.

The breakfast in Walter's home brought everyone in, including Morris and Bainbridge, as well as Yvonne and Aunt Dan. People thoughtfully removed their boots, as a large bootjack stood by the door in the mudroom, aptly named. From there one stepped into the narrow side hall. The floors, clean and dry, didn't feel too cold.

Sandwiches, cheese, fruit, brownies, and hot drink, as well as a bar, kept people happy. As Walter was a bachelor, no one expected him to mount a breakfast. Also it was a Thursday hunt, usually small.

Walter, no cook, had picked up food from Foods of All Nations the night before. Small though the store was, it had high-quality items.

Betty, a whizz at making good coffee, did that while Walter acted as the bartender.

Bainbridge kept away from his uncle but he did keep his eye on Morris happily chatting up Freddie Thomas, Tootie, any woman at all.

In the middle of this he walked over to help Betty.

"I've got it, Morris. Would you like some coffee?"

"How about a cup with milk and sugar for Sharon?"

She stopped a moment, for Sharon had been dead three years, then replied, "Tell you what, Tootie looks as though she could use a cup. Why don't you give this to her and I'll refresh the pot."

As he walked away happy to be useful, Betty motioned for Drew to come over, and she told him of the exchange.

Drew thanked her, walked over to his brother while looking for Bainbridge.

"Did you enjoy the hunt?" Morris asked Tootie.

"Slick as an eel out there, but hounds found."

"Heard them." Morris grinned. "Excuse me. I need to bring a fresh coffee for Sharon. You know how raw air affects her." Tootie simply nodded in agreement.

Then he stopped at Sister. "Where's Sharon? She needs coffee."

"She's not here right now," Sister stated, not as surprised as she might have been.

"She has to be. Sharon always comes to a hunt breakfast."

"Come on, Morris. How about if I walk you out to the car," Sister volunteered.

"No."

Drew, having overheard the exchange, frantically looked for his nephew, now talking to Weevil. "Betty," he called out. "Can you get Bainbridge over here?"

"Of course."

Bainbridge came over as Betty explained to Weevil what was going on. Sister joined Betty, hoping this would go smoothly.

"Come on, Dad, let me drive you home."

"Not without your mother." He snapped his lips together.

"Come on, Dad."

"No!"

Drew took one arm as Bainbridge took the other. "Come on, bro."

"I want my wife."

"Dad, Mom's been dead for years." Bainbridge couldn't think of what else to say.

All of a sudden Morris howled, tears flowing. "No. No. You lie."

Now Walter came over. The three men managed to get Morris out the door, despite resistance from the screaming, crying man.

Sister watched the ordeal.

Betty tapped a glass on the table. She tapped again.

"Folks. Morris was asking for Sharon. He had forgotten she'd passed on. There's nothing anyone can do. I'm sure you understand. This is unfortunate."

Sister whispered to Betty, "Bless you. I was a bit confused."

This announcement was followed by a moment of silence and then people started talking to one another again.

Tootie joined her mother. Aunt Daniella was avidly talking to Sam.

"It must be awful for him to have to relive these events," Tootie said to her mother.

"He's a big man. I'm glad he didn't throw a punch."

"Walter is bigger."

"That he is. Do you need anything?"

"No, Mom. Do you?"

"Yes. If you get by the pet store, will you buy a box of Greenies and maybe some dog crackers for the fox?"

"Sure."

"And when you bring them, bring Weevil. We can all have a visit."

"Okay."

Yvonne put her hand on Tootie's arm. "I can never tell you enough how much I love Ribbon. She is the best present anyone has ever given me. She knows how to sit now. We are working on stay."

They heard more yelling from outside.

Weevil walked out to see if Walter or Drew needed help. Sam followed.

No one really knew what to do. They didn't want to hurt Morris. Finally they hoisted him into the Tahoe.

The men watched in silence as Bainbridge, locking the doors, drove off.

CHAPTER 11

March 8, 2019 Friday

"Happy International Women's Day." Betty, a package in hand, walked into the barn at Roughneck Farm.

Sister looked up from the stand-up desk in the corner of the warm tack room. "A present?"

"Thought we should celebrate being women." Betty placed the wrapped box on the beat-up coffee table in the middle of the floor.

The tack room, filled with cleaned bridles hanging on special wooden mounts on the wall, the saddles aligned on saddle racks, smelled wonderful. The actual size of the room was twenty feet by fourteen feet, not exactly a double stall but close enough.

Betty sat down in one of the director's chairs, "Roughneck Farm" embroidered on the back.

Sister closed the desktop, sat down next to her. One chair was green with gold piping, the other was a reverse. The dark green hid much of the dirt, mud, and saddle-soap smears.

Sister picked up the box, rattling it.

"Something is moving."

"This comes under the category 'useful.'"

Sister smiled at her dear friend. "My favorite kind of gift. Although I have never been adverse to diamonds."

"And I have never been able to get that through my husband's head."

"Those earrings you wore at last year's hunt ball dazzled. Something got through his head."

Betty smiled seraphically. "Hauled his ass to Marion's and stood him right in front of the jewelry case. I did buy him a Tattersall vest. He'd shredded his old one. Anyway, wouldn't you know, earrings from Horse Country appeared on my birthday. So, I suppose something filtered into that male brain."

Sister carefully unwrapped the package. "You underestimate him."

"You know," Betty somewhat seriously replied, "I probably do. Are you going to keep that wrapping paper?"

Sister was folding the paper carefully. "I like the fox masks on it."

"Open the present!"

"All right. All right." Sister opened the box, peeled back the colored tissue. "What is this?"

"You need new paddock boots."

"Oh, Betty." She quickly untied her beat-up paddock boots, seams splitting, to try the new one on her right foot. "Perfect."

"Put the other one on and walk around. See how they feel."

Sister did as she was told, stopping in front of the full-length mirror, which she and everyone else in the barn used to check their turnout. "Real leather. These feel broken in."

"Of course it's real leather. I know you, remember?"

Glancing down at her feet. "So you do. They feel really good."

"Space-age stuff inside. Absorbs shocks and also will help right where the stirrup iron rests. Tell you what, after a long day's hunting, I can feel that stirrup iron on my feet even in the shower."

"Yeah, I can, too. Betty, these are exactly what I need." She bent over to kiss Betty. "I would never have thought of a present for International Women's Day."

"I probably wouldn't either, but Wednesday when we were cleaning tack I realized your paddock boots really had breathed their last."

"I have a hard time throwing anything out that I might be able to use for one more day."

"That day has passed." She leaned back in the chair a bit, tilting the front legs off the ground. "The temptation is to wear out full-length boots, but I've got to make mine last and so do you. The cost!"

Sister sat down, pulled off one paddock boot to more closely inspect the interior, poking her finger into the springy insert. "That's the truth. You know there's nothing like a pair of bespoke boots when you're out there for hours. You and I should drive to Omaha to see rows and rows of lasts. Be kind of fun, say, to call up Ginny Perrin," she mentioned the senior master at Deep Run, "and say I saw your feet."

"Have you ever seen Ginny incorrectly turned out?"

"In forty-plus years, no." Sister took off the other boot, fascinated with the interior.

"You, too. Perfect."

Sister smiled. "Thank you. I really care. When I receive an invitation, the first place I look is at the bottom to see the dress code."

"Me, too." Betty laughed. "And now that I've lost the weight I can actually wear nice clothes."

Betty, with effort, lost over thirty pounds years ago and she fought to keep it off. Her husband, Bobby, did not evidence as much discipline.

"You look good in the hunt field, too. I mean, why do something if you don't do it right?" Sister put the shoes back in the box. "I'm taking these to the house and I'm going to use saddle butter to keep moisture out."

A long sigh escaped Betty's lips. "Miserable year. Worst I can remember."

"We'll get through it. Tootie, Weevil, you, and I walk those hounds in all but a roaring downpour. They are not sitting in the kennel getting fat. Lest I forget, Shaker creeps along in the car." Now she let out a long sigh. "Betty, I'm worried about him. The neck brace is off but the doctor says one vertebra remains slightly out of alignment. He doesn't tell me. I have to worm it out of Walter. That was a hell of a hit he took before Christmas."

"He's damn lucky he didn't break his neck."

"Yes, he is."

"He's been generous to Weevil. You know how hard it must be for him to see a young man hunting the pack. Sister, what are you going to do if he can't hunt anymore? If that vertebra stays out of line, one bad fall and the result could be paralysis. Obviously, that's the worst-case scenario but none of us wants to see someone we have followed and care about come to a sorrowful end."

Sister reached over to hold Betty's hand. "Haunts me. For two reasons. One, I have worked with him for decades. We're like Tweedledee and Tweedledum. Two, I will be the person who must tell him."

"We can only hope for the best. On a positive note, I like hearing Ray's horn in the hunt field." Betty mentioned the horn that Weevil used, for it had been Sister's husband's horn when Big Ray hunted the hounds.

"That deep timbre." She dropped her friend's hand. "Before I forget it, and I can't thank you enough, when did you get these wonderful paddock boots?"

"I called Horse Country after you'd left Monday."

"Sneaky."

"I figured someone had looked at your feet but I know your size is 7½. Easy size to find. Then I called yesterday to tell Jean, who picked up the phone, to send the boots, FedEx Air. Anyway, they got here in time."

"Betty, you never fail to surprise me. Thank you again. I really need a pair of paddock boots. It's easy to muck stalls, tack up, and mount. I will never ride in sneakers."

"Given the tread, it's not very smart." Betty smiled, happy she'd made her friend happy. "Oh, Jean bounced me to Marion. As always, we talked about everything under the sun, then she told me a strange thing. Harry Dunbar's body had been examined, of course. No one has claimed him yet. I expect the authorities are searching for family."

"Did she say anything about the Medical Examiner's report?"

"Well, his fracture, right there at the base of the skull where the step hit him, or more precisely he hit the step, is pretty clean."

"First joint, I recall. Ice on the steps, not mud."

"Marion, insightful as she always is, remarked that he must have hit hard and backwards. A clean break, so to speak."

"Fastidious even in death."

A pause followed this then Betty stretched her legs out straight. "International Women's Day. Do you feel solidarity?"

"Uh, Betty, I never thought of it, so I guess I don't. Well, let me take that back. Women's issues, as long as they stay women's issues, will never be resolved."

"Child-care centers in corporate buildings won't solve anything?"

"Yes, it will make it easier for working women. But keeping women focused on child care, reproduction, child rearing means we are not addressing the military budget, countering the Chinese as rivals, trying to find new ways to produce energy with less pollution. See what I mean? And what about the Federal Reserve? The money supply. Those issues are a long way from child care. Would child care make women's lives easier, help them in the workforce? You bet. Would it bring women one step closer to power, real power? No."

Betty tapped the arm of the chair. "Sometimes I forget how logical you are."

"Some would say cold."

Betty laughed. "Yes, as women we're supposed to emote all over the place and wear our hearts on our sleeve."

"Not this woman," Sister replied. "If there's one thing my own mother taught me that I keep in the forefront of my mind it's 'The secret of success is to watch the donut not the hole.'"

At this they both laughed.

CHAPTER 12

March 9, 2019   Saturday

"Let me drive," Shaker demanded.

"No," Yvonne said with conviction.

"You're going too slow," he complained.

"Behave yourself." Aunt Daniella turned around in the front seat to stare at him.

"Damn, woman. Let me drive."

"I will do no such thing." Yvonne wasn't having any of it. "You are lucky to be in this car with this damned woman."

"Two damned women," Aunt Daniella echoed.

"The pack will hit a fox right about now. They're crossing the back of Tattenhall Station. If they do I predict he'll turn right, go across the road."

"Well, Shaker, they haven't hit yet, and if they do I'll be behind them but out of the way of the field." Yvonne was learning the fox-hunting terminology.

He flopped back in his seat with a groan.

Dragon, nose to the ground, hoped to find a fox right where Shaker predicted scent would be. Turned out, no scent. So the tricolor, vain hound pushed on, forward. He liked to be first, which infuriated the other hounds because he'd rush over if anyone else found scent, to take credit for it.

Aero, in the middle, a young entry and surprisingly steady, kept on. She paused, stern waving, then moved on.

"False alarm?" her littermate Audrey wondered.

"I don't know. This isn't fox scent but it's something, something moving." Aero put her nose down again.

Audrey checked. *"I don't know. Kinda heavy."*

"It's not deer." Aero puzzled over this.

"If we opened on deer, we'd be in trouble." Audrey rolled her lovely brown eyes.

Dragon, stopping a moment to look behind him, saw the two youngsters noses down, trying to work scent out. He rushed to them.

"Got 'em!" His deep voice rang out and the pack ran to him, for Dragon was usually right.

Sister on Matador, a flea-bitten gray, sat a bit taller. Now the whole pack opened, tearing off, but Sister noticed Diana, near the front, lacked her usual brio. Something was up, yet the hounds roared. Matador shook his head, so off they ran.

Behind followed a large Saturday field. The season was drawing to a close, and given that it had been bedeviled with weather so bad it had been lavish misery, lots of people came out on horses not as fit as they might be. Neither were the people.

Yvonne stopped the car when the pack blasted into the woods, heading south. The large pasture at Tattenhall Station offered a lovely gallop. The woods, not so much. The trails, wide enough, forced Sister to improvise, for given the winds of the last few weeks, trees crisscrossed the paths. One could jump a trunk and Sister did, but if the crown fell across the path the branches presented obstacles. She found a way around but had to forge into the woods, fight her way through low-hanging branches from standing trees, then get back onto the path.

Infuriating.

Up ahead, Weevil encountered the same difficulties so he was now far behind his pack. Fortunately, the hound's music boomed through the woods. Betty, on the edge of the right, almost on the road where Yvonne was creeping, was the only staff member with hounds. Tootie, on the left, battled through even more difficult territory than her master or huntsman. Giving Iota a rest today she rode Kasmir Barbhiya's bombproof horse, Nighthawk.

Kasmir and Alida rode a pair of matched bays, looking for all the world like a hunt team poised to win at the Warrenton Horse Show. Neck and neck they rode, exhilarated by the pace and each other.

Behind these two, Freddie Thomas kept her eyes open. In a situation like this a clever fox often doubled back since the ground was in his favor. One need not hurry quite so much.

Drew Taylor rode behind Freddie, with Walter behind him. Usually Walter rode tail but today that task went to Sam Lorillard. Walter had asked him, for he rarely got to ride up near hounds, and Sam readily agreed. Gray rode with his brother. Both marveled at the roar. Behind them came Bobby Franklin, who knew the territory as well as his own kitchen. He had to, as with Second Flight he had to go around obstacles then make up the time.

On and on they rode. They blew past Beveridge Hundred and Yvonne's perfect dependency on the estate, which she had bought and given to the Van Dorns' life estate. Millie, their dog, watched from the window but said nothing. Millie also had life estate. Little Ribbon in the dependency was ferocious.

"Get out of my territory. Mine. Mine. Mine," the Norfolk terrier bellowed.

No one heard her but it made her feel better.

On and on, finally shooting out of the woods across another meadow, this one wild, and back into more woods. If they kept on at this pace they'd be past Whiskey Ridge, barreling into Skidby, the southernmost fixture in the Chapel Cross area.

Then nothing. Hounds threw up. Weevil finally reached them.

"Good hounds." He praised them.

Betty appeared on his right but still no Tootie, fighting her way through a ravine, a small creek running through it.

Weevil waited, as did the field, some breathing heavily. Finally Tootie appeared. He waved her to him, as he did for Betty.

Weevil folded his hands together, dropping the reins onto Hojo, Shaker's horse, a true huntsman's horse; Hojo stood there waiting for the next move. "Ladies, coyote is legitimate game but I can't say as I really want to chase them."

"You want us to whip the hounds off?" Betty tried not to sound incredulous.

"No, of course not, but if you see a coyote wave your crop in a circle around your head. I like to know my quarry. Naturally, I'd like to settle them on a fox."

"Coyote scent is heavier." Betty knew her stuff.

"Yes, it is." He sighed then looked back at the field, smiling. "A few of our people are the worse for wear."

Betty tilted her head over at Yvonne's parked car about one hundred yards away on the road. "So's Shaker, I could hear a few harrumphs when they came alongside me, because Aunt Dan lowered the window and made the V sign. She's incorrigible."

"What now?" Tootie asked.

"We're pretty far from Tattenhall Station. Let's cross the road and hunt back until we reach Old Paradise's corner, then we can cross and get back on Tattenhall Station."

"Was a helluva run." Betty smiled.

"Was." Weevil smiled back, a dazzling smile in a divinely handsome face.

Aunt Daniella, noticing from afar, murmured, "Oh, to be twenty again. Actually, I'd settle for fifty."

Yvonne shook her head. "My money is on you regardless of the decade."

"You sweet thing," Aunt Daniella said, beaming, "but is he not one of the most beautiful men you have ever seen?"

From the backseat, "Men aren't beautiful unless they're light in the loafers."

"Shaker, don't be hateful." Yvonne looked in her rearview mirror at the dispirited man, for he so wanted to ride.

"Well."

"Shaker, my son was gay. Be careful." Aunt Daniella again turned around.

"Mercer never acted gay and—"

"All right, let's agree to disagree." Yvonne now also turned around. "Or how about this? A man can be beautiful to a woman but not to a man. Fair enough?"

"Fair enough." A lightbulb clicked on in Shaker's head. "But here I am in a car with two beautiful women, maybe the most beautiful women of your generations. I mean, how can a guy be with a beautiful woman and not get an erection? I don't understand."

"Please don't tell me you have an erection." Aunt Daniella exploded with laughter.

"You know what I mean." He did have the good humor to laugh at himself.

"Turning back," Shaker noted. "If he has sense he'll cross the road and hunt back on the west side."

"He's doing exactly that." Aunt Daniella watched.

Yvonne stayed put as riders crossed in front of her, most of them nodding or touching their crops to their caps.

Diana, walking next to Trooper, said, *"Coyote."*

"I don't know that I've ever smelled one," the younger hound replied.

Cora, another older, wise hound, now walked with these two. *"Used to be only foxes, reds and grays. But the coyote are moving in and I have never smelled so much black bear. Things are changing."*

"Why?" Trooper asked.

"I don't know," the solid hound replied. *"Sometimes when the humans are talking and we're in the feed room I like to listen. I remember once Sister and Shaker talking about what it must have been like when the Blue Ridge was full of wolves and elk, huge elk. Before our time and theirs."*

"Lift your heads," Diana instructed.

"*A faint whiff.*" Cora now put her nose down. "*If we can reach the shade, might pick it up on the ground.*"

"*But it's a cold day. Why has scent lifted?*" Trooper sensibly asked.

"*Trooper, if I had the answer to that I'd be a genius.*" Diana moved a little faster, and sure enough, the line now stuck.

The run lasted fifteen minutes, which doesn't seem like a long time but fifteen minutes when you've run hard for a good forty minutes began to separate some riders from their horses. People were tired and didn't know it, and those who didn't know their mounts were tired were in worse shape.

Staff horses were not, as staff kept their horses fit, riding them to do so in sleet, in snow, in bitter cold, and worse, in cold rain.

Sister pulled away from her field, looked around, then slowed down a bit.

Hounds made it to Old Paradise, where their fox disappeared. Weevil crossed the road, took the coop in the fence line, and they rode back to Tattenhall Station, some walking their horses. People straggled in for the next half hour.

Drew rode with Freddie as they replayed the day's hunt. His top hat gleamed. Being a gentleman, he helped her untack then did so for his own horse. Some women would refuse the help but Freddie, born and raised in the South, believed a woman should allow a man to assist and thank him for it.

Southern men needed to do for women. It's the way their mommas raised them, and you don't cross Momma.

Drew walked over to Freddie to chat her up as they approached the station.

"Sometime I must tell you about my trip to Patagonia. Freddie, it's incredible, unspoiled."

"I'd love to see it but it's so far. An expensive trip."

"Worth it."

"You've been traveling a lot these last few years," she noticed.

He smiled, looking down at her, revealing perfect teeth thanks to a good dentist. "Turned sixty a few years back and decided it's now or never."

He held the door for her as she asked, "Next trip?"

"St. Petersburg. I want to see all those treasures."

"Thank you, Drew. If I had some extra money I'd go to Wyoming for the summer. Different kinds of treasures." She smiled and walked forward.

A moment's pause, then Drew walked up to a visiting guest, introduced himself, and got her a drink. Drew never missed a pretty girl nor did they miss him in his scarlet.

As usual Kasmir and Alida opened the station for the breakfast, wonderful odors from the kitchen enticing everyone to move faster.

Kasmir had remodeled the station for events and dances and the place was perfect. All the old Victorian bric-a-brac filled the outside and inside. A big potbellied stove kept the place warm. Of course, there was electric heating, too, but that old stove threw out the heat. The bar was mobbed. Gray brought Sister her usual tonic water with lime.

The mood was high. Being able to go out put everyone in a good mood and the runs lifted spirits.

Betty, Weevil, Aunt Daniella, and Yvonne chatted, while Skiff

Kane, Shaker's lady friend, had slipped away from work to see him for a moment.

Sister, who only ate an English muffin before hunting, usually returned famished. She sat down at the long table, set with winter berries, creative arrangements all done by Alida. Gray put a full plate in front of Sister then sat next to her with his own.

"Thanks, honey. I was too tired to get my own food today."

"It's the cold. A raw day. Beats you up." He clinked glasses with her as others also sat down, plates loaded.

Betty and Drew sat across from each other as Yvonne, Aunt Daniella, and Sam sat next to Betty. Soon the two set tables were full and the kitchen staff buzzed in and out, seeing to the guests. An attractive female guest sat at the end of the table. She and Drew exchanged glances.

Yvonne watched this with a knowing eye. Kasmir, very rich, fulfilled the responsibility of someone with means; he entertained. While this was also part of noblesse oblige, it brought people together. Entertaining fulfilled a communal as well as political function. More good things came out of dinners, cocktail parties, foxhunting, golf, sitting under an umbrella at the beach with friends, than ever came out of a legislative or business meeting. Smart people knew the real business was always done elsewhere and Kasmir was phenomenally smart as well as well educated. Oxford.

Cecil and Violet Van Dorn, the former owners of Beveridge Hundred and former foxhunters, who still lived at Beveridge Hundred on life estate, were there, along with the Bancrofts, both couples in their eighties. While the Bancrofts still rode, the Van Dorns did not, but neither wanted to ride in bad weather anymore. The place was filled with hunters and what Betty Franklin called muffin hounds, the people who showed up for the breakfasts and were always welcome.

Betty asked Drew, "Did things settle down?"

"Oh, finally. Got Morris home. He has moments where he realizes his memory is gone. What surprised me was Bainbridge taking him to the hunt. He really is trying to make amends with his father."

"Is he going to rehab?" Betty bluntly asked.

Drew shook his head. "No."

Aunt Daniella, sensitive, said, "Bainbridge might do better on his own. Some people aren't made for the talking cures. Clearly not your problem, Betty." She laughed.

Betty laughed at herself. "Oh, I know. Me and my big mouth. Which reminds me. I was talking with Marion at Horse Country and Sister can vouch for this because she had been talking to Marion as well. We were wondering how Harry died. Was it a fall or did something trip him up?"

"Oh, Betty, don't start," Aunt Daniella chided her. "No murder theories."

"I'm not saying that. I'm only saying it's unusual."

"If it was murder I would like to congratulate whoever did it," Drew ungallantly said.

A moment of silence followed this, then Sister quietly replied, "Drew, that's beneath you."

His face flamed crimson. "I—I'm sorry."

Aunt Daniella piped up. "There isn't a person at this table who hasn't been angry enough at someone to kill them. Human nature. Fortunately, we didn't do it."

Yvonne, holding up her glass, said, "There's still time."

They all laughed, then Yvonne surprised everyone by tapping her fork on her glass.

All eyes shifted to the shimmering beauty, who stood up.

Lifting her glass she proposed a toast. "To the hounds."

The room reverberated, "To the hounds!"

CHAPTER 13

March 10, 2019   Sunday

Macbeth's witches stirred their cauldron. Great as Shakespeare was he misapplied their object with "Double, double, toil and trouble." What they were truly focusing on was the weather. Why pinpoint kings and the ambitious when you can make all humans miserable? Yesterday's bout of moderate warmth had been reversed to thirty degrees Fahrenheit, medium winds, now snow showers.

Target, a handsome red who sometimes shared quarters under the log cabin with Comet, a gray, at Roughneck Farm wandered three miles away from the den. By vehicle, Pitchfork Farm rested seven miles from Roughneck Farm. Reposing at the end of a tertiary state road, then one drove on stone.

The Taylors had owned Pitchfork Farm since the 1920s. However, it wasn't until after World War II, 1950, that Frederick Taylor's son, Quentin, started the insurance company bearing his surname.

As funds rolled in, Pitchfork Farm transformed into an inviting place. The old frame farmhouse, clapboard, gained another addition, a wraparound porch. New outbuildings for storage plus a small stable had been built by Quentin's son. Business boomed.

Target, well fed, evidenced curiosity more than hunger. He hadn't been back here since cubbing, when he'd given Jefferson Hunt a terrific run from Roughneck Farm over hill and dale, strong running creeks, and one nasty ridge. He had dumped them but sat on the ridge looking down at Pitchfork Farm while he rested a bit.

On the other side of that nasty ridge was Beasley Hall, Crawford Howard's home base, majestically situated. No expense was spared in impressing the locals, which had the reverse effect. Crawford, who had made his first fortune building strip malls in Indiana, misread Virginia. Little by little he learned, but not before enraging Sister, storming out of the hunt club, forming an outlaw pack. He also managed with stealth, guile, and patience to buy Old Paradise, in ruins, 5,000 acres at Chapel Cross, acres across the south-north road from Tattenhall Station, itself 2,000 acres, plus or minus.

The restoration, breathtaking and accurate, brought him respect. He was paying homage to Virginia's heritage, including rebuilding slave quarters, doing his best with a researcher, Charlotte Abruzza, to find and repair the slave cemetery which also, given careful excavations, contained some bones from the earlier occupants, the Monacan Indians. Old Paradise was originally built during the War of 1812, business exploding at that war's conclusion. The owner was Sophie Marquette, young, lovely, who robbed British supply trains.

People assumed that sooner or later Crawford would sell Beasley Hall, move to Old Paradise. The Taylors prayed it would be sooner, for even though Crawford's grand estate sat on the other side of the rough ridge, he was a difficult neighbor.

Plumes of smoke spiraled upwards from the two chimneys at the frame house at Pitchfork but were then pushed down, spreading out like smoke pancakes. The small dependency, Bainbridge's quarters, an imitation of the main house, also had a fire in the fireplace. Bainbridge did help with Morris as well as farm chores. A part-time stable girl took care of the horses, sometimes hunting as a groom. Bainbridge need not do that work.

The fox, always curious, watched as the son walked with his father in circles. Why a human would wish to walk in circles, Target couldn't fathom, but there was much about humans he couldn't fathom. They appeared to have little sense.

If he could have heard the conversation between father and son his analysis would have seemed correct.

"I like the snow." Morris brushed flakes from his eyelashes.

"Good." Bainbridge picked up the pace a bit, for his father was slow.

Left to his own devices, Morris would have simply sat watching television. He no longer could formulate projects. Taking the keys to the Range Rover, ill-advised as it was, had been a time when the older man wanted to do something and did it.

Bainbridge had moved into the dependency after a long discussion with Drew. It also alleviated him from paying rent. He reminded Drew he was Morris's heir. Some of that pension money should come to him now. He was broke. Twenty-four-hour-a-day nursing would put most people in the poorhouse. Drew kept the nurse but only from 9:00 to 5:00 and no weekends. Bainbridge picked up the slack, which really was helpful. As to the sizable pension funds, Drew avoided a heated argument by agreeing but not specifying how much.

This arrangement didn't mean father and son effected a rapprochement. But Morris's disappointment with his son flickered on and off. Mostly, those disappointments faded but Morris could live in the here and now and didn't like being told what to do, for he still knew Bainbridge was his son, most times.

Bainbridge walked to the barn, Morris in tow, then the son trotted a bit.

"I can't go that fast and I have to go." Morris stopped, unzipped his pants, removed his member, and peed on the barn siding. Snowflakes attached themselves to his part so he brushed them off, returning same to his pants and zipping back up.

It was the need to go to the bathroom that had ended Morris's diminishing social life eight months ago. Drew took Morris with him to visit Liz Taylor, no relation to the actress, a tall blonde for whom he nurtured hopes of a romance. Liz, hospitable, served the two drinks while Morris listened. He didn't speak much even before the dementia. Then he stood up, unzipped his pants, and urinated into the fireplace, to the horror of his brother and the surprise of Liz Taylor.

"I am so sorry." Drew grabbed his brother by the elbow as Morris was trying to rearrange himself, propelling him outside.

Liz heard the car door slam then her front door opened. "Liz, if you get me a pail of water and soap, I'll clean this up."

Cotillion never covered such an emergency but it did teach its victims to stay calm and carry on. Which Liz did.

"These things happen," she replied.

Well, they did not, but they had happened to Liz and Drew.

He left because Morris was honking the horn. Drew had locked him in the car, taking the key.

So Liz cleaned it up herself and, being a lady, never brought it up to anyone. However, no romance was kindled. Extinguished, you might say.

But Drew babbled to everyone, which was the first clue people had to Morris's increasing troubles as well as Drew's exhaustion. No longer could any party deny that Morris's mind was going, going fast. After this episode, Drew no longer took Morris with him, even to the supermarket, unless someone, like the nurse, could stay in the car with him or walk and monitor him.

For a time Drew thought seeing things might stimulate mental activity but it didn't. The mental activity devolved into towering arguments with Drew and also Bainbridge, who foolishly argued back. The last straw was when Morris forgot to pay his bills and creditors showed up at Taylor Insurance.

Target watched the two men below circle the barn four times. At last, Morris sat down in the snow.

"I'm tired."

"Okay." Bainbridge reached down to pull him up.

The snow fell more heavily, a lovely snow but still snow.

Reaching the back door of the main house, Morris opened it, slamming it in his son's face. Bainbridge cursed, pushing the door open.

As Morris took off his coat, bent over to remove his boots, he said, "Amateurs built the Ark. Engineers built the *Titanic*."

Bainbridge nodded, as his father used to say this to all and sundry. Usually got a laugh.

Target, losing interest when the humans repaired to the house, turned to lope back to Roughneck Farm.

Had he known, he might have wondered, did foxes suffer from Alzheimer's or senile dementia? If they did, they wouldn't live long. Humans could keep one another going no matter how useless or in despair the afflicted might be. To a human this is compassion. To a fox it would be hell.

Fortunately, no such thought crossed Target's sharp brain. As he approached the log cabin, which took him thirty minutes at a lope, he noticed Yvonne's SUV. Whenever Yvonne visited her daughter she brought food. Happy, Target slipped into the den, where Comet lay flat on his back on a pile of old towels.

He turned his head.

"Goodies." Target grinned, his teeth white.

"Love that woman." Comet smiled back.

Sure enough, when Yvonne left, the snow still falling lightly, Tootie brought out a tray of pork bones, two biscuits, and strawberries.

Tootie knew foxes love fruit.

The taillights hadn't disappeared down the farm road as the the two foxes devoured their repast.

C H A P T E R   1 4

March 11, 2019   Monday

Two brilliant emerald eyes peeked above a pavé diamond tail draped over the end of the fox's snout. The divine Erté ring rested on Marion's desk while the Faquier County detective, a competent, attractive-looking woman, sat opposite her.

Knowing she was coming, Marion had suffered a brief fit and tidied up her office, which wasn't a mess but by her standard it was.

Officer Serena Neff often had to slide through the unacknowledged prejudice of whoever she was questioning. This reserve, if you will, would have been there anyway. No one really wants to talk to a law enforcement detective. Add race, a bit more reserve. Marion factored in race, class, all the now so important divisions, but cared little for any of it. She focused intently on the individual in front of her and saw Detective Neff as an individual. An individual she was discovering knew her job.

"Fifties?" Detective Neff looked at the piece of jewelry.

"Perhaps the forties. I have no record of its creation but I do have records of where I purchased it, from Georgia Untergraf's estate." Marion slid a folder over to the middle-aged woman.

"I remember my grandmother nattering on about Miss Georgia." She smiled. "Apparently a lady one did not cross. Imperious and rich."

"I barely remember her but I do remember her shoes, hat, and gloves matched even walking down Main Street." Marion recalled a tiny powerhouse with a big step.

"Owned half of Waterloo," Detective Neff murmured. "Can you believe what's happened to it now?"

Waterloo, an area west of Warrenton, once home to large estates, had been developed. Parts of Warrenton, again to the west, had held firm, but not so much Waterloo, although it remained quite pretty only with more homes.

"Here." Marion handed her another folder, with detailed reproductions of some of Erté's jewelry.

"I confess I know nothing about him. When I started researching his output, wow, impressive. Paintings, jewelry, scenes for theater. Quite the dandy, too."

"Lived almost to one hundred. He was born in St. Petersburg, Russia, in 1892 and died in 1990. Nicholas II was Czar when he was born. Erté got out in time."

Detective Neff flipped through more pictures. "Lucky for him. Lucky for us."

"Same with Poland and all those countries. Those who got out, whenever they got out, brought us so much. Detective Neff, you aren't here for politics but I hope we don't forget who we are."

She smiled, a warm smile. "Me, too. My husband and I sent off for the 23andMe DNA kit. A complete surprise. I am twenty-three percent North African, which could mean Egyptian, thirty-eight percent Dahomey, or a close West African tribe, and the rest is British Isles. We laughed about that."

"What's he?"

Detective Neff waved her hands. "Mostly Scandinavian with a hint of French. Odd, not one of us has Native American blood and I thought we would." She returned her gaze to the ring. "It's a sure bet Erté had none of it."

Marion laughed. "No." Then she leaned forward. "I have no idea why this was in Harry's pocket."

"Well, neither do I, which is why I'm here. How long have you had items from Georgia Untergraf's estate?"

"The family brings it in whenever." Marion paused after *whenever*. "The ring came in a month before Christmas. Just got it into the catalog."

"Interest?"

"Yes. But, as you can surmise, it's quite expensive. If I had a store in New York City like old Knoud's on Madison Avenue I would have priced it for, oh, ten thousand."

"You could do that on the Internet."

"I could but I like people to come into the store and I know my people. We do sell online but I know two people who would love this ring and I was rather hoping. So I priced it at seven thousand four hundred dollars, which is still costly."

"Even with all these pavé diamonds and the emerald eyes?"

Marion nodded. "The young don't know who Erté was. My fear was a dealer would buy this ring, pop out the stones, weigh them, and create another, more modern ring. I couldn't do that. I truly want his work to stay intact and in a way it's my small gesture to a great lady, impossible as she was reputed to be."

"I understand." And Detective Neff did, coming from a line of impossible, demanding ladies. "You and Mr. Dunbar both sold to the public, in your case the antique jewelry and the silver. For him, furniture."

"Oh, Harry Dunbar could talk a dog off a meat wagon, but Detective Neff, people come into my store because they need something. They might see something they now want that they are seeing for the first time, but in Harry's case his customers were driven only by want."

"Ah. Do you think he had a customer who wanted this ring? Obviously he sold to the wealthy."

"I don't know. When I put the ring in the catalog, he called and asked did I have more of Georgia Untergraf's estate? I said no. Then he asked had I seen any of her furniture, for she had pieces going back to George II. I told him no. I don't do furniture, which he knew. He was fishing."

"Did you like him?"

"I did. I can't say I was close but we had years to know each other."

"I see. We all have enemies. Did you know his?"

A long pause followed this. "Well, I knew a few people who felt he bought low and sold high when they were in need. The Taylors in Charlottesville, the Blys in Culpeper, and I heard once he was hoping the Wadsworths outside of Rochester, New York, longtime masters of Genesee Valley Hunt, might part with valuable items. They didn't, and it was one of the few times when Harry couldn't wheedle a few pieces to sell. Old families often need money."

"Do you think these people held a grudge?"

"Not the Wadsworths. I don't know them all that well but Harry wouldn't be an irritant to them, an amusement perhaps. As to the Blys and the Taylors, there was bad blood there."

"Bad enough to kill him?"

"Oh, I can't answer that, but if either family were to kill him it would have been years ago when he first bought their furniture, when tempers were hot." She shrugged. "I don't believe in gouging anyone up or down but the basis of capitalism is knowing when and where to buy or sell and value. Harry knew value and the truth of the matter is neither the Blys or the Taylors did."

"I see. They simply needed money."

"The Blys did. The Taylor heirs didn't want what they considered old furnitrure."

"Back to this ring. Do you know anyone who collects Erté?"

"No. Again, the young don't know who he was and anyone owning a painting or a piece of jewelry isn't going to part with it. There isn't any more."

"What about when they die?"

"My generation may be the last to know Erté but Harry used to talk about this, too, how the young don't like what they call brown furniture. In time that will shift. Their children may come back to appreciate the exquisite workmanship. Nothing stays the same."

"Isn't that the truth. The women who work for you . . . each of whom has been most cooperative, by the way . . . each one said she liked Harry."

"We all did. He was a man who paid attention to women in a gentlemanly fashion. Of course, he'd sell ice to the Eskimos, as I

said before. However, none of my girls are in the market for five-
and six-figure pieces of historic furniture."

"You know what I think about? Here you have a valuable, extremely valuable, piece of furniture, someone sits on it and, boom,
the dog eats a corner."

"There is that." Marion laughed. "At least the dog wouldn't
wear this ring."

"Who would?" came the key question.

Another long silence followed that. "I wouldn't say a hundred
percent but close to it, it would have to be a woman who foxhunted.
Who attended hunt balls, big fundraisers, maybe not disgustingly
rich but well off."

"One last question. Jean and Roni said the expensive items,
the jewelry, the silver hunting horns, might be put in the safe or
locked up at night."

"Now that I have the latest security system we don't have to
always put everything in the safe but we lock the cases. As for the
jewelry, it is so easy to misplace or knock off a shelf, we usually do
put that in the safe. Here, let me show you the jewelry."

Detective Neff's eyes lit up, for she was not immune to beautiful things. Marion walked her to the front of the store, where they
both faced the lighted glass case.

"See those crystals? Painted?"

"The hounds heads, fox, what do you call them?"

"Masks. Older ones tend to be more expensive than newer
ones and they usually come from England. Martha!" Marion called
to Martha back in the small accounting office, "come here for a
minute."

Martha did, smiling at Detective Neff. "Yes?"

"Hand me those clear crystal earrings and the ones with the green background."

Martha carefully extracted the earrings, placing them side by side on the top of the glass case, where they showed to good effect.

"See these clear ones?"

"Yes," the law enforcement officer said.

"These are new. About one thousand dollars. Part of the reason being, it's not easy to create this, to paint on the crystal," Martha filled in as Marion moved the earrings closer to Detective Neff.

"Okay. Here, these green ones are from the, mmm," Marion flipped them over, "1890s. Before World War One for certain, but like everything else, colors, stuff like that, can give you hints. This green background, popular then, fell out of fashion after the war. These are worth two thousand dollars, give or take. As they are in good condition, two thousand." She dropped them in the detective's palm.

"Are the earrings always round?"

"Usually, the bar pins, say with a running horse, those can be even more expensive because some of them have the colors of the owner's horse painted on the jockey. Also, more gold for the pin."

"Did Mrs. Untergraf have crystal jewelry?"

"She did. Still in the family. Jewelry is often so personal it's the last thing to go. Which is why I was surprised when the ring became available."

"Did the Untergrafs know Harry?"

"Everyone knew Harry." Marion smiled. "As far as I know, no problems. Of course, he would not be inquiring about jewelry. He knew while the fortune had eroded the furniture stayed put."

"I see. What about a woman scorned? Any of that?"

"Harry squired ladies to all the balls, but I don't think he ever became serious about one."

"Gay?"

"Well, Detective Neff, usually I can tell. Harry, he never spoke of it, pro or con, if you will, and he always noticed a pretty or rich woman."

Having heard part of the exchange while she hung up her coat, Jean, back from lunch, smiled devilishly. "Harry was sneaky. I think he had women all over the East Coast."

"Jean, he wasn't rich enough to keep them." Marion laughed.

"Maybe they kept him." Jean winked.

Detective Neff smiled. "I can see I have more work to do. We left the ring on your desk. If we need it, say for a court trial later, we will come to you."

Marion waved her hand. "Keep it in your safe. Better than here."

The word *murder* did not escape Marion's lips but she knew the detective wouldn't be here if the department felt Harry's death was simply an open-and-shut accident.

Best to be silent and vigilant.

CHAPTER 15

"*There's leftovers in the fridge. I could help you eat the chicken,*" Golly offered, her fluffy calico tail slightly lifting and falling.

Sister, knowing the cat shouldn't be on the kitchen table, never could resist her company so she reached across to tickle her ears.

The Doberman, Raleigh, under the table, lifted his head then dropped it back again.

Rooster, the harrier, did likewise, for the dogs knew there was no hope of ever resting on the table. There was hope of food falling off of it, however.

But Sister wasn't eating, rather drinking hot green tea.

As the heat rose, Sister stared down into the cup. "I can't help it. I am suspicious of green tea. But it is restful."

"*So is chicken,*" the cat retorted.

Humans deluded themselves into thinking that animals did not understand language but they did. Studies had proven that a dog can have a vocabulary of perhaps up to a thousand words, depending on breed. And studies in a Hungarian university revealed that animals recognized different languages, and being like humans did not necessarily understand them, but they could hear them.

Golly wasted no time on this. Humans, lovable as some may be, were a lower life-form than herself. The dogs, occasionally likable, were beneath contempt. Her tail lifted and lowered at a faster pace.

Sister took a sip. Her kitchen phone, an old dial landline, rang.

Rising, she picked it up then sat down. "Hello."

"Are you busy?" Marion's distinctive voice came through.

"Drinking green tea. I don't like this stuff but it helps me sleep."

"So does bourbon." Marion laughed.

"What's cooking, babydoll?" Sister asked.

Marion launched into the visit earlier by Detective Serena Neff. "It was all very low-key, but still."

"Mmm. She interviewed the girls, I assume."

"She did. Once again, Jean reported that she and Harry left at closing but she had emptied the jewelry case, putting the items behind it, on the shelves with the sliding doors."

"Not in the safe?" Sister queried.

"Takes a lot of time and all these years we have never had a problem. Anyway, Roni checked everything out, locked up. That's it. No contradictions or even, umm, discomfort. But after Detective Neff left, Martha was the first to say something is not right. We all agreed."

"I assumed he fell. But if he was killed the big question is, why would anyone kill Harry Dunbar?" Sister wondered. "Doesn't seem likely, strange as some of this is."

"And why was the Erté ring in his pocket?" Marion replied.

"Did Roni know if the ring was on the shelf when she locked up?"

"No," Marion quickly answered. "Jean swears she put it there and I expect she did. Closing up is a routine we all know, and again, there would be no reason for Roni to check if the case was empty of the jewelry. She would assume it was on the shelves, locked."

"I guess there's the word, *assumed.* Would Harry have known of its location?"

"No. Plus no one was in the store."

Sister took a sip of tea, placing the cup on the saucer. "You don't know that."

"What? Both Jean and Roni said no one was in the store."

"He could have been hiding. You have two bathrooms plus the back storage room. He could have been in there, Marion."

"What? To steal an Erté ring, which he really couldn't have known where it was? Plus Jean said he left with her."

"Did he know how to get back into the store? Do you hide a key?"

"No."

"He observed Jean closing up," Sister logically posited.

"Possible. Not probable but possible. Then again, Sister, why the Erté ring? A man steals an Erté ring?"

"I agree. Even if Harry were a jeweler, I can't imagine anyone stealing the Erté unless a devotee of the man's work or even a scholar. Well, I take that back. A scholar isn't going to steal a ring."

"This will drive me crazy," Marion stated.

"Well, thanks a lot. Now you're driving me crazy." Sister reached over to hold Golly's paw; the cat was patting at her teacup.

"I wonder if anyone has Erté's prints or paintings, around here, I mean."

"You'd know or Nancy Bedford would know. She has a keen aesthetic sense and knows everyone." Sister mentioned an officer of the Museum of Hounds and Hunting.

"He lived in Albemarle County. Sniff around."

"I will," Sister replied firmly.

"I know I've dumped this on you but you sometimes see things I don't."

"And vice versa."

"How was your hunt?" Marion finally asked.

"Cold. Spring is sort of now you see it, now you don't, and it's mostly don't. We were over at Little Dalby, a smaller fixture. Not much going on though we had a small run."

"Warrenton and Casanova are adding a week to the season since there really wasn't a season thanks to all the rain and snow."

"I'm thinking about hunting to March 31. As you know, we stop on the Saturday closest to St. Patrick's Day. I don't want to run a heavy vixen, but breeding got delayed this year. Foxes didn't want to go out in the downpour any more than we did. I've only seen a few traveling in pairs."

"But even if they had bred on schedule, doesn't the vixen stay near the den? Not too much chance of running her down."

"Usually, but I'm already taking care of next year's fox cubs in my mind. Still, I think I will extend the season. For all I know, the rains will continue."

"How is everything else? Members okay? No hot gossip?"

"If there were hot gossip no one would tell me. Weevil stepped up to the plate. He's doing a lovely job with hounds." She then told Marion about Shaker's crooked vertebra, Morris Taylor smashing through Cindy Chandler's fence. Crawford Howard having hired a historian for Old Paradise. Stuff like that.

"Morris Taylor. Didn't he run an insurance company with his brother?"

"No. He tried to do that to please their father but hated it. Became a nuclear physicist, which makes his slide more unsettling somehow."

"It was the Taylors who blew up at Harry Dumbar over the eighteenth-century furniture, right? Did I get that right?"

"Right. Years ago."

"Well, I know Drew because he comes into the shop, and I've seen his brother once or twice years back. I did mention the Taylors and the Blys from Culpeper to the detective, as enemies. Perhaps that's too strong a word."

"Oh, not with the Taylors but it seems unlikely that Drew Taylor would drive to Warrenton to kill Harry even if he knew he was there. That whole mess was a long time ago. Can you imagine people killing over furniture?"

"No. But I can imagine them killing over money."

"Or an Erté ring?"

"Then the killer would have taken the ring," Marion sensibly added.

"You'd think. You'll get the ring back, won't you?"

"Once this case is settled."

"And I'll make you a ten-dollar bet. The ring will be snatched up for more money. Maybe even a bidding war. People are weird about stuff like that."

"How about if we leave it at people are weird?" Marion laughed.

CHAPTER 16

March 12, 2019   Tuesday

Switching the light on, Kathleen Sixt Dunbar looked around the shop. A large grandfather clock stood against one wall. Furniture from the eighteenth century glowed. She could smell the lemon polish. Fair to good paintings adorned the walls but all paintings dated at least to the late 1700s or early 1800s, with a few odd pieces of tapestry earlier than that. Those clocks on the wall also reflected the period . . . banjo clocks, more modest clocks, the pendulums still swinging. Harry had paid attention to such things.

Kathleen listened to the ticking, knowing she should wind those clocks, but first she needed to take in this elegant shop. The heat had not been turned off. The interior proved cozy.

A small room off the main showroom contained a simple farmer's table, which Harry had used as a desk. At a right angle to it, in front, two comfortable chairs seemed poised for a transaction. All the sitter would need to do was hand across a check.

Along the wall behind the desk, a large computer screen reposed. All was organized and quite clean.

Sitting behind the desk, a file cabinet by her right side, Kathleen opened the top drawer, pulling out a folder. Bills. Electric had been paid. All was in order.

Then she pulled out a folder containing invoices. Again, all was in order. A few bills remained outstanding.

The bottom drawer of the file cabinet reminded her of how smart Harry was. Folder after folder, organized by decade, contained names, addresses, and often photos of furniture, paintings, ephemera of value. These pieces, still in possession of the owners, of old estates in some instances, interested Harry. Some, like a sideboard from 1730, cherrywood, not usual for sideboard wood, caught her eye. No price or valuation had been written on any of the folders she glanced through. Again, this reminded her of how smart Harry had been. Values change, sometimes dramatically.

She would study those folders assiduously in time. On some, in the upper right-hand corner was written the name of the hunt club to which the owners belonged. Other notations included museum affiliations, opera organizations, and the like. Quite a few noted supporters of local animal shelters as well as the names of their pets and horses. She smiled, for some of these folders, carefully updated, had lists of animals going back to the early 1990s, with today's much-alive animals noted as well as their favorite treats.

Her curiosity peaked when she found a folder of what she considered ephemera, although technically it was not. This contained photos and accurate descriptions of jewelry, especially hunting-themed jewelry.

The only jewelry in the shop was a slender stock tiepin. A model in evening scarlet stood against the wall. The pin did not pierce a stock tie, since evening scarlet was actually white tie, but rather it had been pinned to the left sleeve. The only reason Kathleen could come up with for this oddity was that Harry didn't want to lose it and perhaps forgot it.

The two pieces that most pleased her were the Louis XV desk against one wall, a soft overhead light bathing it, revealing the richness of the colors, and a stunning Louis XVI ebony cabinet with a green marble top, the two drawer handles golden heads of an unidentified demigod with a mass of curls on his head and beard.

Left to her own devices Kathleen would have specialized in French furniture from Louis XIII to the unfortunate Louis XVI. However, central Virginia was not the best place for such treasures. A few good pieces would be sold but Harry knew his people and his people reveled in the eighteenth and early nineteenth century, English. Was there a Virginian alive who could refuse anything Georgian or even Federalist?

Driving from the airport yesterday, she was again reminded of how steadfast the state was in its devotion to its own history. Outsiders focused on the politics and the battles. Insiders focused on what she called the living arts. And Virginians knew how to live.

If Harry could have put an Audubon on the wall he would have been in his glory. However, he had some good Alfred de Dreux, a French painter born in 1810 who did quite nicely by horses. As for Stubbs, well, Harry could and did dream, but his focus had to be furniture because when you specialized in painting you ran up against museums constantly and their budgets could overwhelm most private citizens'. That left him furniture and some clocks.

Again, a stunning and rare piece could find one up against The Metropolitan Museum of Art, but usually he could find those mid-range very good pieces that he could afford and so could his market.

The trick was getting the furniture before an estate sale. Harry was a master at it.

Harry and Kathleen had married right out of William and Mary in 1987, dreaming there as Harry began working at Williamsburg in the carpentry shop, where visitors could watch items being made. This proved better instruction than anything he soaked up at William and Mary, great university though it is. The hands-on experience added to his already sharp eye. For one thing, he could spot a fake quickly, having spent so much time creating accurate reproductions. The fakes usually took shortcuts. Once in business, he started with accurate reproductions because people could afford them. By that time they were separated, the marriage having lasted a desultory six months.

In 1987 when they got married, they had made a will. Kathleen didn't think about it after the divide. She wanted to get out of Virginia, flee the eighteenth century, so she went west, young woman. Oklahoma City beckoned. She opened her own store, a little flower shop that grew. They never divorced officially. Occasionally, they would talk. Sometimes a few years would go by. She did not mention him to her circle of friends in Oklahoma City nor did he mention her to his friends.

On February 27, she had received a call from April Fletcher. Years ago Harry had moved his estate planning to another fox-hunter, specializing in same. April was bold in the hunt field, prudent and insightful off of it. They worked well together. Not only did Harry not change his heir, Kathleen, he willed the business to her and the building that housed it, a stone two-story structure with gable windows, which also housed him. Harry literally lived over the shop.

When he passed, April notified Kathleen immediately. Harry's wife didn't pretend sorrow but she was shocked. Harry, a vital man, would live for decades, so she and everyone thought. Kathleen asked April to check in on the shop, see to security, and hire someone to clean the upstairs. Harry was fastidious but the refrigerator, etc., would need cleaning.

She then informed the ultra-capable lawyer that she would be taking over the business. She needed a bit of time to sell or rent her own shop but she would be there as soon as possible.

Oklahoma City, being on the rise, meant Kathleen need not wait long. Her business, successful . . . she had the contract for special events at American Express and other corporations . . . sold in three days. Even she was stunned. The buyer, a young woman, ambitious, who worked for Kathleen, lost no time putting together investors and, boom, Mrs. Dunbar was enriched and freed. She also sold her house with all the furnishings within ten days. Granted, that would take some time to close but it was a cash offer.

Clearly, some people did not need banks in Oklahoma City.

She packed up her Welsh terrier, Abdul, flew to Charlottesville, and picked up the keys to Harry's car and shop from April, who offered to escort her but Kathleen politely declined.

When she opened the door to the upstairs, which she did before going downstairs, she knew she had made the right decision. Harry's living quarters reflected his eye for color, value, and comfort. All she needed were her own clothes, which she had brought. A few odds and ends were being shipped. The paintings on the walls, mostly sporting art, harmonized with the Sheratons, one Hepplewhite credenza. She didn't know if they were accurate reproductions or originals but when she had time to study his papers, she would. In the front hall, his crop, silver collars, hung over the corner of a Ben Marshall painting. His hunt gear, brushed, was inside the front hall closet. She noticed his frock coat was torn, the seams worn.

"Hard riding," she thought, then said to Abdul, her Welsh terrier, "We're home."

Home was wherever Kathleen was, so the jaunty fellow was happy.

She wandered through the shop then she sat at the desk perhaps an hour after unpacking personal items upstairs.

At fifty-four, a few vagrant thoughts about age had crossed Kathleen's mind, starting really when she turned fifty. Forty had flown by. She noticed only because her friends teased her, but fifty stuck. Here she was fifty-four, having a nest egg from her own efforts augmented by the estate of a shrewd absent husband. In short, Kathleen was rich.

Placing the folders back in the file cabinet, she resisted the urge to turn on the big computer. Lots of time for that, which she assumed would be full of furniture pictures as well as auctions at the various American and European auction houses.

Walking into the showroom, she sat down on the large sofa, a fireplace directly across from it, a pile of hardwood neatly stacked to the side. Once secure here she would make certain that fireplace glowed on cold days, a welcoming sight and smell.

She would carry on.

Furious as she was when she had walked out of the marriage,

young as she was at twenty-two, she realized Harry had hit on the perfect formula for what would become his business. Woo older women. Become friends with them. Talk to them about what interested them. Which is why so many people thought Harry was gay. He was not. He was finding out everything about their furniture, their paintings, and even their expensive ceramic vases from the 1700s. Sometimes he would sleep with them, a discreet affair. That's what had set her off. He had slept with another woman not two months after they were married.

"It didn't mean anything, Kathleen."

"It does to me."

And that was the sum of it. She eventually got over it. He clearly continued on his quietly effective path. So far as she knew he never got caught.

A knock at the door alerted Abdul, who barked.

Kathleen rose, walking to the door.

She opened it to face a tall, at least six foot, woman with gorgeous silver hair and a fit body. This was an imposing figure until she smiled and held out her hand; in the other she held a large gardenia bush in a pot.

"Forgive me for coming unannounced. I'm Jane Arnold, the master of Jefferson Hunt. Harry was a stalwart and adored member."

"Please come in." Kathleen looked at the pot.

This was a good healthy gardenia, which Sister handed to her. "Welcome."

Kathleen took the pot while Abdul sniffed Sister.

The two women walked to the sofa, where Kathleen placed the pot on the table, motioned for Sister to sit in a wing chair.

"Again, forgive me. I had no number for you but I do want you to know you are welcome. Like it or not, you have inherited many of Harry's friends as well as this beautiful shop."

"Thank you. How did you find out about me?"

"I didn't exactly. Harry's death was announced on February 27 in the news. Nothing more was heard about it, no service. Well, we all waited, as such details fall to next of kin. There seemed to be no next of kin. Most of us do use April Fletcher as our lawyer but I did not trouble her. She is very closemouthed but she did tell my treasurer, one of the world's nosiest men, that Harry had an heir and that individual would be taking care of a funeral if there was one. Well, Ronnie Haslip, the treasurer, kept digging, and how he found out about you I don't know, because I do know April didn't tell him. Then the tiniest obituary appeared in the local paper, only giving his birth and death dates with a line that he left a wife and that details of a service would be forthcoming."

"Ronnie should be a reporter."

"In his own way he is. I call him the Town Crier."

They both laughed.

Abdul left Kathleen to come over and lick Sister's hand.

"Abdul," Kathleen reprimanded him.

"I'm surrounded by hounds and two worthless house dogs. He's a handsome fellow."

"Welsh, of course. A Welsh Muslim."

At that both women laughed again and Sister warmed to Kathleen and vice versa.

"You might be needing firewood for the shop and upstairs. My gentleman friend and his brother will bring some by."

"Oh, don't, you needn't do that."

"It's not a bit of trouble. I have a decent-sized farm and trees come down. Nights stay cold here sometimes until early May."

"I went to school at William and Mary."

"Ah, you know."

"It's where I met Harry. I know it's a surprise, that I'm a surprise. We married right after graduation and it was a mistake. We found our way to a friendship but never divorced. Being legally married, quietly or not, is a form of protection."

"It can be," Sister agreed. "Let me give you my card. Don't hesitate to call. I do mean it. You have a lot on your hands."

And Kathleen did, although neither woman could have known that meant murder.

CHAPTER 17

March 14, 2019 Thursday

While it was still cold, the footing had improved. Few felt the cold, as they'd been running for thirty minutes at Mousehold Heath, a farm fifteen minutes east of the kennels. The miles of pasture from Mousehold Heath through After All then Roughneck Farm sometimes produced a track-and-field fox. On the other side of the ridge rested Foxglove Farm and Cindy Chandler's neighbors. In theory, a fox could surmount the ridge to run north. However, many opportunities to dump hounds and humans existed on this side, so thus far no fox had ever taken advantage of the hard climb.

Hounds, fit, pushed hard but the fox, a visiting one, proved fit, too. Mousehold Heath, first cornerstone laid in 1807, sported a few fences but mostly the land was open. Hounds blew through it ten minutes after the first cast. They were now circling the main house at After All, the Bancrofts' large estate. Mousehold Heath began as a modest farm and remained one now, being brought back to pristine condition by Jim and Lisa Jardin, a young couple doing much of the work themselves.

After All, by contrast, had begun as a large estate, undergirded by first tobacco money then railroad money. It remained a sumptuous place, having never fallen into disrepair. Money couldn't buy everything but it certainly could maintain grand old estates.

The main house, stone with white pillars, a bit unusual, allowed the fox to give Sister, Weevil, and the whippers-in fits. Of course they couldn't gallop close to the house. Winter may be hanging on but impeccable lawns would soon revive.

Sister rode quickly to the western corner of the main lawn, standing where she could view the house and outbuildings but be close to the covered bridge in case the fox decided to use that. Not only did he decide to use it, he stopped to assess Sister and her field.

After inspection he sauntered across the bridge while the hounds could be heard circling the house.

"Devil," Sister thought as she smiled.

Sister never tired of fox behavior, rooted, it seemed, in a sense of superiority. She thought that in some ways foxes and cats held similar opinions of themselves. Nothing she could do but sit as her quarry walked through the bridge, then walked along the creek bank. Walked. Not ran. Not even trotted.

The field, of course, bellowed, "Tally-ho," hats off, pointing in the direction of Mr. Fox's path.

She could have killed them. For whatever reason, humans can't resist "tally-ho." If they count to twenty, all's fair. Flushed from their ride, curious as to hounds circling, then dazzled by the appearance of the star himself, half the field shouted, "Tally-ho."

Weevil heard them, but wisely did not lift his hounds. They would hunt their fox sticking to scent and move off soon enough, for clearly the fox had tired of circling the house.

Giorgio, a hound of smashing beauty, not the best nose in the pack, but good, plus he had drive, stopped by a boxwood lining one of the walkways into the main house.

"He turned here," Giorgio called.

That fast, Dreamboat reached where the sleek fellow had paused. *"Come on!"*

Fifteen couples of hounds, full throttle, moved off, with Giorgio in the lead.

Weevil carefully followed from a distance, for he didn't want to tramp close to the house. This walkway's English boxwoods had to be at least from the mid-1800s. One doesn't mess with such ancient boxwoods, no matter what hounds are doing.

So the lean, broad-shouldered fellow trotted alongside the main drive then reached the drive to the covered bridge. Hounds were already into it.

Sister and the field awaited him, hats off, horses' noses pointing in the direction the fox had gone.

Ripping out an encouraging shout, Weevil pushed Gunpowder, another of Shaker's horses, through the bridge, hooves reverberating loudly. Gunpowder didn't twitch an ear. An old hand, he knew his task and wanted to get on terms with this smartass fox.

Once they were on the other side, Sister then walked through the bridge. She knew the noise of all those hooves would be deafening, an opportunity for a green horse or a rider not so tight in the tack to bolt, fall, or embarrass oneself.

Betty galloped on the right side of the creek. She did not ride through the bridge. If the fox crossed back, Betty would be the only staff member who could stay close to fox and hounds.

Tootie went through the bridge after the field. She'd gotten behind, for she correctly waited on the other side of the house, far enough from it not to be a problem but close enough so that it would not be a problem for her.

She held up her whip hand as she passed Sister and the field. Quite proper of her but a few greenies grunted as a Thoroughbred blasted by them. That's the whipper-in's job. Get used to it.

Now Sister squeezed Rickyroo. They flew along the creekbed. This fellow could have veered farther west, run through leftover corn stubble, and wound up on Roughneck Farm. That would have been a lovely run but one in the open. He may have been a visiting fox but he had perused the territory before at some time.

They moved at least twenty feet in from the creekbed edge. Given all the rain and snow, the ground might give way. Ice hugged the edges of the flowing creek.

Onward he ran and ran. And then, oh how low, he wiggled underneath vines and old bushes, heading straight for Pattypan Forge. The master couldn't follow nor could the huntsman. The undergrowth was impenetrable.

Weevil hit the narrow deer path first. Within a few minutes Sister followed. No one had been on this unattractive path for weeks thanks to the weather. Each time Sister fought her way to Pattypan Forge, a true forge set up after the Revolutionary War and allowed to discontinue after the First World War, she cursed, for the path had never been widened to tractor width. Nobody even wanted to do that. The vines had minds of their own. You couldn't get back to the forge without scratches on your face, vines grabbing your leg, practically pulling you out of the saddle.

Then there was a medium-sized pine that had fallen over the path. Fortunately it was jumpable.

Over she and Rickyroo went, Weevil's scarlet coat up in the distance. Within minutes, barring another impediment, she and the field would be at the old forge, still impressive. Hounds screamed.

As she reached the opening where the building stood, the large stones as tight as the day they were laid, hounds had leapt through the floor-to-ceiling windows. Weevil was in there with them as Gunpowder stood staring into a window long broken and open.

Hounds gathered around a den opening. Terrible words could be heard from within, for the chased fox had dived into Aunt Nettie's den. She had many openings at Pattypan Forge. He wisely used the closest one, as hounds grew near.

"Get out! Get out!" Aunt Netty spat.

"No. Not until hounds go."

Giorgio, still in front, stuck his head into the den opening. *"Who are you?"*

"It's not him you need to worry about, Giorgio. I know where you live and I can get you," the old vixen threatened.

Giorgio pulled his head back while the other hounds dug at the entrance. They knew Aunt Netty. She had tunnels everywhere, but one had to make a show of it.

Weevil blew "Gone to Ground."

"Finally. Those jerks will leave." Aunt Netty eyed the interloper. *"You can go when they do."*

"Not so fast. That's a smart pack."

"Who are you?" she almost shouted.

Outside the den it sounded like barking, which it was. Weevil smiled at the window, walking with his hounds as he praised them.

"Aunt Netty?" Gunpowder asked.

"She's in there giving that fox hell." Zorro laughed.

"We'd be easier to deal with than that old bag." Twist, humiliated by Aunt Netty countless times, hoped she was miserable.

She wasn't but she was putting this young fellow in his place.

"I am Colby."

"Colby, you can get your ass out of my den."

"Ma'am, I can't do that until all is safe, but I can then tell you where fresh fried chicken bones are."

Her nose twitched. *"And where might they be?"*

"Behind the big house back there. Someone knocked over a garbage can. Didn't finish the job. I would be pleased to escort you."

Colby smiled at the old girl, who became quiet. He was attractive. He promised fried chicken, a favorite. This would take a bit of thought but not too much.

"All right." Weevil, now mounted, glanced down at his proud hounds. "Let's see what we can do."

The way out of Pattypan if one headed straight east wasn't too awful. Within five minutes of slow going Weevil and hounds walked out on the farm road connecting After All to the Old Lorillard place. Betty, in perfect position, waited for them.

Weevil had learned much of the territory last year when he whipped-in, but a refresher wouldn't hurt.

"Think I should head to the Old Lorillard place?"

Betty replied, "It's that or go back to the bridge. It's been a long, hard run but another forty-five minutes won't hurt; even if we don't find the fox, it's a good day."

He smiled then called to his hounds. "Come along."

Sister emerged from the path as hounds headed toward Gray and Sam's clapboard house, the old graveyard, tombstones intact, to the side of the house. Generations of Lorillards and Laprades rested there.

Tootie also came out from the bracken, decided to trail the field then flank them on the west once things opened up, which they would.

Noses down, hounds moved into the cleaned-up woods across from the Pattypan path. Nothing doing.

Once at the Lorillard place, a whiff of fox scent curled into their nostrils. They opened, followed it around the graveyard, a stone wall setting that off, then came back to the road down almost to the Pattypan path.

Weevil decided to walk them to the bridge. They were now on the house side, having needed to cross the creek to move away from Pattypan Forge.

Upon reaching the bridge he waited for Sister.

"It will take about a half hour to walk to Mousehold Heath. It's been a wonderful day. Let's go back."

"Yes, Ma'am." He nodded, thinking that was the right decision.

Most people in the field managed to hang on but they weren't really fit. Why make a mess?

The mercury climbed to the mid-forties, not warm but not

nasty cold either. The sun peeked from behind clouds and when one walked into a sunny patch the temperature felt like a warm hand on your back.

Finally, at the starting fixture everyone dismounted and took care of horses while Weevil, Betty, and Tootie loaded hounds, checking each one off the list as he or she boarded.

The Jardines were at work so a tailgate had been set up literally on tailgates. Those with director's chairs pulled them out. Others stood. Walter kept the bar on his truckbed. Drew, Freddie, and Alida had a feast on their tailgates.

Sister, drink in hand, dropped in a chair.

Alida dropped next to her. "Good day. Would you like a sandwich? Chili?"

"Maybe a sandwich, but here comes Gray. He can do it."

"He can sit next to you. I would be delighted to serve my master." She smiled her beguiling smile as Kasmir, having changed into a tweed, came next to her.

Everyone fed themselves, hungry. Alida and Kasmir pulled up chairs. Soon a tired, happy group sat down.

Weevil, Tootie, and Betty grabbed some food but wanted to get the hounds home.

"I'll see you at the stable," Betty called out, waving to Sister, who waved back.

A half hour of this pleasurable time passed then Sister, who usually left the speeches to Walter, stood up, tapped a bottle.

All heads turned to her, a few tears in her britches and mud on her boots.

"Ladies and gentlemen, I'm so glad we could share this day." She paused for affirming murmurs. "I ask you to visit Harry Dunbar's shop. His wife," she paused, for this created more than murmurs, "has taken it over. None of us knew he had a wife, but I did go down, having heard she was coming, to visit. I invited her to hunt club functions and I encourage each of you to drop in, welcome her and her handsome Welsh terrier. With any luck maybe we can get her to ride. But do go." She sat down.

A flock of people now pressed upon her for more information. What did she look like? Was she really going to run the shop? Where did she come from? Etc.

Drew stood at the edges looking as though he had swallowed a pickle. As the crowd cleared, Sister crooked her finger to him. He came over as Alida, Kasmir, and Gray observed.

"Drew, your past unhappiness did not involve this lady, who I am sure knew nothing. You ought to go and," another pause as she used the Yankee phrase, "make your manners."

Four sets of eyes bore into him and those were four important sets of eyes.

"Well—you're probably right."

"She's attractive and likable. All you have to do is welcome her. I trust you to do so and I thank you in advance."

"I will." He then turned and left.

Gray tapped the wooden arm of the folding chair.

"Let's hope he doesn't make an ass of himself and bring it up."

Kasmir agreed then added, "And let's hope he doesn't take Morris."

"Yes," Sister said with conviction. "What's the point of hanging on to things that went wrong?"

Gray sighed. "Because people define themselves by the shit that happens to them."

At this the others stared, openmouthed.

Finally Kasmir muttered, "Gray, I hope not."

"I do, too, but look at your nation and Pakistan? Will anybody ever forgive and forget? Hell, you don't even have to look that far. Look here."

Alida smoothly said, "You're right, Gray, but we can try to overcome and move forward. I mean, look how Europe has stabilized itself after World War Two. It is possible."

"With American money and leadership. And remember that's when India gained her independence." Kasmir knew history and would always love his country of birth.

"Anything emotional takes time, but it's worth trying." Alida smiled at the man she adored. "Maybe marriage is the beginning. Think about it. Men and women are different." She held up her hand. "Whether it's biology or society. We fall in love, live together, and have to learn about each other. Maybe that's the true beginning. One has to start somewhere. Who knows, maybe same-sex couples have as much to learn as we do. One has to bend."

All were quiet for a moment then Sister reached out for Alida's hand. "You've given me something to think about. I would never have put it that way." She looked at Kasmir. "What a special woman you have found."

"Now, Sister." Alida blushed.

Kasmir reached for Alida's other hand. "I am the luckiest man on this earth. You know, anyone who refuses love is a fool. It's what makes us better than we are."

Gray looked from the couple to Sister then smiled. "Why does it take so long to learn?"

CHAPTER 18

March 15, 2019   Friday

Friday, supermarkets were packed as people prepared for the weekend. Bainbridge rolled a cart along the aisle at Harris Teeter. He'd meant to shop yesterday but a clogged pipe under the sink in his small house at Pitchfork Farm took up much of the day.

Drew still employed the male nurse part-time which fortunately gave Bainbridge the time to run back and forth to the hardware store then take over for the nurse until his uncle returned from work.

Today, however, he was on duty. Pulling the nurse back to three and a half days already saved the Taylors seven hundred fifty dollars a week. Registered nurses and nurse practitioners proved very expensive. While Morris didn't need a nurse practitioner he did need a nurse. Given his size, male muscle power came in handy. Also, getting Morris's drugs from the doctor's office or the pharmacy was easier with a nurse.

Morris endured a monthly appointment to get a new script,

which then was carried to the pharmacy. The time this took was irritating if not exhausting.

So Bainbridge had to take his father to the supermarket. The son rolled the cart while he told his father what to put into it. So far Morris was cooperative, cheerful even, and didn't run the cart into anyone else.

"Crackers." Bainbridge pointed to a package on the shelf.

"I don't like that kind."

"Grab what you do like."

Morris snagged a box of Triscuits.

They rolled on. Bainbridge wanted to get out of there, but then so did everyone else.

They reached the bread section, some shelves not high, in front of cold cases filled with made sandwiches, sushi, ready-to-eat things.

Morris grabbed a sandwich, starting to unwrap it.

"Dad, you can't do that. Wait until we get home."

"I'm hungry."

Bainbridge walked in front of the cart, took the sandwich from his father, started to rewrap it.

Morris, furious, grabbed a long loaf of French bread, hitting his son over the head. The bread broke in half.

"Gimme my sandwich," the older man yelled.

Looking around, Bainbridge picked up the bread, tried to guard the cart as his father kept reaching for his sandwich. He got into line but Morris attacked the cart then attacked him.

People in front of them in line huddled up. No one came behind. The lady behind the register picked up the phone.

Within a minute, two men appeared to handle the situation.

Morris swung at them. Fortunately, they ducked.

"He's got dementia," Bainbridge said louder than he'd intended.

"Shut up. You shut up," Morris hollered.

"I'll get him out." Bainbridge slipped behind his father, swinging at the two supermarket employees, and as he did so Morris turned, hitting him in the face.

Bainbridge held up his arm to protect his face but Morris, enraged, pounded on him.

Exasperated, the young man let fly a right cross, catching Morris on the chin. He wobbled, mouth bleeding, hanging on to the cart, which now rolled back in the line.

That fast the two men grabbed Morris's arms, pinning him as they hustled him to the store exit.

Bainbridge reached in his pocket for cash as a policeman hurried through the door.

"He's got dementia and lost his temper," Bainbridge tried to explain.

"Come on, buddy." The cop pulled Morris's arm up behind him, propelling him out into the parking lot.

Bainbridge managed to pull out more bills, stuffing them in the employees' back pockets.

"I'm not crazy. Let me go," Morris hollered.

"Officer, if you help me get him to the car I can take him home."

"Who are you?"

"I'm his son."

"Is this your son?" the cop asked Morris.

"I never saw that bastard in my life."

When Drew reached the station both father and son languished in adjoining cells. Of course, Bainbridge had a record for possession of drugs. Morris simply screamed bloody murder in the next cell.

Drew, overwhelmed, called his personal lawyer, who came down, filled out paperwork. Bainbridge was released to his uncle. At first they weren't sure what to do with Morris, who by now demonstrated to all and sundry that he suffered from senile dementia and was in a rage, which is not uncommon. Not every dementia patient loses their temper. But enough do that it is one of the things a medical person or a law enforcement officer would perceive.

"I can take him home." Drew and Edward, his lawyer, stood together in front of the discharging officer.

"If he becomes violent again, I don't see how you can," the officer replied. "I can't release him to you."

"He can't stay here. He's sick," Drew pleaded.

Edward, calm, placed paperwork in front of the policeman. "This is the name and number of Morris's doctor. Would you release him to the doctor, who would place him under observation for a night?"

Reading the paperwork, the officer agreed, and called Dr. Frank Gericke.

By the time Drew and Bainbridge got back to the farm it was almost ten o'clock.

Bainbridge disappeared into the bathroom, emerging with a washcloth, wet, at his split lip.

"Dammit, this will cost." Drew sagged in his chair. "What in the hell did you think you were doing taking him to the supermarket?"

"He seemed fine. How was I to know he would go off?"

"Sit down," Drew commanded. "What set him off?"

"He picked a sandwich out of the case and started eating it. I told him to put it in the cart, he could eat it when we left the store. That was all it took."

Drew rubbed his hand over his eyes. "You can't cross him."

"I didn't think I was. I was trying to get out of the store without food all over him or on the floor."

"We'll pick him up tomorrow. Maybe Dr. Gericke can prescribe something to keep him calm."

"That can't be too difficult, but Uncle Drew, meds wear off. How will we get more into him?"

"He's been pretty good about swallowing pills."

"But what if he isn't? Do you hold his mouth open and I cram them down his throat?"

"I don't know. And I don't think a nurse will be any better at it."

"I don't either."

As uncle and nephew worried, news about the uproar in Harris Teeter spread. The place had been packed and this was gossip too good to be true.

Eventually Sister heard about it from Betty, who had heard about it from Freddie Thomas, whose best friend, Karen Sorenson, had been in the store with her mother.

Sister did not think this was any of her business. On the other hand, she was glad Betty alerted her so no one would run up to her in public or try to bag her after a foxhunt. This way she could prepare her response, which simply was, "This is a terrible problem and I hope Drew and Bainbridge can see to Morris's safety and everyone else's."

She resisted the urge to call Gray, over at Old Lorillard with his brother tonight. However, she thought a call to Walter Lungrun might not be out of order.

Once on the phone, he told her he had heard of it about fifteen minutes ago from Ben Sidel, who would make sure neither Drew nor Bainbridge nor Morris were prosecuted. As far as the sheriff was concerned, it was a medical issue and should be handled as such.

"Good man," Sister said. "Ben."

"He is. However, there is no way back from dementia."

"Does that mean Morris will be increasingly violent?"

"Not necessarily. People with these conditions reach plateaus and can remain there for some time. As to episodes of violence or terror, they're very difficult to predict. Frank Gericke was called down to the station, Ben told me, so I called him. This is his specialty and right now Morris is at UVA University Hospital for observation. He can't get out. Drew will need to pick him up in the morning if Frank thinks he's stabilized."

"I see. Walter, is it time to put him away?"

"You know, that really is a medical and family decision. But Frank did tell me Drew has power of attorney, thank God . . . Morris gave it to him a year ago . . . or this kind of thing could drag through the courts, in and out of hospitals. There isn't really a safety net."

"I am sorry to hear that."

"For one thing, Sister, a family can't exactly hide someone with dementia but they can keep them at hand. Would it be easier to put them away? I think so, but emotionally many people can't."

"Or won't." She thought a moment. "I would assume that in some cases there is financial gain."

"Well, again that depends on the circumstances, but the family or a trustee does have control over the patient's worldly goods."

"People fight over the damndest things, like a car, a large silver bowl. There is no fight as bad as a family fight."

He replied, "True. Although it doesn't appear this is a family fight; I mean, apart from fisticuffs in Harris Teeter."

"Let's hope so."

CHAPTER 19

March 16, 2019 Saturday

Neither years nor neglect had erased the purity of Bishop's Court, an abandoned tiny Catholic chapel. The small stained-glass windows remained unmolested, as did the gilded cross on top of the chapel. Blue double doors faced each other, the paint so old it was mostly powder. This house of worship over the decades had protected the homeless, both human and fox.

The pack of hounds waited for their religious fox to come out. However, this gray, with a tight den in the office as well as places under the structure itself, wouldn't budge.

"Come along."

"He's in there," Aces correctly spoke.

"Come along," Weevil sang out again as he turned Kilowatt away from the dignified church.

"Mass," Pickens cheekily told the youngster.

"What's that?" Aces wondered.

"Humans kneel and chant things," Dasher filled him in.

"Is there anything to eat?" Angle, Aces's brother, piped up.

"I don't think so." Dasher followed Weevil, as did the others.

Low clouds, mid-forties, not good golfing weather but good hunting, had given the pack a bracing run when Weevil first cast them from Little Dalby, a fixture at the edge of Jefferson Hunt territory.

The gray, young himself and surprised, ran for all he was worth to home, which took him fifteen minutes but the field a good twenty-five, for they traversed abandoned land, charged into the church land, also abandoned. Bishop's Court, owned by early Catholics, endured, but unappreciated people back then built this small chapel for themselves. A streak of pride or rebellion or both provoked them to name their holdings Bishop's Court two hundred twenty years ago.

Small as it was, so was the Catholic population in western Albemarle County. The faithful did come, a priest was found, and over time improvements were made, such as the stained-glass windows and a big brass door knocker for each door, a brass cross.

The church's membership dwindled as prejudice against Catholics waned and a large church was built in Charlottesville, and then as the faithful grew, more churches appeared in surrounding counties.

Bishop's Court finally closed in 1938 but even with peeling paint it looked as though it would stand for centuries more. From time to time an elderly person, remembering their youth in the chapel, would return. Some of their progeny did clean up the graveyard once a year as well as inspect the chapel.

Riding by, Sister considered all the strands that made Virginia. People did not necessarily believe the same things but they were tolerant. The new system of government held.

"We are a miracle, in our way," she thought to herself then felt Keepsake twitch a tiny bit. He heard and smelled what she didn't, a whiff of fox which the first-time lead hound, Pansy, had picked up.

Soon all the hounds surrounded a spot, noses down, sterns wagging. Then they opened and, boom, were off.

Keepsake needed no encouragement nor did Sister. The brief respite at Bishop's Court was enough to restore them.

The field had reversed, running back in the direction from which they came, so once again they found themselves in the middle of Kingswood, an old land holding but a new fixture right next to Little Dalby. The field felt like they were in the back of the beyond. Almost.

The house, under construction, had the roof up and sides closed in. A blessing and one the construction crew, Robb Construction, had busted their butts to get done before the weather turned. Turn it did and no one could do squat until the incessant rain and snows passed. Even a temperature in the mid-forties seemed promising.

Fortunately, the new owners, from Raleigh, hunted down there with Red Mountain, so they couldn't have been more helpful and Sister looked forward to when they would move in.

Given the straight run, a bit of a zigzag once into the woods, Weevil and Sister both thought they were on a red. The hounds knew they were, but they didn't know this fox. They really didn't know this territory but their task was to follow their noses.

A steep incline up ahead slowed the field, not because people couldn't gallop downhill, First Flight could, but because the footing was so unreliable, why test it here in a place no one knew well at all?

Sister slowed, picked her way down, then squeezed Keepsake once on the other side. By now hounds had flown a good quarter mile ahead of her. The going, tricky in the woods, didn't help. Finally she came out on East Chapel Cross Road. She was six miles from Chapel Cross itself.

Creeping along, two vehicles followed. Skiff drove Shaker in her truck. This territory, old in history but newer as fixtures, meant both huntsmen observed everything and mostly shut up. For Shaker this was unusual because if the hounds hunted on territory he knew there was an endless stream of corrective, ideas, the occasional curse.

Behind these two drove Yvonne, with Aunt Daniella in the passenger seat and Kathleen Sixt Dunbar in back. Yvonne had stopped into the store although it wasn't formally opened, introduced herself, and offered Kathleen a Saturday's ride. As she was learning hunting, the county, she thought the two of them could profit from Aunt Daniella. It was a nice gesture.

"What an incredible sound." Kathleen had cracked her window.

"They're roaring. I wish I could tell you what was happening but this is uncharted territory. Hounds are on but where we'll end up is anyone's guess." Aunt Daniella also had her window down a tiny bit, for it was cool.

Yvonne slowly drove on the two-lane macadam highway obviously ignored by the state. However, apart from potholes, it held up, as did the old church.

Suddenly silence.

"Damn!" Shaker shouted as Skiff stopped first, followed by Yvonne, who turned off her engine.

"Hounds have lost the line," Aunt Daniella told Kathleen.

"What's a line?"

"A line of scent. Scent from different animals smells different, that's obvious, but what nonhunters don't realize . . . and many who do hunt, I am sorry to say . . . is that certain species throw off a stronger scent than others."

"Like perfume." Kathleen nodded.

"More or less." The nonagenarian now put down her window a bit more, clutching her coat collar tighter around her neck. "For instance, bear scent is heavy. Coyote scent is stronger than fox, and if you smell fox it's like a sweet skunk. Only way I can describe it. It's not an unpleasant odor but it is very noticeable. But it can drift with wind and can evaporate fairly quickly in warm weather. I believe the fox has some control over his or her scent, but that's me. For instance, during mating season scent is stronger, as it is for deer."

"Kind of like 'Hey, Baby.'" Kathleen laughed.

"Exactly." Yvonne laughed with her.

"And now what has happened is the hounds have lost the scent," Aunt Daniella told her.

"But they were screaming. How can it just stop like that?"

"Kathleen, if I knew that I would be the smartest person ever. For centuries, since Xenophon and Arrian, people have tried to figure that out."

Kathleen, educated, knew who these two men were. Xenophon, a major-general and passionate hunter, was born in 430 BC and died in 354 BC. Apart from being a highly successful man, once his military career was over Xenophon retired to his estate, building a temple to Artemis, goddess of the hunt. He wrote about his pack, about breeding, about Celtic hunting customs. He was a traveled and highly intelligent man. What he wrote is as true today as the day he wrote it.

Arrian was born in 86 AD, a man of genuine charm, which comes across in his writings.

Of course, both men, writing before blood typing and advances in medicine, had ideas about rabies, things that proved untrue, but they paid attention to so much and did the best they could for their hounds.

Xenophon did his best for Artemis, too. He believed one should leave an offering at her temple if you hunted on his land. He was generous to others in that respect.

"You know about Xenophon and Arrian." Aunt Daniella, who had mentioned them, was pleased.

"Classics major at William and Mary."

"Ah, how did you wind up in Oklahoma City?" Yvonne was now fascinated.

"That's a long story but I hasten to add there are people in Oklahoma City who read Latin and a few who read Greek. It's not the cultural backwater East Coasters assume."

"We are terrible," Aunt Daniella agreed. "But I am delighted you know these early hound men."

"Well, not like you do, Aunt Daniella."

"Call me Aunt Dan. Everybody else does. What you call me behind my back I need not know."

"What people say behind your back determines your place in the social firmament," Yvonne sagely noted.

"Where did you study, Yvonne?" Kathleen asked.

"Northwestern."

"Ah, a smarty."

"If only that were true." Yvonne laughed.

"Don't let her fool you, Kathleen." Aunt Daniella had grown enormously fond of the transplant. "As for me, no college. Education for girls was not important when I was young. I would have gone to Howard or Grambling or Alabama State; black schools, to be blunt. Good schools, too. Never doubt for one minute that people could and still do get a superior education there. But in our family it was my brothers who were important. All gone now."

"Less distracting, I think. I mean, Northwestern was wonderful. Still there's that edge if one is not white, you know," Yvonne said.

"I don't," Kathleen honestly replied. "But I am sorry."

"Don't be. We all adjust, fight as best we can so the next generation has it easier." Yvonne shrugged.

Aunt Daniella leapt right in. "But I think that's the problem. Why do we make it easier? Oh yes, I believe one should have the chance of a good career, education, live where you please, but to truly make life easier, that's how you make weaklings."

The other two women didn't know what to say.

Kathleen, not disagreeing, changed the subject a bit. "Xenophon wrote, 'No one should admire those whose only aim is to fulfill personal ambition, in private or public life.'"

"Clearly, no one is reading Xenophon today." Yvonne grimaced slightly.

"Oh, honey pie, it's always been this way. It's that now, thanks to the nonstop media, we can examine the vulgarity of others at our leisure." Aunt Daniella looked out the window, to see Tootie fly by.

"You know more than I do and I went to college," Kathleen said admiringly.

"You're very kind. I'm old. There's a lot upstairs." She tapped her head. "And I am a reader."

"What is my daughter doing?" Yvonne saw Tootie stop on a dime.

"That's your daughter?" Kathleen beheld Tootie at her best.

"Out of hunt gear you'll see how alike they look. Two gorgeous, gorgeous girls." Aunt Daniella also peered at Tootie, who now had her cap off. "She's viewed."

The two in the front seats explained this to Kathleen, now completely enchanted with the hunt.

Tootie shouted, "Yip, yip, yo!" for all she was worth.

"What happened to 'Tally-ho'? That much I know," Kathleen asked.

"Actually, one should not shout that but people can't help themselves. Must count to twenty first to give your quarry a chance." Aunt Daniella took a breath. " 'Yip, yip, yo' is the old call of the night hunters, which was then used as the rebel yell. Jefferson Hunt staff uses it so the huntsman knows staff has viewed. No one in the field is allowed the night hunter call."

"You're kidding." Kathleen now sat on the edge of her seat.

"Oh, no. When I was a child the old men, the ancient, and I mean ancient, night hunters, used it. A few of them were veterans. The last veteran of that war died in the 1960s, I think. It's been just recently that the last veteran of World War I died. God, what we do to one another."

Before anyone could answer, Weevil and the pack charged up close to the car. Shaker, of course, had his head hanging out the window. Weevil could not stop to listen, which Shaker understood but that did not shut him up.

Yvonne and Aunt Daniella explained to Kathleen what had happened to Shaker and who Skiff was and that they quite liked her.

Weevil watched where Tootie pointed with her cap, where Iota's head was pointed, and he laid hounds on.

"Got him!" Zane called, and then all were on.

"My God, I can't believe this. I have chills up my spine . . . or down. Can't remember which." Kathleen had the window lowered all the way and the music poured in.

Next Sister barreled by, then the field, then Second Flight. They thundered on.

"But didn't the fox just come from this direction?" Kathleen was confused.

"Yes," Yvonne confirmed.

Aunt Daniella closed her window, as the cold began to bother her. The others did, too.

Skiff turned the truck around. Yvonne waited for them to go first. They could see Shaker gesticulating in the cab.

Now rolling, Yvonne checked her speedometer. "Fifteen miles per hour."

"We won't miss anything at that pace." Aunt Daniella turned back to Kathleen. "Everything you've read about foxes in stories, how clever they are, it's true. Granted, some of the stuff like *Reynard the Fox* is more about human behavior, but tales of foxes outsmarting us, hounds, other animals, they are uncommonly smart. Fiction may gild it but whatever goes on between their ears goes on much faster than what we think and their senses are sharper.

This may be our fox and he's turned back. It could also be another fox."

"But why did it get so quiet?"

"Hounds lost the scent. There are a lot of tricks a fox can do to destroy its scent. Chances are, our fellow pulled one out of the bag," Aunt Daniella replied.

Yvonne drove a little faster. "They are moving."

Were it not for scarlet coats, the ladies in the car would not have been able to see the field. Then everyone burst out of the woods, flying back to the abandoned chapel. Again, a full stop.

Diana trotted to the chapel, checked around it. Walked to the double doors. Sniffed. Not a hint of scent. She rejoined the others, filtering through the tombstones with Irish, Polish, and Italian surnames. Many of these had gone AWOL from the English troops. Others arrived on our shores after the war. Here and there an English surname appeared. Perhaps someone sick of Catholics not being able to hold office in England.

Again, Yvonne cut her motor. They watched, silent.

Hounds made good the ground. Weevil walked with them, from time to time encouraging quietly. Betty followed, as did Tootie, on their respective sides.

Finally Weevil stopped them, for Sister sent up Gray to tell him they were out of territory. At the end of the back pasture they would be intruding on land rented by a deer hunting club. Even though deer season was over, many clubs forbid anyone on their land. For the actual landowner this could be a welcome bit of income on land unproductive or land they could no longer manage.

Weevil turned Kilowatt, hounds obediently followed.

"*I hate when he gets away,*" Pansy complained.

"*Me, too, but this is the first time we've been back here. Next time we'll know a bit more,*" Diana wisely counseled.

It was one-thirty. They'd been out three and a half hours, much of that hard running. So the walk proved slow, everyone catching their breath. At Little Dalby all loaded up and drove to Tattenhall Station, where Kasmir and Alida hosted another breakfast. The owners of Little Dalby, awash with in-laws this weekend, couldn't really do it. But this was fine.

Once in the station, Kathleen sat next to Aunt Daniella, for the older lady told her to do so. She said that everyone would come up to pay their respects and then she could introduce Kathleen. And they did.

Yvonne caught up with Sam, who hunted Ranger, a new green horse that Crawford had bought. He was buying a lot of horses lately.

Drew was there, having changed into tweed for the breakfast, fielding questions about Morris. He declared he had to get out of the house. He needed to hunt and he had hired the nurse for today to give Bainbridge a break, too.

The breakfast, like everything Kasmir and Alida did, was perfect.

Finally, Aunt Daniella, Yvonne, and Kathleen left. Pulling up to the stone house, Kathleen invited the two in for a moment.

"I want you to meet Abdul."

So she introduced them to her sparky Welsh terrier then on a whim said, "Come downstairs for a moment."

Dutifully, the two ladies trooped down.

Kathleen cut on the lights. "You know everybody, Aunt Dan, and you, Yvonne, have wonderful taste. Look at how you've turned out for the hunt."

"That's clothing, not furniture," Yvonne demurred.

"Tell me, what can I do to improve?"

"Oh, Harry pretty much thought of everything," Aunt Daniella praised him.

"What about an open bar, a place for coffee and tea? A place to sit down at the back? You know, so people would have to walk through the shop to get there."

Yvonne, a media person, hadn't thought of that. "There's an idea."

"You know how a supermarket puts milk in the back so you must walk down aisles to reach it. I mean, everybody needs milk."

"Kathleen, here's the rub," Yvonne shrewdly realized, "everybody doesn't need fabulous antique furniture."

"No. Which is why I want to find ways to get people in here. Much of this stuff will sell itself."

They chatted on, then Yvonne walked over to the Louis XV desk, a soft light shining down on it. "Gray told Sam, who told me, that Harry hoped to sell this desk to Sister."

"Ah. I had no idea," Kathleen murmured.

"Her uncle had such a desk and it was stolen over twenty years ago." Aunt Daniella remembered it well, because it was such an unlikely thing to happen but it did. "This is beautiful." She walked over, touching the inlaid leather top, running her forefinger over the ormolo on the corners. Two squarish drawers made up the sides, with a long narrow drawer in the middle.

"Do you think people know how to build like this today?" Yvonne joined Aunt Daniella.

Kathleen came over. "Maybe it's like classical music. There will always be people willing to study, to take the hard path for beauty. Surely there are a few workshops even in our country where men are fashioning such treasures."

"Men," Yvonne said without rancor.

"Give the girls time. If they can become Marines and firemen, some ladies will begin to make beautiful things with their hands, I mean things like this, not pottery or something on a loom, not that I don't notice pretty fabrics." Aunt Daniella laughed. "Hell, we only got the vote in 1920." Then she snapped her fingers. "Minutes ago."

"May I open a drawer?" Yvonne respectfully asked.

"Of course," Kathleen said.

Yvonne first opened one of the drawers on the corner. She peered at the two woods joining each other. No nails, nothing like that. These drawers were perfectly fitted pieces. Then she opened the middle drawer. A light blue envelope, dark blue handwriting, a man's handwriting, on the face of it.

Kathleen reached in and picked it up. "That's Harry's hand-writing."

"Addressed to 'Mrs. Jane Arnold, MFH,'" Yvonne read out loud.

"It's sealed." Aunt Daniella put her hand on Kathleen's, turning over the envelope. "Expensive paper."

"Kathleen, I drive by Roughneck Farm on my way home, would you like me to deliver it?"

"Yes, Yvonne, that would be thoughtful." Kathleen, like the other two, was mystified.

Forty-five minutes later Yvonne pulled up to the stable, for Sister, Betty, Tootie, Weevil, and even Gray were in there. Tootie and Weevil had seen to the hounds, coming in to clean their tack with their last reserves of energy, but Betty, bless her, had already done it. Tired, they had collapsed on tack trunks, director's chairs in the tack room for a moment.

Gray stood up when Yvonne entered, as did Weevil.

"Oh, please sit down, gentlemen. You've had a full day."

Weevil smiled. "Terrific day."

"Yes, it was," Sister, Betty, and Tootie echoed.

Yvonne relayed how she and Aunt Daniella had stopped for a bit to visit Kathleen's living quarters, meet the dog, then had gone downstairs, where Kathleen had asked for advice. Yvonne told how the envelope was found. She had dropped off Aunt Dan and stopped by with Kathleen's permission to personally hand over the letter.

Sister rose, fetching a pocketknife from the stand-up Jefferson desk in the tack room. She slit open the seal, carefully removing the paper. Her face registered shock. She handed the paper to Gray while Betty leaned over his shoulder. Then Yvonne, Tootie, and Weevil read it.

Dear Jane,

  Thank you for years of hunting, for breakfasts, for inspired chats. In the event of my death, this desk is yours.

            Love,

            Harry

His bold signature filled up half the page.

Sister sagged into her chair, her eyes moist. "Dear God," she gasped.

Gray bent over her, placing his hand on her shoulder. She covered his hand with hers.

Betty blurted out, "It's as though he had a premonition."

CHAPTER 20

March 18, 2019 Monday

"You hear that, that people sometimes know when they're going to die." Suzann stood books upright on the round table across from the cash register.

"My grandmother always said she would die when she was eighty-three." Roni, behind the counter, double-checked her Post-it notes by the side of the register.

"Did she?" Martha, listening on her way to the small accounting office, inquired.

"No. She made it to eighty-nine." Roni smiled.

"Close enough," Jean said. "I think people know."

"Guess some do. I mean, if you've had a heart attack or something like that maybe you become more sensitive." Suzann wasn't sure she wanted to entertain such a premonition.

"There are perfectly healthy people who tell others maybe a week or two before they die." Jean came out from behind the counter, a clean cloth in hand, to wipe down the books that Suzann had stood up. "Fingerprints. People pick them up. I can't stand it."

"So I see," Suzann wryly observed.

"Do you think Harry had a premonition? Marion said Sister read her the note," Roni asked.

Marion, in the store early, had gone to pick up new velvet pillows for the zebra-covered chair at the entrance. One of her Scotties had chewed the corner of one, which wouldn't have offended most people but Marion wanted things perfect.

"Yes," Jean said with conviction. "How many years have we all known Harry?"

"Ever since I started working here, thirteen years ago," Roni added.

"And I knew him years before that from foxhunting. He had a feeling. It was in keeping with his character that he would leave the desk to Sister." Jean finished her wiping.

"And if he had lived he would have finagled the money out of her somehow." Roni laughed. "A born salesman."

"Look who's talking!" Suzann teased her.

"I'm not a born salesman, but if something looks good on someone, I tell them. Now, Jean, there's the born salesman. Can you imagine if she and Harry owned a business together?" Roni pointed to Jean.

"What you do is notice what people wear, how they talk, jewelry. If it's a man, look at his watch. Does he wear a signet ring? Nothing born about it. Who doesn't want to look good? Some people have no idea about colors. So hold the color up to their chin. You all can do that." Jean put her hands on her hips.

"Not as well as you can. You probably took one of those color lectures." Suzann laughed.

"What is a color lecture?" Roni was confused.

"Oh, she's talking about years ago when there was this 'what season are you?' fad. Winter color or fall color? Red, pink, stuff like that was assigned to a season. Well, all you have to do is look at someone's hair color and skin color. Nothing seasonal about it. You don't pop a dark-haired person in beige usually. That's for blondes." Jean returned to behind the counter.

"Well, Jean, what do you pop a black-haired person in?" Suzann was having fun with this.

"Red. All dark-haired people look good in red and blondes rarely do. It's not difficult."

"For you, Jean. I get sidetracked on the fit. I mean, I can't stand baggy coats, baggy hunt coats. If it fits across the shoulders, if you can move your arms forward with the horse, then I tell the person to consider tailoring the sides. A nip, you know," Roni said. "Unless it's a side-saddle. That has to be perfection." She mentioned warm weather coats.

"Hear, hear," Martha called out from the small office.

"Oh, Martha, you can wear anything." Roni laughed.

"That figure." Suzann, herself well made, nodded.

"Back to Sister's letter. What do you think truly?" Roni, having seen Harry, wanted feedback.

"He knew." Jean didn't hesitate.

"Knew he would have an accident?" Roni asked.

"Maybe not that. Maybe he felt his time was close. You don't need to know how. I don't think so anyway. Someone suffering in the last stages of cancer, that's different. But he knew." Jean folded her arms across her chest. "I think Dad knew."

"Speaking of someone who could talk a dog off a meat wagon." Roni smiled. "You had to like Mr. Roberts. He'd come into the room and you were glad he was there."

Jean, who loved her father, smiled broadly. "You had to like him because he liked you. He liked people. Wanted to know all about them."

"You're like that," Martha called out.

"I don't know, Martha, the older I get the more doubts I have about the human race."

"Don't we all." Suzann shrugged. "But I like to think people are trying their best."

"Pollyanna." Roni flipped a rubber band at her.

"Oh, Roni, you're a mushball," Suzann teased her.

"There's a song about her. 'I'm just a girl who can't say no,'" Jean teased her more. "Not about sex. But you can't resist a hard-luck story."

"Look who's talking?" Martha again called out, couldn't stand it so she joined the group.

"Well, none of us could resist Harry, that's for sure. We chatted away when he left the store with me. How he could make me laugh."

Roni nodded. "A man who can make you laugh is already on second base."

"Maybe third." Jean smiled then changed the subject. "I don't think winter is done with us."

"Don't say that." Suzann took the cloth Jean had to wipe the top of the glass case. "I have had it."

"We all have." Jean thought she would scream if she saw another snowflake.

"While we're talking about liking people, about selling to people, who do you like better to sell to, men or women?" Suzann knew that would arouse them.

"Men. Women are too picky." Jean laughed.

"Well, when it comes to clothing, women are raised to be picky. Looks are everything. Most men have no idea about color, your expertise." Roni was right.

"You'd think they'd learn." Martha laughed. "Actually, it is interesting, in that many great designers were men. Balenciaga, Worth, even today, many more men are designing than women."

"Halston. Versace. All gay." Roni liked fashion, not that she wanted to spend a fortune on it.

"Givenchy wasn't gay. I don't think so. But I'm willing to bet they learned that stuff from their mothers." Jean paused. "But hey, Charlotte Ford. Jil Sander. Women are moving in. Diane von Furstenberg, Donna Karan. Granted, I haven't named any young women."

"Young women have to be out there. We're showing our age," Martha teased all of them.

"Okay. Would you rather work with men or women?" Suzann bedeviled them.

"Suzann, we're all women. We work together fine." Martha liked the "girls," as she thought of them, and vice versa.

"We do get along. We can talk about anything." Suzann sighed.

"And do," Roni shot back at her.

"Harry was like that. Not that he was one of the girls but you could talk to him about anything." Jean's voice softened.

"Isn't that something about him having a wife? No one knew."
Roni leaned on her elbows on the case.

"Marion said that Sister liked her and she, Kathleen, said
nothing bad about Harry. They didn't fit but neither one felt like
dragging the other through a divorce. I believe that," Jean replied.

"Think about it. If you marry and it's not what you wanted but
it's not awful, okay, you separate, but not being divorced you aren't
tempted to marry again. I think for all his charm Harry must have
lost his confidence. This was a form of protection. He wouldn't
make a mistake." Suzann had thought about this obviously.

"I wonder." Jean wrinkled her brow for a moment. "If we were
logical, no one would take the chance. Love has to override logic."

"And when it works, it's great," replied Roni, happily married.

"We delude ourselves. I don't think humans are all that logical. We parade it but look at what we do, look at who we elect to
public office, only to find out we've been betrayed?" Jean picked up
another cloth to wipe the glass case on the other side of the cash
register from Suzann. "We want to believe, you know."

"What's life if you don't take chances?" Martha wondered.

"Exactly." Roni backed her up.

"I wonder if I'll have a premonition about my death." Suzann's
voice drifted off.

"Oh, bull, Suzann. If you have a premonition it better be
about the winning lottery ticket." Jean flicked her rag at her.

CHAPTER 21

March 19, 2019 Tuesday

One day from the vernal equinox added needed light to the evenings. Drew pulled into his home, sunset ahead but still he could do some chores in light.

He changed clothes, passing Morris, who sat in front of his computer, nose almost touching the screen. His computer skills seemed mostly intact, if he could remember what he was curious about in the first place. He didn't greet his brother.

"Bainbridge?"

"Who cares?" came the sour reply.

Drew walked into the large kitchen, copper pots and pans hanging from overhead hooks. "I'm going out to the barn for a bit."

"Okay."

Drew opened the kitchen door to the outside, walked across well-laid flagstones to his four-stall center-aisle barn. To the side of this lovely taupe-painted building sat his brand-new three-horse trailer attached to a year-old Dodge Ram 3500, dually. The bed of the new truck was so high that he traded in his old trailer at Blue Ridge Trailers for a new one that had a nose to accommodate the seven-inch rise in floor beds. Why truck-makers raised the floor bed was anybody's guess. Made climbing into the truck cab an adventure, too. Even a tall man like Drew now needed a sidestep.

A stable girl picked out stalls, cleaned out buckets, cleaned tack, worked horses during the day. All Drew had to do was feed in the evening, which he enjoyed. It wasn't that he felt above physical labor, but the agency sucked time. He hated the dead of winter because he arrived home in cold dark. Then he would lead in his two trusted hunters.

Today, sun almost at the horizon line, he put his fingers in his mouth and whistled. Two eager horses galloped up. He opened the outside doors to each stall and they walked in, ears forward, heads immediately in the feed buckets he had filled before calling them.

The sound of horses eating calmed him. Not that his day had been bad, only one fender bender, on the off-ramp of Route 64 at the Shadwell exit. His team would take care of that. The adjuster from the large insurance agency with which his agency had placed the account would go over the car, an Altima, at the garage where it had been towed. A good adjuster could keep costs down. Naturally everyone thought they were being screwed by their insurance company and many times they were. He kept an eye on it and if something seemed really out of line, Drew called someone at the mother company, often housed in another state. The insurance agency was his job, the only job he knew. That didn't mean he liked it. He preferred the land insurance, houses, which was also part of the business. Drew knew the county intimately, as his father or he had insured much of it.

He'd been spending money like water the last two years. Trips, cruises, the truck last year, the trailer. A new Vulcan stove. But his accounts were in order. Drew liked having what he wanted when he wanted it. Unlike Crawford he wasn't showy. Of course, people noticed the new truck, a new trailer, but foxhunters needed those things. He wasn't driving a Bentley. He did want the brand-new BMW X7 but he would wait a bit. Also, he did not show photos of his trips nor brag about them. If anyone asked he would discuss where he visited. The last big trip was to Patagonia, which he loved.

And he loved Binny and Ugh, his two hunters. The night would cool off so he put a blanket on each horse as they ate. Tuesday, a hunt day, was one where he worked because Monday always spilled over onto Tuesday. However, with a bit of luck he'd hunt this Thursday and Saturday also. That was the great thing about owning Taylor Insurance Agency. He could set his own hours. The day his father died he did exactly that, for the old man had worked him ruthlessly.

Latching the stall door behind him he opened the door to his tack room. A thick sisal rug covered the floor, no tack trunks inside. They lined the center-aisle walkway next to the stalls. Two over-stuffed chairs of uncertain vintage took up the middle of the large room. Leaning against the wall were folding chairs in case more people showed up. He wanted to host a hunt, as Sister had extended the season to March 30th, Saturday. He'd been busy with Morris this season, plus the traveling, and hadn't hunted as much as usual. He picked up the phone and dialed his master.

She answered the phone. He discussed an added hunt at Pitchfork Farm.

"Drew, you have a lot on your plate. Hosting a hunt breakfast is a lot of work."

"I can lock up Morris."

A pause followed this. "I do hope it doesn't come to that, but I have an idea that is halfway to your own. Perhaps we can hunt Fairies Bottom, next to you. That way we can park there. Maybe we can have a tailgate there. We'll probably reach Pitchfork."

"Never know where the fox will go."

"That's the fun of it. I'll need to run this by Walter. I appreciate the offer." She made her goodbyes and hung up.

Morris had walked into the tack room. "When is supper?"

"Bainbridge is making it now. Let's go into the house."

"I want to hunt."

"Morris, we're at the end of the season and you haven't been riding. You aren't fit."

"I can ride. I've been riding since I was a kid."

"Come on, let's walk to the house, wash up, and we can talk about this at the table."

Morris looked around the tack room, then went out to the center aisle, reluctantly following his brother to the house.

"I heard you say there would be a hunt. I want to go."

Drew glanced at his nephew making stir-fry. Bainbridge looked up and shrugged.

"Why don't we see how you feel later?"

"Don't put me off. I'm not stupid." Morris's temperature rose.

"I'm not putting you off. I need to see how I feel, too." Drew kept his voice even.

"I'll see how I feel, too." Bainbridge reached into the cupboard for three bowls.

"You can't ride," his father complained.

"Well, I can, but I haven't in a long time. What I can do is ride us both around in the car."

"I want to ride!"

"Morris, relax," Drew said.

That fast Morris stood up, grabbed his spoon, throwing it in Drew's face. He stomped out of the kitchen. They could hear him thumping up the stairs.

"Has he been like this all day?"

"No," Bainbridge replied to his uncle. "He's spent the day in front of the computer."

"Doing what?"

"Watching movies. Science fiction. Dragons. He can watch the same film over and over but it keeps him quiet."

"I guess that's something."

Thump, thump, thump, Morris came down the stairs, opened the front door. Out he went.

Drew hurried after his brother, who was heading for the car. The keys were not in the ignition. Both Drew and Bainbridge had that down.

Morris opened the car, searched for the keys, then slammed the door.

"I want my books."

"What books?"

"The books I kept in Mother's secretary."

Those books had been on one shelf of a secretary the color of honey. It was one of the pieces that Harry had picked up and sold.

"You took those books out after Mother died."

"Where are they? I want to read *Catch-22*."

"You must have put them in a carton."

"Drew, where is Mother's secretary? I want to look."

"Sold. We sold the secretary."

"I never sold Mother's secretary. I loved her secretary. I liked the cubbyholes." He narrowed his eyes. "Don't lie to me."

"I am not lying to you. We sold her things years ago. Twenty-some years ago."

"Never! I would never have agreed to that. You've been stealing from me. Those things belonged to me."

"Morris," Drew's voice rose slightly, "we both decided, and our wives decided, it was old-style. Not what we wanted in our houses."

Morris stepped toward Drew, took a swing at him.

Ducking, Drew doubled his fist, stood up after Morris swung wildly, hitting him hard on the chin. Morris dropped.

"Bainbridge!"

Bainbridge didn't hear him so Drew dragged Morris by the arm to the back kitchen door.

"Bainbridge," he called as he opened it.

The tall young man came to the door. "Shit."

"Let's carry him to his room. And I'll need to lock the door. He accused me of stealing from him and lying to him."

"Over what?"

"The books he had in Mother's secretary."

Bainbridge took Morris under the arms, Drew took the feet. Sweating, they reached the top of the stairs, walked down the hall, tossed him on the bed. Drew closed the door, locking it.

"He'll throw a fit when he wakes up," Bainbridge predicted.

"Better a fit than come at me."

"He was docile watching his movie."

"He's not docile now. He's only going to get worse. For all I know, he'll set the house on fire in a fit."

"Well, I don't know."

"I don't want to find out. Even if he wakes up, pounds the door, smashes furniture in there, don't open the door."

"He needs his meds."

"Go get them. We'll stuff him full. Then we can see how he is in the morning, because he'll need another dose."

Bainbridge ran down the steps, opened the medicine cabinet, grabbed the pill bottles, one being a tranquilizer. Once upstairs they pried open Morris's mouth, shoved the pills down his throat like a dog, then poured a bit of water in his mouth. He reflexively swallowed.

Then they left him, locking the door.

Bainbridge shook his head. "We can't live like this. Even his nurse would have a hard time."

They could hear a chair being thrown against the wall, the door being pounded upon.

"If he kills himself, that's one thing. If he kills one of us, that's another. The violence is sporadic. We'll probably need to put him on even more drugs."

"How do we get them in him?"

"I don't know. He'll calm down. We have time to think about it."

CHAPTER 22

March 20, 2019   Wednesday

Slap. Slap. Slap. The huge waterwheel at Mill Ruins turned, throwing water outward, the long rays of early-morning light not yet fracturing the water into millions of tiny, moving rainbows.

Sister, next to Walter, watched the wheel, giant gears still working as they had for over two centuries.

"That sound." She breathed in the quite cool morning March air. "For centuries that sound was as familiar to people as their own breathing. Now few have ever heard the rhythm."

He kept his hands in his fleece-lined pockets. "Funny you bring that up. As a doctor I see new technology advances so much in medicine that I like, and yet on other fronts it can be a loss, can't it?"

"Yes, to me it is. Who brings grain to be ground anymore then takes home the fresh corn, oats, whatever, placing it into their wagon, inhaling that odor? The odor of life, if you think about it. For centuries those grains kept us and our stock alive."

"Still does, but God knows what's in it." He grimaced.

"In that respect I envy the horses. If you can get fresh crimped oats, they're exactly what they're supposed to be." She thought a moment. "But on the other hand, the commercial feeds have vitamins and many of the brands have the protein content, the fat content, etc., printed on the bag. That certainly helps with feeding the hounds, because we can adjust according to their workload and the cold. Everyone needs more calories in the cold if you're working out in it."

"Cold beats you up. And I'm getting cold. Let's go into the kitchen."

"Walter, one last thing. The fox that lives behind the mill. How about if I put out another feeder for him and add a few more near the other outbuildings? Because you're getting a bumper crop of foxes here."

"Fine with me." He looked up. "I wonder why they built the wheel side of the mill facing west. The wind comes from the west. I'd think that would be a problem."

"Could be, but the stream runs through the property, strong running. If you walk backward to the mill run where it cuts into the stream, this is easier, closer than trying to reroute the water. They cut those banks straight and clean. Our ancestors possessed incredible skills without gasoline-powered equipment."

"Ah." He nodded then they turned to walk into the kitchen.

Once sitting, Sister placed papers on the smooth small oak table. How many decades had she sat at that table absorbing Peter Wheeler's wisdom about many things, but especially hunting?

Placing a cup of tea before her, one for himself, Walter read the papers.

"Drew offered Pitchfork Farm for next week. How about Thursday?"

Walter nodded. "I'm not opposed to Pitchfork Farm but I think we should end our season's extension on March 30, Saturday, at the kennels. Go out with a weekend blowout."

"Gray and I talked about that. I think you're right."

"Well, five hunts to the end. Only if the weather cooperates. Maybe we will close this season with a few good runs. God, what an awful year."

"Mother Nature will do as she pleases. Okay, I'm with you on the Saturday for closing meet. How about if I call Drew back and ask would he consider a Thursday?"

"You can, but then he'll need to take off work." He picked up his mug then put it down. "We can't park easily at Pitchfork Farm. Never could. Did Drew mention that?"

"He'll call the Ticknors. I'll call as a follow-up, too, obviously."

"Whatever happened there? We haven't hunted that part of the county for years."

She shrugged. "Mrs. Taylor liked having us hunt at Pitchfork and we did. She'd created a roundabout at the end of the drive, all grown over now, so we could get the trailers in and park on the field with decent drainage. Anyway, we hunted there for years until she died and Drew and Morris sold her furniture to Harry Dunbar."

"Really?" He didn't know this part of the story, but it had been years ago and he didn't really know the Pitchfork area well.

"The entire affair descended into endless acrimony. If we had hunted there with Harry in the field, Drew and Morris would have created a scene."

"Wait a minute. I thought a landowner couldn't deny a field member access for a hunt. Isn't that part of the MFHA rules?"

"Yes, it is, but you can't enforce it without tearing apart a club. Most people don't care about the rules and it's difficult to get some of them to understand the traditions."

"True," he mumbled.

"Harry paid his dues. He had a right to hunt wherever we cast. I let it fade away. That's why Drew's call somewhat surprised me. Then again, Harry is dead."

"Good Lord." Walter exhaled.

"You've lived long enough to apprehend how petty people can be, vain, egotistical, but then again it was an ugly, ugly fight."

"But Drew rode in the field with Harry at other hunts."

"He had no choice. That wasn't his land and they never, ever spoke. Not once since the furniture debacle."

Walter took a deep sip. "Well, then I guess we have to hunt Pitchfork if we can start from Fairies Bottom. Think the Ticknors will be okay?"

"As Drew has probably already called them and he hasn't called me to say it isn't okay, I think it is, but of course, as I said, I will call, and since this is the reopening of territory, basically, we should bring gifts for the Taylors."

"Right." Walter put his chin on his cupped hand, elbow on the table, which would have driven his mother wild. "What?"

"Can't be bourbon. Bainbridge."

"I don't think he's an alcoholic."

"I hope not but there have been times when he's put on a good show. Then again, Drew and Morris could knock it back.

Maybe a bush that can be planted. Winter can't last forever. One for the Ticknors, too. Everyone likes a flowering bush."

"All I need is one daffodil and I'll believe." Walter laughed.

"Walter, I called you about Harry's letter, and Marion. Since then I've been thinking."

"It is a tremendous gesture on his part. An act of love, really."

"I couldn't believe it. We all had such good times and you never do know how what you do affects others. Actually, you know better than the rest of us. You save lives."

"Oh," he fumbled a moment, "I try. Our diagnostic abilities, our operating techniques, are so much better than even a decade ago. We can repair a heart without sawing through a ribcage. Most times. There are still problems where you have to do that to someone. But we have pinpoint lasers now. I can literally cut with light."

"Amazing."

"And it gets better and better. What I can't do anything about is a person's health habits. That's why Chalmers at Heron's Plume is such a great example. If I have a heel dragger but someone who is in our circle, so to speak, I bring up Chalmers Perez."

"He does look good. Younger."

"Health does that for you."

She folded her hands together, looked him in the eye. "Walter, is there something about Harry that I should know? Did he have some kind of condition? Something for which there was no hope?"

"Oh, Sister, the only way I would know that is if I were his personal physician or on a medical team called in to consult and treat him. Also, I'm a cardiologist. I would only be consulted if the issues involved the heart."

"Betty said she thinks his personal physician is Mark Derrick over at Augusta Hospital."

"He is."

"Would he tell you?"

"No. Nor would I ask. Patient confidentiality is important, and thanks to the Internet, fragile. I'll spare you my worries about the wrong people getting hold of your information and then selling it to insurance companies. That's for starters." He held up his hand. "But Mark wouldn't tell me unless I were part of the team."

"Well." A long pause followed this. "Let me come at this another way, did you have an inkling something might not be right with Harry?"

"No. I could see sometimes after dismounting he'd be stiff or he'd drag his left leg a few steps. We all have, as you put it, 'jewelry.' If he had, say a cancer, I would think it would show if it were one of the more obvious ones, like lung cancer."

"Are there cancers that aren't obvious?"

"Yes. For women, ovarian. Often by the time we find out it may be too late. Certain forms of colon cancer. Even with a colonoscopy, you can miss a tiny, tiny cell, and by the time you know, a major operation may fix it, but then again, the cancer may have metastasized to show up later."

"Okay. But if he had regular checkups, wouldn't his doctor know that his red blood cell count was up, I guess that's a stroke signal, I don't know. Or what about white blood cells?"

"Sure." Walter nodded. "But, Sister, there are an unfortunate number of things that give no warning. Like a massive stroke."

"Yes. I think I understand but if someone was vital, full of life, maybe they wouldn't want to wait for that. Go out on top."

"Is that what you think Harry did?"

"I don't know, but that note about the desk makes me wonder."

"Don't quote me on this, but that is a decision I understand and respect. And between us, if anything happens to me, that's what I'm going to do."

"Well, I'll be long gone by that time. I don't want to see you go."

He smiled. "Oh, Sister, you're tough as nails. You might outlive us all."

She smiled back at him. "Walter, I don't know that I would want to. It's hard enough to lose those who are older than you, then your own age, then younger people. I don't know that I want to live without at least some of my friends."

"Years ago, I wouldn't have understood that, but I do now. And I will miss Harry. We weren't that close but what good company he was and he knew hunting."

"Yes, he did, bless him." She finished her tea. "I called, also. Put the schedule on our website. Oh, I'll ask Betty to send out an email, as well. And remind me to change the color of the fixture card for next fall."

"Whatever you say. Fall's far away."

"Walter, September will be here before you know it. We're good?"

"Yes, ma'am."

"Think of Pitchfork Farm as a homecoming."

CHAPTER 23

March 21, 2019   Thursday

Ground fog hovered over the two ponds at Foxglove. The running water could be heard out of the pipe from the higher pond to the lower but Sister couldn't see it.

Mid-forties, light rain off and on, she wondered why the fog hadn't dissipated. With a light rain the ground fog wasn't going to lift but it could disperse. Fortunately her densely woven hunt coat dispersed the rain, but for how long?

The hunt, an hour into it so far, kept her tight in the tack. Hounds hit one fox after another although the runs proved short. But the undulating ground, the wetness of it, meant you'd better keep your leg on.

Sister waited as hounds cast again, a few raindrops dripping off her cap brim, clouds seeming to dip lower. A hard rain washed scent away fairly quickly if hounds could initially pick it up. The great thing about foxhunting was that textbooks, lectures couldn't help you. You figured it out or endured it on your own. The field, only fourteen today, heads down to ward off the moisture, had time to consider this.

Hounds moved deliberately, noses down.

A little tickle made Tattoo pause. *"Georgia."*

The others walked over to him, now all hounds walked slowly up the rolling pasture to the schoolhouse, where Georgia listened. Hounds didn't speak, scent wasn't heavy enough, plus they knew where Georgia was and they knew she wouldn't come out. Still, they moved in a single file, stopping at the house then looking up at Weevil.

"Good work." The blond fellow smiled down at them. Sister and the field waited perhaps forty yards off and Second Flight, only five people today, rested behind them.

Weevil turned toward the west, walked out on the farm road to cast on the other side of this road, where a woods gave some protection. The rain stayed light but the longer one was in it, the wetter one got, and now they'd been out perhaps an hour and fifteen minutes.

Hounds filtered into the woods, as did Weevil. Sister waited on the farm road. Her string gloves, while wet, allowed her to keep her hands on the reins. If she'd worn leather the reins would have slipped constantly.

Comet must have kept a calendar in his den because Wednesday nights Cindy Chandler often left gummy bears and bits of little honey cakes by the feeder boxes that Jefferson Hunt kept on her farm. The purpose of the boxes, which had an entrance and an exit too small for a hound but perfect for a fox, was to feed. However, during terrible weather those feeder boxes saved many a fox from hunger. Throughout the fall, wormer was spread on the kibble to clean out tapeworms and roundworms. Hence the very healthy Jefferson Hunt foxes with splendid coats. But good as all that was, sweets sang a siren song. Cookies, gummy bears, Jolly Ranchers, bits of candy bars, and every now and then a few peppermints lifted from the horses created a vulpine foodie heaven.

Comet had climbed the ridge between Roughneck Farm and Foxglove, descended, trotted through the lower weedy meadow. Then he crossed Soldier Road to hurry on to Foxglove. He ate too much and waddled home, leaving scent, too much scent because he wasn't that far away.

Pookah, a bit to the side of the main pack, found his line first. *"Comet."*

Hounds knew their foxes. Mostly they knew where all the burrowing animals lived as well as the larger animals, some of which they avoided. No point irritating a deer in rut. Besides, if they even looked at a deer, Tootie or Betty would call their names. If any hound was foolish enough to ignore a whipper-in naming them and naming them loudly, the human would ride up close and crack the whip over their head. It was embarrassing. So deer could be damned.

The pack opened. The ground in the woods, firm, offered some relief but soon enough hounds charged out into the huge wildflower field, now barren except for creepers here and there. The footing began to deteriorate. Not so much that staff worried, but as the grade dropped toward Soldier Road, time to slow a bit.

Comet, hearing the pack, disgusted with his piggery, picked up speed. Full though he was he could still run like the devil.

Fortunately no traffic filled Soldier Road. As this road took traffic far west including over the Blue Ridge on an old winding road as opposed to perfect I-64, the only time cars rolled along it was to get to work and to get home, for there were other farms beyond Foxglove.

Looking both ways, Comet shot across. Hounds within five minutes also shot across. One can't really stop hounds on a good line without cracking whips or firing .22 pistols in the air. No one wished to do this except in the case of danger, but no staff member ever really wants to cross a paved road, especially a wet one.

Weevil crossed on Midshipman, a four-year-old Thoroughbred learning the ropes who would eventually be ridden by the master herself. Sister prized a Thoroughbred or an Appendix, which is a Thoroughbred/quarter horse cross.

She stopped at Soldier Road holding Matador, not happy. Then she clucked and they crossed too fast for comfort but all was well. The two fields followed soon, fighting their way through the untended lower meadows on the north side of Hangman's Ridge, which loomed up ahead like doom itself.

Thorns never died. The worst blizzard couldn't end their nasty lives. Those creepers reached out, scratching boots, or worse, scratching thighs in a few cases, pulling the threads right up from the thick material.

Comet had reached the high flat ridge with the huge hanging tree in the middle toward the west. Most of the animals hated that tree, as they could feel the spirits, which the humans ignored or denied. Such things weren't logical and humans were hagridden by logic. Not Comet. He put on the afterburners.

Within another four minutes he was sliding down the south side of the ridge. A good mud farm road led up to the ridge while a few navigable deer trails snaked down, as well as one that circled the ridge.

Hounds closed then skidded down the southern trail. The trees, many of them conifers, created a few barriers but they also slowed down the rain now picking up. Sister followed but wisely chose the farm road, muddy though it was.

Comet flew down now on the farm road, which ran by the orchard. Inky, the black fox, popped her head out of her den, said nothing, then popped back in. Why Comet needed to go to Roughneck Farm when there was plenty of food at After All, she didn't know, but she lacked his sweet tooth.

Comet reached Tootie's cabin, paused, then crawled underneath, finally going down into his den. Target wasn't there, as he had gone back to After All. Target liked second and third homes.

Panting and wet, Comet nestled into the blanket he'd stolen from the barn. Dragging that back was a feat but he was glad he had. Snuggling in he flipped his gray tail over his nose, no white tip.

Then he listened.

First to the den was Dragon, out today and as offensive as usual.

"*Chicken. Show yourself,*" the arrogant hound complained.

"*Comet, you're slowing down.*" Ardent also insulted him.

A high-pitched voice called out, "*I ate like a pig and still you couldn't get near me. You didn't even see my tail, you were so far behind.*"

"*If we're so slow, why did you move out so fast?*" Diana sagely replied.

"*To get out of the rain.*" Which was partly true.

By now Weevil had reached the cabin. Betty was already in the field between Roughneck and After All Farms, having cleared the stiff coop in the north corner while Tootie stood on the farm road, down near the kennels. She had figured out where everyone was going and had reached the ridge before either Weevil or Betty. If hounds surged forward, she'd be there.

Weevil dismounted, knelt down, gloves wet and rain pattering on his back. All the hounds wanted to kiss him.

"Good hounds." He stuck his head under the stone foundation, for the entrance underneath was big enough. The odor of fox filled the air.

Comet could smell Weevil. Humans give off a distinctive scent, often heavy and often laced with cologne or perfume, especially if they've been sweating. The fox was tempted to stick his head out of his den.

He did.

"Ha!" was all Comet said, but it sounded like a bark.

"Cheeky devil." Weevil laughed then stood back up, patting each hound on the head. His knees shone with red clay. Rain, a trickle, managed to find its way down the back of his boots.

Sister rode up. "That was a surprise."

"Cheeky devil," Weevil repeated himself to Sister.

"Life's good here. Why he went all the way over to Cindy's I'll never know, but I suppose foxes like people enjoy a change of scenery."

"A better day than I thought it would be." Weevil reached Midshipman.

"Why don't you walk him to the barn? We're here. No point in riding back over the ridge and crossing the road again. I hate that road."

"Yes, Master." He took Midshipman's reins, the young fellow stood patiently, clearly a good student. Weevil reached down again to touch those beautiful heads. "Come along, come along. You were such good hounds."

"I did the heavy lifting," Dragon bragged.

His sister, Diana, snarled, *"Hell you did."* She walked alongside Pookah. *"Good work."*

The older hounds congratulated the younger hound, a few brushing next to her so that they walked shoulder to shoulder. A hound pack is a society. This was a step up for Pookah. She was a very happy hound and wiggled her way to the kennel.

Betty and Tootie dismounted, held the big double doors to the draw pen open as Sister and Gray stopped to take their horses' reins, walking them to the barn.

Sister told everyone to leave their horses in her paddocks if they wished. Each paddock had a run-in shed. They could all be driven over to Cindy's, then after the breakfast drive their rigs back here. No point riding and getting soaked.

Everyone was grateful.

Shaker, who could drive now, rolled down the farm road. Sister told him the decision so he began to load people in his truck. Yvonne and Aunt Daniella also showed up, as they had followed the hunt as best they could.

Sister and Gray wiped down their horses, Betty and Tootie's horses, then put them into their stalls with a thin cotton sheet, which would soak up the wet. Upon returning they'd swap it out for a blanket but not a heavy one. Nights were warming up. Maybe not as much as one would wish, but on the other side of freezing was good.

At Cindy's, people dripped even though they'd hung their coats in her mudroom.

"Don't worry about it. That's what mops are for," the hospitable blonde told them.

Freddie and Alida discussed politics. No one else had the stomach to do so. Drew was catching up with Betty. He'd told her about Morris's latest moment.

"Can you predict these outbursts?"

"No. He trashed his room after I locked him in. All I need is for him to find the keys and take off again. I've actually put the keys in a small metal lockbox."

"I can understand why you don't want to put him in a facility—"

He interrupted her. "Betty, they'd drug him insensate. You've seen what happens, or maybe you haven't, but I've visited a few of these, checking them out, you know? It's not a life. Morris at least is on familiar territory."

"Thank God he made a good living. Can you imagine what this is like for someone who hasn't?"

Later, driving back to Roughneck Farm, Betty relayed the conversation to Sister and Tootie, jammed into the cab of the truck, for Sister had allowed Weevil to use her Jeep to drive others back.

"What a mess." Sister turned up the speed on the windshield wipers. "I need a new car. The Jeep is, what, four years old, and I've beat the hell out of it. Thank the Lord, the truck's held up."

"You have. I'm sure you've checked out prices and what might you be looking at?"

"I'm torn between a Highlander and a BMW X5. I think either

one can handle what we have to go through out here. The price difference is, um, unfortunate."

"Is there any such thing as car prices lowering?" Betty asked.

"Probably not." Sister sighed. "You're smarter than all of us. You kept your Bronco. Goes through hell and high water. Sure, it sucks gas but the money you've saved in not cycling through cars makes up for it."

"I've been reading that gas prices will spike this summer. Way up. If so, then the car lots will be crammed with SUVs, and those little cars, good on gas, will fly off the lots."

"Maybe I should wait." Sister considered this.

They slowed to a crawl as a line of rigs clogged the Roughneck Farm road.

"What would you do if you had a Morris in your life? If Gray began to lose his marbles?"

A long silence followed this. "I'd talk to him before the inevitable and do what he wishes while he could still make good decisions. I'll tell you what to do for me."

"I'm all ears."

"Shoot me."

CHAPTER 24

March 22, 2019   Friday

The light reflected off the gilt ornament of the Louis XV desk as Sister positioned it in the center of the kennel office, where the original desk had been placed by Uncle Arnold.

"To the left." Betty wiggled her hand.

Tootie and Weevil moved the not terribly heavy desk two inches to the left.

"Looks good to me," Sister said.

"Is." Betty stepped back a bit. "It's odd to see such a beautiful piece of furniture in this office, but I remember the other one. Ray's uncle sat in this office more time than in the house so I suppose he liked his luxuries."

"Come on. Tootie and Weevil, you, too."

They followed her, raincoats on because the rain never stopped, to the house, into the kitchen, where the aroma of vegetable soup greeted them.

"Betty, you're in charge of putting out the sandwich meats.

Tootie, you can cut the bread. Weevil, you can sit down. I'll take the drink orders."

Given the raw day, the orders involved coffee or tea. Once settled they chatted about tomorrow's hunt, whether it would go off.

"Rain's supposed to stop tonight but the ground will be soaked," Betty reported.

"I know, but we can hunt. Maybe we won't be able to do anything but walk but we can go."

"Sister, why don't you make that call in the morning. You can't trust the weather reports. This entire season has been a mess," Betty wisely counseled.

"You're right," Sister agreed.

Weevil, a good cook himself, tasted the soup. "Perfect."

Sister smiled. "I think anything hot today would be perfect."

"What was Uncle Arnold like?" Tootie asked.

"Firm in his beliefs." Sister smiled. "He became a bit frail at the end and that's why Ray and I gave up our little place to move here. He was easy enough. All you had to do was go to the kennels with him, talk hounds. Made him happy."

"Was that when my grandfather carried the horn?"

"Yes," Sister answered. "Uncle Arnold was careful about who he hired. There was little turnover on his watch. He loved the big hound shows. I don't think he ever missed the Virginia Foxhound show or Bryn Mawr. Our hunt won classes, even the pack class once."

Weevil politely inquired, "But you didn't show once the hunt passed to you and your husband?"

"Actually, Weevil, we didn't really have the time. I was still working when we took over Roughneck Farm, as was Ray, of course. He hunted the hounds, which saved money. He was good. I didn't interfere with his decisions but if we were going to show we wanted to do a good job and we didn't think we could. Then when my son was born I had even less time."

Betty reached for the mayonnaise. "Uncle A, as he was often called, was gone by the time I hunted seriously. Of course, I heard the stories. He knew his bloodlines, Big Ray continued his breeding program. I came on board when Ray carried the horn." She passed the mayo to Tootie then said to Sister, "Bet the desk brings back memories."

"Well, it does, but it brings as many memories of Harry."

"Kathleen was gracious about that," Betty replied. "She could have hinted for money or been less understanding."

"She strikes me as a decent soul and she sent the desk over. I didn't do a thing. Gracious. That's how I would describe her."

"Did she say anything about the letter? You know, she knew him, um, differently than the rest of us," Betty wondered.

"She never indicated that he was prophetic, if that's what you mean." Sister tasted her own soup. "I did okay."

"Better than okay." Tootie smiled then added, "Maybe he had a feeling."

"Actually, I think we knew Harry better than Kathleen. People are usually forthcoming about their entanglements, marriage. Harry, odd for an antiques dealer, didn't look back." Sister then laughed. "Not even in the hunt field."

They chatted about who they might breed once the season ended and who would come into heat at the right time, always a crapshoot.

Then Betty, clearing the table even though Sister told her not to do it, opened the refrigerator door. "Aha!"

"I was going to do that."

"Don't you fib. You were going to keep the brownies for yourself." Betty pulled out the plate while the dogs sprang to life at the sound of the refrigerator door opening.

Golly, wiser, waited for Betty to put the plates in the sink before scraping them. Golly cleaned them as Betty put the brownies on the table.

"You know, these are good, if I do say so myself." Sister laughed as everyone grabbed a brownie.

"Didn't Kathleen receive the coroner's report on Harry? She's his wife. Wouldn't she be the first in line?" Betty wondered.

"I suppose she'd be after the authorities. She did."

"Well?" Betty raised an eyebrow.

Sister replied, "No drugs. A high red blood cell count but nothing to indicate a stroke. He had an accident. For whatever reason, we don't quite believe he could slip and fall and crack his head, but he did."

"It's the letter," Betty simply stated.

Weevil piped up. "Maybe he was planning to surprise our master anyway. He was working up to it."

"Given that he quoted me twenty thousand dollars, that would be quite a work-up."

"Twenty thousand?" Weevil was astonished.

"If the desk were original, from the time of Louis XV, it would be worth far more than that. For one thing, think of all the beautiful objects, even church art, destroyed in the French Revolution. Much of what we have was either hidden in the provinces or from the British Isles or other countries. Can you imagine how terrible that time was? They damn near killed anyone who had an education."

Tootie, who liked reading history almost as much as the sciences, replied, "Was there another way?"

"Oh, good question." Weevil smiled. "Destruction before construction."

"The king, not the brightest, wouldn't give way . . . but then, if you had to deal with that Parliament, you probably wouldn't either. Oh, I don't know. I'm not a historian but I do know once people start bitching and moaning it never comes to a good end." Betty grimaced then laughed. "Show me one place where life got better."

"For whom?" Sister fired back then looked up. "I can't believe this."

The rained poured.

"There's no way we can hunt tomorrow." Betty shook her head.

"Tootie, you have your phone attached to your kidneys." Sister pointed to her. "Dial up The Weather Channel."

Tootie, accustomed to Sister teasing her about technology, pulled her phone from her hip pocket. "The radar has changed. Rain and even tornado warnings, as this is coming up from the Gulf."

"What about tomorrow? It was supposed to end tonight." Sister was frustrated.

"No. Now the hourly forecast is that the rain will end at nine tomorrow morning."

"Dammit to hell!" Sister cursed.

"We could go on foot." Weevil wanted to hunt.

"You know, Weevil, we can do that for snow, but to get people out in saturated conditions is harder. Dammit. I'll have to cancel."

"I have an idea." Betty put both hands on the table, palms down. "Cancel, of course. But then add a closing hunt party Saturday. Sweeten cutting yet another hunt with a blowout for the last one."

"Well—all right. Betty, send out an email. I'll change the huntline. Now, Weevil and Tootie, here is a lesson about human pack behavior. Most of our members will like that we've thrown in a celebration. But some will say we should hunt Thursday, Friday, and Saturday if it isn't raining, to make up days."

"Oh, for Chrissake," Betty exclaimed. "Who will have enough horses? We've hunted so little this year thanks to . . ." She pointed to the roof, where the rain hammered.

Tootie said, "Their horses aren't fit. Who could go three days in a row, no matter what?"

Betty nodded. "Doesn't mean they won't pretend they could do it."

"You know what, we'll just deal with it. I am not extending the season into April. My prediction is many people will hold off until Saturday, even with keeping to our regular schedule."

"So they'll skip Pitchfork Farm?" Weevil wondered.

"Maybe. Dear God, I hope the ground is dry by then. You think?" Betty asked.

"If it isn't, it will be a mess, but if it's not raining, I'm going."

Betty thought then responded, "It probably will be a little messy, no matter what."

She had no idea.

CHAPTER 25

March 23, 2019   Saturday

Rain, steady but not torrential, continued to fall. The weatherman lied, but then forecasts along mountain ranges lean toward the inaccurate.

Sister drove while Aunt Daniella rode shotgun and Yvonne and Betty sat in the back.

"Are you sure Sam isn't going to be upset?" Aunt Daniella called back to Yvonne.

"No. I told him I won't buy a hunt kit without him but I wanted a Saturday with the girls."

"How nice that you called us 'the girls.'" Sister glanced into the rearview mirror.

"Well, we are." Aunt Daniella leaned on the armrest. "Betty told me you're thinking of buying another car?"

"Actually, this is Gray's. My Jeep wouldn't be as comfortable as his Land Cruiser for the drive. He's at the home place with Sam.

They're building something. Those two ought to start a contracting service for older homes."

Aunt Daniella agreed. "You know how precise Gray can be. When I wanted new marble for my entrance, the green veined kind, the expensive kind," her voice dropped, "Gray measured and re-measured. They installed it. Saved me money, but what a fuss. Does cast an allure when you walk through the front door."

"You cast the allure," Sister complimented her.

"That's very sweet of you. There was a time." Aunt Daniella smiled broadly.

"You can still reel them in." Betty laughed then turned to Yvonne. "You and Aunt Daniella are women of such beauty. Now, don't deny it. We're all old friends here. Granted, you're a new friend but no one pussyfoots. Do you think, and you, too, Aunt Dan, that beauty gives power?"

Yvonne stretched out her long legs, which she could do in the Land Cruiser. "It does and I did not use it wisely. And I didn't un-derstand what I could do, really. All I ever knew was men making fools of themselves. I was actually repelled."

"Different times. I knew it was a way up and out, and now you must remember, Yvonne, that the Lorillards and the Laprades were free blacks. I knew I could attract another well-to-do black man to marry. Which I did. My sister, Graziella, beautiful herself, wasn't logical. I knew I had to think for both of us."

"So you married for money?" Betty knew she had but had never said it out loud.

"I did, but then I realized I hadn't married for enough." She laughed. "Yvonne, you and Victor made a fortune. You may not have been as single-minded as I was but you considered the bank balance."

A long breath followed that, then Yvonne replied, "I knew he was ambitious. I'd been courted by football players and basketball players, famous, rich, but something told me they would not fare well once the playing days were over. I was right. Also, they have been petted and protected even in high school. They expect everything to come to them. At least that was my experience. I wanted someone who would make something of himself through his mind."

"You found him," Sister simply affirmed.

"I thought I loved him. We built a fabulous business."

"And?" Betty prodded.

"I never factored in what middle age does to men . . . or women, for that matter. But how can you when you're young?" Yvonne wondered.

"Oh, I think you pick up a whiff. You know, the man who preens before every woman, the woman who has her first face-lift at thirty-five," Aunt Daniella said.

"Well, I suppose. You all know what happened. But as to power, your original question, yes, beauty supersedes logic. But I don't think it affects women the same way."

"Yvonne, you mean a beautiful woman, let's say she's gay, isn't undone by another beautiful woman? Or what about women in general? We notice but . . ." Betty shrugged.

"You'd have to ask a gay woman, but for straight women, when have you heard a woman say, 'I saw him and knew I'd marry him.' Or 'It was love at first sight.' Think. How many women have said that to you?" Yvonne answered.

"Uh, I've heard women say they noticed a man was handsome."

"Sure, but love at first sight?" Yvonne stuck to her point.

"I never have and you know how old I am. I think women are more logical. Now, I have seen women made a fool by a man once they've decided they love him. It's funny because men accuse us of being more emotional. I think they're the emotional ones." Aunt Daniella looked out as they crossed the Robinson River, not a big river.

"I have a type. Maybe we all do, but I have to be able to talk to a man. Don't you?" Sister asked.

"I do," Yvonne agreed.

"I . . . well, I think I can size men up easily." Aunt Daniella added, "But then, I wasn't looking for love."

"You found it though. You loved Mercer's father." Sister remembered him.

"I did. He grew on me. I liked him. I would have never married him if I didn't like him. He was my second husband, Yvonne. I learned to love him. He was a good man." She snapped her fingers. "Heart attack. Fifty-six."

They rode on, talking about everything. Sister drove to Horse Country's front door. "Ladies, disembark. I'll park in the lower parking lot. This one is full. You won't get wet."

"You will." Yvonne leaned forward.

"No. Betty, tell whoever is behind the front desk to unlock the downstairs door. Sometimes it's locked. Sometimes it's not. Then I can dash in."

"Will do. Come on, girls." Betty opened her door, then opened the door for Aunt Daniella, escorting her into the store.

Yvonne made a dash for it then stopped right inside to take in the store. She hadn't expected it to be so sophisticated. She'd been dragged to enough tack shops by Tootie before she left Chicago to go to Custis Hall.

Betty, making sure Aunt Daniella's shoes weren't slippery, turned to Yvonne. "You could spend an entire day in here."

"That's what I'm afraid of." Yvonne laughed.

"Hello, ladies. Betty, didn't see you at first." Jean Roberts was behind the counter.

"Sister's coming up from downstairs," Betty informed her.

"Good. I'll tell Marion."

Marion came out from her office, greeting everyone, and immediately took Aunt Daniella by the elbow as Yvonne followed.

"I haven't seen you in years. You look wonderful."

"Marion, so do you, and you probably should know this is Tootie's mother."

Yvonne laughed. "Ever since I've moved to Virginia I've been introduced as Tootie's mother."

"She's a beautiful girl and so talented. Sister updates me on her riding, and she's almost finished with UVA. She compressed three years into two."

"Driven. Tootie has always been driven." Yvonne smiled and Marion could imagine her on the runway, especially a runway for a hunt fashion show.

"Let me show you the hacking jackets I just got in from England." Marion steered them to the rear of the store, where she guided Aunt Daniella to a small wing chair. "As I recall, you are partial to a bluish tweed."

"I am." Aunt Daniella fingered the fabric. "Oh, Marion, I won't be riding anymore."

"That doesn't mean you can't wear tweed to a hunt breakfast and show everyone up." Marion laughed.

Jean joined them, pulling off the rack a gorgeous medium-weight windowpane jacket, which she held up under Yvonne's gorgeous face. "Hmm." Jean pulled a more honey-colored one. "Ah, what do you think?"

If there was one thing Yvonne knew, it was clothing, but hunt clothing was a new category. The fabric brought out her luscious skin.

"You can buy ratcatcher but you can't buy formal wear. Sam would be crushed. He truly wants to be with you for that." Aunt Daniella nodded her approval of the coat, which Yvonne slipped on.

To Marion and Jean, Yvonne explained, "My trainer is Sam Lorillard and I'm a beginner, but I am determined to hunt next year. He wants to bring me here and put me together, so to speak."

"Of course," Jean agreed, for she knew Sam; she knew most of the state's horsemen.

"However, you can buy a tweed coat and you can wear it everywhere but especially to a hunt breakfast," Aunt Daniella encouraged her.

As the two tried on jackets, ogled vests, Sister walked outside in the rain to see where Harry had fallen. The steps were steep and in the rain she could well imagine a slip. She dashed back in, a bit damp. Then Betty did the same thing. They looked at each other, clasped hands, and then let go. His death wasn't exactly a sorry end, for it was swift. It seemed too early an end, though, but when you like someone, it's always too early.

They walked back to Aunt Daniella and Yvonne.

"What do you think?" Yvonne had the tweed on, looking divine.

"Perfect." Sister smiled.

Marion touched the sleeve. "You will probably ride in this next season, so don't shorten the sleeves. They are long but when your arms are forward, hands on the reins, the cuff will be at exactly the right place."

"Okay." Yvonne pushed her arms forward to see for herself.

"Will you put this behind the counter? I want to see every-thing." Yvonne was fascinated.

"You go ahead, honey." Aunt Daniella rose, following Marion and Jean back to the front, where she sat in the zebra wing chair.

Roni, now behind the counter, asked, "Would you like a drink? Tea? Coffee? Cold drinks?"

Suzann, beside her, winked. "We do have spirits."

"I'm sure you do. I would like a Coca-Cola. The caffeine will pick me up. Rain makes me tired."

"Me, too," Roni agreed.

Saturday was always a big day at the store, and it filled with people. Martha Kelley took over behind the counter so Suzann could go downstairs to answer questions about some bridles. Ladies had come in from a hunt all the way in Michigan, and Suzann shep-herded them happily.

Finally Yvonne returned, discovering the jewelry. She had al-ready swooned over the silver and china, as had Sister. Both women evidenced a weakness for table settings. Why, they didn't really know. They blamed it on their mothers.

Sister stood next to her as Jean pulled out ravishing gold, diamonds, crystals, jewelry from the late nineteenth century through the 1920s, captivating Yvonne.

"The workmanship. Oh, how could I miss that?" She pointed to the fox ring, now back in the case.

Jean pulled it out, saying nothing. Serena Neff had brought it back at the beginning of the week. No foul play seemed to be at issue. Serena couldn't help it, she wore the ring to Horse Country then slipped it off. That fox ring cast a spell.

"Erté," Marion stated.

Yvonne knew who Erté was. "Why would anyone part with this? It's a piece of art."

"You know, tastes change. And of course, finances change." Marion placed the ring on a small piece of black velvet on the countertop. "Here."

Yvonne held out her hand as Marion placed the ring on her third finger, left hand, then noticed the St. Hubert's ring on her right hand, little finger. "That's stunning."

"I hope Saint Hubert protects me. Now, I wouldn't wear both of these rings at the same time. The fox ring is a nighttime dazzler. Don't you think?"

"I do," Marion agreed as Yvonne took it off, placing it on the velvet.

"While I'm here I'd like to buy something for Sam. He's been so good to me. His chaps are worn."

"Allow me to suggest you not buy ready-made chaps." Marion looked into her eyes. "Sam is a professional. He lives in chaps, boots. He needs a pair of chaps made specifically for him. You can't do better than Chuck Pinell, who has his workshop in your county.

Sister will take you there. I could sell you chaps, but really, he needs a custom order."

Yvonne realized why people remained so loyal to Marion. She could have sold her chaps. She gave her good advice rather than make money off of her.

"Marion, could you suggest something I could purchase from you?"

"How are his paddock boots?"

"Worn to pieces." Sister now leaned on the counter. "As you know, Betty bought me a new pair for International Women's Day. So comfortable."

"All right." Marion came out again from behind the counter, leading them to the rear of the first floor, where the paddock boots and Italian formal boots were lined up. As the ladies were back there Betty sat on a step, a riser sort of, next to Aunt Daniella. Roni had thoughtfully brought Betty a drink as well.

Sister and Yvonne returned, each with paddock boots, tough ones. Sister liked her boots so much she was buying a second pair. Yvonne and Sister readied to pay their bills. Yvonne bought a tweed jacket for herself and winked, so Jean ran back and picked up the blue one for Aunt Daniella, who wouldn't know until later. Roni started ringing up the order. Jean was sorting out Sister's boots as well as a book she had to have, which Jenny found, a Moroccan-bound volume from 1919.

Yvonne, card in hand, paused. "I have to have that ring."

Sister looked up from her order, she'd pulled a lovely colored stock tie for Betty, which she didn't want her to see. "Yvonne. Stunning."

"I have to have it."

Jean reached for the ring before Roni could, placing it in a velvet ring box. She had tears in her eyes. Then she gave the box to Roni and walked back into Marion's office.

Marion of course noticed the tears. She knew Jean well.

"It will be beautiful on you." Marion meant it. "Excuse me. Roni, I'll be back in a minute."

Marion walked into her office, where Jean leaned against the desk, tissue in hand.

"I'm sorry," the blonde woman apologized.

"At least we'll know where it is. We'll never know why it was in his pocket."

Jean simply nodded, wiping her eyes.

Turning to go out to the counter, Marion looked back as Jean pulled herself together.

"Jean, what do you know that I don't?"

"Nothing," came the soft but swift reply.

CHAPTER 26

March 24, 2019   Sunday

"Ten." Betty brought down the back rear door of the old Bronco.

"Small boxes, for which I am grateful." Sister climbed into the passenger seat. "How many cards in a box?"

"Fifty. And a piece of tissue paper between each card. Then the inside of the boxes have tissue paper. The tissue between the cards covers the card when you send it. Takes time."

Betty drove into Charlottesville to Water Street. They parked, lights flashing, and before they could reach the door of Taylor Insurance, Drew opened it, walked out to the car. "Don't worry about a ticket. Sunday. Hardly any traffic. Hello, Sister."

"Hi, Drew. Your invitations are quite proper. Lovely." She grabbed a box, as did Betty and Drew.

Walking into the plush office they passed two women, both middle-aged, going out to fetch boxes.

Within five minutes the boxes sat on a long table.

"You ladies are working on Sunday. He'd better be good to you," Betty joked.

"This is our annual handwritten invitation to clients." Loretta Giordis sat down, picking up a true fountain pen.

Drew sat down and pulled one out of his pocket. "Dad's."

"That pen has to be fifty years old, Drew. It's a Sheaffer White Dot. I love stuff like that."

"Betty, you and Bobby recognize anything having to do with papers and pens because of your business."

"The good stuff lasts, doesn't it?" Betty noticed Sister staring at the pen in Drew's hand.

He held it up for her. "Gold tip."

"Ah, like a Montblanc." She marveled at the old pen.

"Somewhat. More gold in the Montblancs." Drew remembered his manners. "Can I get you ladies a drink?"

"Oh, no thank you," Betty declined. "I wanted to bring the invitations down here in person to thank you again for your business."

He smiled. "Two years from now the invitations will be printed in gold. How about that? Our seventieth anniversary."

"Drew, I applaud any business that grows throughout generations." Betty did, too. "I don't want to pick up the phone and talk to someone in India or even Dallas. I want to walk into an office and see a neighbor or at least someone who has lived here."

"Drew, congratulations on your sixty-eighth anniversary. Before we get out of your hair, would you mind if Betty and I drove down the lane to your farm? We haven't hunted there for years. I need a bit of a reminder."

"Go ahead. I'm looking forward to it, and the Ticknors will come to the tailgate. It will be like old times."

"Good times." Sister smiled.

As the two drove out of town, turning west, Sister inquired, "How expensive is it to print a true invitation? You give us the invitation to Opening Hunt for free. I actually have no idea, which says something about my social life."

"Three factors. One: the quality and size of the invitation paper. Two: the color of the ink. There is a slight price difference, for some inks are easier to use and clean from the presses once used than others."

Sister interrupted. "I had no idea."

Betty smiled. "No reason you should. Kind of the same for people who don't know much about horses. They don't realize a horse's feet must be trimmed even if not shod, those hooves need tending. Okay, third factor: the number of invitations. And there can be a third and a half if it's a rush job."

"So a small number of invitations is cheaper? That would make sense."

"Not necessarily. You actually save money if you leap from, say, seventy-five cards to one hundred. Now, for a wedding invitation or what Drew is doing, celebrating the birthday of Taylor Insurance, that's not relevant. But let's say you want Bobby and me to create special hunt club stationery. And you wanted to sell the stationery to club members. It would be cheaper to print up, say, five thousand sheets and envelopes. That sounds like a lot of paper, given there are only one hundred of our true hunting members. Obviously when you factor in the social members, adjacent hunt members, there are more people, but stick to one hundred. It's easy to figure. So one hundred members buy five hundred sheets apiece. That's the standard of what you would buy at Staples for a ream of paper."

"Vaguely, I know you're right. I dimly remember seeing the amount on the plastic wrap of the paper I buy for the printing machine."

"And you go through it fast. Anyone running a business or a club like we have goes through paper. So five hundred sheets isn't really that much."

"Wedding invitations and Taylor Insurance, that's a set number."

"Right. No point in buying extra, but for the hunt club a large order would create more profit for the club. Are you thinking about it?"

"I am now." Sister smiled. "I'm not the fundraising person, and Walter, well, he doesn't have as much time as either of us would like, but he tries. His hours can be brutal sometimes."

"God bless anyone who goes into medicine." Betty turned on the road parallel to Crawford's, the one where Beasley Hall was located, with the ridge between Beasley and the Ticknor Farm and lastly Pitchfork. Betty drove slowly so they could study the terrain.

"Stop a minute, Betty."

She did and both women cast their eyes upward, for the ridge loomed behind the Ticknor outbuildings.

"They've kept the place up. We should be able to at least move along the bottom of the ridge if we have to. Oh wait, don't start yet. What about over there for parking?"

"Given yesterday's rain, it's somewhat drained. You'll call them, of course."

"I will and I figure Phipps Ticknor will put out an orange cone or a bucket so we'll get it right. We're the first people there. Usually." Sister hit the window button, sticking her head out.

"Can I go now?"

"Oh yes, sorry."

They trolled along, the ridge on their right, open fields on their left, with reasonably secure fences in need of painting.

"If we hit a fox and he heads across their fields, no telling where we'll wind up."

"Given the roll of the land . . . well, we can pull out a topo map when we get to my house, but I don't think we'll be all that far from Mousehold Heath," Sister guessed.

"You might be right. Love those topo maps. You can see so much territory in one glance." Betty, too, put down her window, throwing her scarf back around her neck, for it was fifty degrees at best and the wind cut that down.

Reaching the corner of the black fencing, a three-board slip fence took over. They were now on Pitchfork property.

"If the fox goes right, we're going to be at Beasley Hall. The climb, mmm, maybe about as steep as Hangman's Ridge," Betty conjectured.

"Right. I'll call Crawford tonight and prep him for Thursday. And I'll invite him, of course."

"What's that?" Betty stopped in time to see a large coyote cross the road up ahead.

"Damn," Sister cursed.

"If we get that line we will be at Mousehold Heath."

"No joke." Sister peered at the disappearing marauder.

Betty drove toward the house, tidy barn to the left three hundred yards away.

"Morris," Betty noted, seeing a figure run from the barn to the house.

"Too far away but it must be Morris, he doesn't want to see us."

They reached the barn, got out, did not go inside but did walk around to the back to see if any of the old trails were visible back there.

"Doesn't look too bad." Betty reached the end of the barn. "I think our coyote was here."

Sister came up next to her. Betty pointed down at a small pool of blood on the barn floor.

"Did you notice anything in his jaws?"

Betty shook her head. "He wasn't that far away but I can't say as I looked."

"Well," Sister paused, "whatever he killed wasn't small."

"Could have gobbled it on the spot." Betty knew of a coyote's voraciousness.

"You'd think there'd be fur or feathers. This is only a pool of blood."

As they rode back they discussed casting possibilities. Then they decided to show Weevil and Tootie the topo maps and go over same. Those two had never hunted back there and neither had many of the members. Sister focused on the task at hand, but the blood bothered her.

CHAPTER 27

March 26, 2019   Tuesday

A finger of wind kept punching down the side of the Blue Ridge Mountains. Not a sweeping, moaning wind but one steady puff riding a ravine, which bottomed out a mile west of Old Paradise's carriage stable being refurbished.

Given the weather and the odd run they'd had last week, Sister had changed to Tattenhall Station for Tuesday.

Cindy Chandler breathed a sigh of relief, since a pine tree had fallen over Clytemnestra's paddock fencing. A crew had worked on it Monday and how Cindy got that stubborn giant and her equally huge son to follow her to the adjoining paddock was a miracle. She'd considered walking them into the barn, food shaken in a bucket being the enticement, but if Big Momma grew restive in Cindy's beautiful stable, the damned cow could take out a wall. Cindy was always helpful about using her place for a last-minute fixture change. She was, however, glad they were at Tattenhall Station.

Also Sister didn't want to overhunt Foxglove Farm. It was tempting because it was close and if the unpredictable weather socked them again, it was easy to drive in and out of the place. Not always the case with other fixtures.

As Cindy unloaded Booper from her two-horse trailer, she and the girls laughed about her tribulations. Sister asked her dear friend to ride up with her, which Cindy accepted. So she'd be up front with Kasmir and Alida. The Bancrofts, still wary of the footing, chose to remain at After All.

For a Tuesday there was a crowd. Only two hunts left, the sun was shining, people found a way to wiggle out of work.

Weevil, hat under his arm, waited for Sister to nod. He clapped his cap on his head, walked behind the train station.

The large pasture rolled down on the east side toward the railroad track, on the south toward woods. Norfolk Southern had abandoned the station decades ago, as well as much of the land they owned. Trains did run from time to time, though, and Weevil kept clear of the tracks.

However, he wanted to slip over the lip of the rise to be out of the wind. His plan was to hunt forward, which is to say south.

Riding with him on her day off was Jean Roberts, former huntsman at what was then New Market Hounds. Retired some years back before the merger with Middletown Valley, like most huntsman she may not have been carrying the horn but her mind never left the hounds.

Weevil, knowing Jean's history, felt a trifle nervous but she smiled at him, encouraged him, and he relaxed a bit.

That odd wind wouldn't abate. Weevil stopped, allowed the hounds to think a bit. Instead of staying out of the wind, over the lip of the land, they moved right up onto the pasture, now moving crosswind.

Seeing Weevil hesitate for a moment, Jean observed, "It's a tricky wind but my experience is if hounds draw crosswind, sooner or later they will turn into the wind. Scent will carry depending on wind speed, of course."

He nodded, grateful for her experience.

Still adjusting to Virginia's conditions by the Blue Ridge Mountains he could be baffled sometimes by how quickly conditions shifted. At Toronto and North York Hunt he didn't need to factor in mountains or how ravines could create wind tunnels and funnels. Also the soils were rich in Canada. Here, one could run through Davis loam, some lovely alluvial deposits, and then clatter on clay, awful for holding scent. One needed versatile hounds, hounds with glorious noses. Given the thick forests, one also needed hounds with cry. How else would you find them?

Marty Howard had kindly loaned Jean her hunter, a good match. The two huntsmen walked along, the wind now perhaps twelve miles an hour. Jean, like most Mid-Atlantic huntsmen, could peg windspeed. One had to, as you'd be riding across a pasture, calm, mountains to your right, and in a blink, whoosh. And equally as fast one would go from bending trees to silence, nothing.

"Trust your hounds." Weevil repeated this to himself, a mantra.

Ardent lifted his head. Then Dasher, Thimble, and Taz followed suit. Four hounds standing stock-still, noses in the air. Then without a yelp they trotted west, occasionally rising on their hind paws.

Hounds may run silent when very close to their game but it is unusual otherwise. It's not something staff particularly wants, yet here were four solid hounds running without a peep. The pack followed them to the fence line between Tattenhall Station and Old Paradise, the two-lane Chapel Cross South Road in between.

Hounds crossed the road, leapt over the stone fence, stopped.

Weevil and Jean got over first, followed by Sister.

Now two fingers of wind smacked them in the face.

Weevil put his horn to his lips. Jean intervened.

"Forgive me, but wait a moment. You were going to move them a bit off the wind, right?"

"Yes, Ma'am."

"This wind is like a thin blade. It's not spreading, it doesn't cover territory to the sides. Your hounds picked up the scent high. If you wait a bit, the wind may drop for a moment. Then speak to them, for scent will have dropped with it."

Hounds waited, lifting their noses but not moving forward. Weevil waited, too, a moment or two, and as wind often does, it slacked.

"Get 'em up." He smiled at the hounds.

Diana, nose down, needed no encouragement. Scent settled. She opened, for she now had little doubt, plus it's hard to open when you're running with your nose high in the air, occasionally standing on your hind legs, which is what set Jean to rights.

The pack roared, heading straight for the elegant original stable. Now finished, the old stable looked like something out of a nineteenth-century print. The copper roof gleamed, verdigris not yet in evidence. The three huge cupolas also gleamed, and the middle one had a large copper flag, created to look as though it was waving. It was the Union Jack.

Earl, resident of this architectural gem, had already ducked into his den in the next-to-last stall. He also used the tack room for his lazing about, but if he needed to escape, the stall was the answer.

Hounds rushed into the center aisle, then into the stall, as all the doors were open. No horses were yet at Old Paradise and would not be there until the entire estate was regenerated.

Everyone sang at once.

Weevil dismounted, throwing the reins up to Jean, walked in, blew "Gone to Ground," and praised everyone. Then he leaned down and called into the den opening. "I know you're in there."

A bark greeted his hello. *"Yes, I am. Time to find another fox."*

Smiling at the response even though he didn't know what the fox said, he walked outside, the entire pack around him, swung back up in the saddle, taking the reins from Jean.

"Thank you for that advice."

She smiled at him. "I was born and raised in these parts and I'm long in the tooth," she mocked herself.

"Madam, if you were long in the tooth you wouldn't be riding with the huntsman."

She laughed, happy to be up, happy to be with hounds, and while the run was short, the music was good.

Weevil cast southward from the stable and carriage stable, past the newly discovered slave graveyard along with remains of Monacans, for this was once Monacan territory.

Dutifully, hounds kept noses down. Not until the woods' edge was there a bit of speaking. The pack fanned out. Scent would appear then disappear, frustrating.

Sister noted footing was better on the woods' path but hounds then turned east, moved toward the road. They crossed over to Beveridge Hundred, began working back north toward Tattenhall Station. All opened at once, charging north.

A stout coop divided Tattenhall Station from Beveridge Hundred at this point. Yvonne, Aunt Daniella, and Ribbon sat in the car in Yvonne's driveway. Once everyone was over the coop or through the gate, she crept out onto the road.

This turned into a straight shot, no maneuvers to throw off hounds. Scent, relatively fresh, was in a straight line as though laid down by a drag, which of course it wasn't. They threaded their way through the woods, which covered the rear of Tattenhall Station starting about a half a mile from the coop. So there was a burst over the meadow then the woods, and of course trees had come down in the high winds earlier in the week . . . the whole season, really.

Cursing, for all were losing time, Sister did her best to keep up, but even Weevil couldn't. Hounds easily negotiated the obstacles. Not so horses.

Finally out in the open again, she galloped toward Tattenhall Station, which was visible a mile and a half away. To her right, low, ran Broad Creek, the same waters that flowed through After All. The fencing behind Tattenhall Station was zigzag, as it was in colonial times. The entire fence line behind the station where everyone could see it was zigzag fencing. Along the road it was three-board. Sister picked her spot, over, pushing on, for this fellow had passed the station, crossed Chapel Road East, and moved into Tollbooth. There hounds stopped, for Gris, the gray whose scent they had picked up, was in his den in the outbuilding. He could easily get into the outside entrance. Hounds could not.

It was now two and a half hours since the first cast. Had this been a normal season Sister would have stayed out another hour, at least, but given the footing and the season it had been, no one's horse was truly fit for such a full day.

Tattenhall rested across the road, rigs parked there, so all walked back.

Within twenty minutes everyone had a drink in their hand, some sat with a plate of food at the tables. A buzz filled the room.

Jean and Cindy Chandler relived old days of hunting with the late Jill Summers or the late Bobby Coles of Keswick Hunt. They remembered great masters from Maryland, wonderful whippers-in.

As those two caught up, Yvonne sat down with Sam, Tootie joining her.

Kasmir, as always, saw to the comfort of his guests.

Marty and Crawford attended although they didn't hunt. Skiff was with Shaker. Those who hunted spoke of the odd wind currents. The great thing about hunting is one never runs out of things to discuss.

"Strange. A pool of blood perhaps the circumference of a plate," Sister recalled how she and Betty had been checking out their fixture for Thursday. Pitchfork had everyone wondering how it would be. The weather reports kept Sister running to the TV and The Weather Channel. Drove her and everyone else crazy, but she was determined to finish out March and sidestep yet another downpour.

Sam, sitting across from Sister, who was starved, said, "Betty said you all saw a coyote."

"We did," Sister confirmed as Betty now sat next to her.

"They're out there and they'll kill anything." Sam had heard them howl at Beasley Hall at sundown.

"You'd think he'd be carrying whatever it was," Sister puzzled.

"Who knows? And you don't know how many of them there were. You only saw one. Usually there's more than one." Sam watched wildlife, especially coyotes and foxes.

"True," Sister agreed.

"Pray we don't get one on Thursday. The last thing we need is a coyote hunt on a fixture we haven't hunted in years."

The breakfast, with people eating, talking, drinking, not wanting the season to end when they were so close, went on for two hours. Finally folks trickled away.

Jean bid her goodbyes, complimented Weevil, and pulled Sister aside to tell her he was young and good, all he needed was time on the target.

Then she got in her car, headed back through Charlottesville, pulling off Route 250 to Dunbar's Antiques.

As she opened the door, Kathleen looked up. "How was the hunt?"

"Pretty good."

"Could I get you something to drink? I'm Kathleen Dunbar, by the way."

"Jean Roberts. Here for a day with Jefferson Hunt. I hunted with Harry and thought I'd see the store. Looks wonderful."

"Thank you. These are all his acquisitions. In time I hope to add things I find. There's a hand-tinted old hunt print on the wall." Kathleen walked over. "1850s. Don't you like to look at the clothing?"

"I do." Jean walked through the store, picked up an ashtray from the 1930s with a sculpted fox on the outside. It was a deep ashtray, the kind that used to be in expensive hotels.

"How do you like it here?" Jean asked.

"So far so good." Kathleen smiled. "Did you hunt often with Harry?"

"Until I retired six years ago, I did. I occasionally fill in at Horse Country and a few of the other girls there hunt. We all would go out together and Harry," she smiled, "would take each of us to a different hunt ball annually. He could have started an escort service."

"He could talk to anybody." Kathleen wrapped the ashtray.

"None of us knew he had a wife until he passed," Jean confessed. "Do come up sometime to Warrenton. You'll like Horse Country and I see you have a Welsh terrier. Two Scotties run Horse Country. They are our best marketers."

"Hear that, Abdul? You've got a lot to learn."

When Jean left, Kathleen sat down at the desk in the back. She knew Jean had come in to look at her, but then many people did. She'd turned into a bit of an attraction.

CHAPTER 28

March 27, 2019   Wednesday

"Jean, you walk Bunsen, I'll walk Aga. Let's have a walking lunch." Marion carried two leather leashes in her hand, waited by the front door.

"Where's your scarf? The sun may be shining but it's not that warm." Jean grabbed her own cashmere scarf, soft. "I'll get yours from the back."

Marion slipped on her coat as the two Scotties looked up, ready to go.

"Why does it take them so long?" Aga grumbled.

"No fur," Bunsen, beard perfect, replied.

"Here." Jean handed Marion her own scarf, which she had bought in Scotland years ago.

Marion, while not a Scot, displayed an affinity for Scottish terriers and vice versa, plus her keen eye for fabrics prized those tight Scottish weaves. She handed Bunsen's leash to Jean as she knelt down to clip their leather collars onto them. Nothing plastic for these two.

The two women stepped outside. Sunshine made old town Warrenton bright again. Winter had dragged on, gray skies plus all that snow and rain. The day seemed a tonic, although the mercury had only nudged into the low fifties and the slight breeze made both women glad they wore their scarves and gloves.

"Let's walk up to the Courthouse," Marion suggested.

Alexandria Pike, the road on which Horse Country sat, ended at the Courthouse door. The building, a soft yellow, originally constructed in 1764, glowed. The polished walnut doors appeared bright in the early-afternoon sun, although perhaps not welcoming. One did not usually go into any courthouse in a good frame of mind.

The two humans and two dogs turned left, nodding to people they knew, as a few were out shopping. Mostly people blinked, for it was a long time since the sun had shone this brightly, or so it seemed.

"I miss the old work-clothing store. They carried Red Wing shoes. Lasted a long time, those old work boots." Jean looked into the large plate-glass window now offering fancy stuff.

"When you consider how many new people, people with money, have moved here it's surprising so many of the old stores are left. At least the buildings are undisturbed, even if the goods have changed."

"More restaurants." Jean looked across the street.

"True. People who don't know the area can walk to decent places. I'm hooked on that wonderful place down at the old train station. I think of it as the Station Restaurant."

Jean smiled. "Do you have a destination in mind?"

"I do. First Baptist Church."

"Oh. Well, okay."

The church, clean lines, red brick, built in 1867, added to the allure of Main Street.

If someone time-traveled from the nineteenth century, they would know where they were. They might be surprised at the contents of the stores, but Warrenton remained Warrenton. The difference now was that with such improved highways people could commute to Washington, D.C. The nation's capitol was forty-eight miles away. It wasn't the distance that got you, it was the traffic, the subdivisions, the two airports.

"Over there." Jean stopped, pointing across the street to where the old insurance agency once stood. "That's where Fred Duncan, hunting Warrenton's hounds, wound up, his whole pack inside. I would have given anything to see it. Pack ran right down Main Street in the middle seventies. Made the papers, made the TV news. They'd switched to a deer, who ran down Main Street and turned into the store. As did the pack."

"I think Fred told me that story." Marion remembered with affection the late Fred Duncan and his irrepressible wife, Doris, both missed.

"Well, the deer actually crashed through the front window but lived. Made it to wherever home was. And Fred, mortified, snapped back when Melvin Poe," Jean mentioned another famous huntsman now also gone, "told everyone that Fred and the Warrenton Hounds got foxhunters more good publicity than they would have gotten otherwise."

"Ah." Marion turned onto the walkway to the church, opening the front door.

"Can Bunsen and Aga go inside?" Jean wondered.

"They're Christian dogs. Being Scots, they're Presbyterian." Marion smiled. "We can sit in the back. They'll be quiet." She opened the door.

Jean glanced around. "No one is here. Is it always this empty?"

"That's one of the things I like about Catholic churches. There's usually someone in the pews, or lighting candles. The Protestant churches, not so much."

"You were raised Episcopalian, right? Why do I remember that?"

Marion smiled. "Because my last name is Italian, people think I was raised Catholic. But I find comfort sitting in a church, any church."

Jean slid into a pew, Bunsen also, and being a good fellow he lay down. Aga showed more curiosity about the altar but Marion convinced him to also walk into the pew and rest.

The four remained silent, then Marion spoke. "How long have we known each other?"

"Decades." Jean felt the years fly by.

"Do you think we know each other well?"

"Given that we've traveled overseas together, worked in the store for years, I'd say we know each other as well or even better than our own families." Jean smiled.

"You are one of my best friends. I want to make sure you're okay."

This startled Jean. "Why wouldn't I be okay?"

"Your health is good?"

"Of course it is. Maybe I should ask if you're okay."

Marion nodded that she was. "Harry's death has affected you.

You cover it well but you can't hide your feelings from me. You two were old hunting buddies."

"We were." Jean wondered where this was heading. She looked down at Bunsen then up at the altar. A long, long silence enveloped the two dear friends.

"Jean."

"He left the store with me. He knew I had an Ashland Basset meeting so he left a bit before I did."

"Go on."

"We agreed to meet back in the lower parking lot in two hours. He said he'd take me to dinner after my meeting. It was dark, pitch black and cold. One of those nights."

"And?" Marion waited.

"I parked next to his car, got into his passenger side. He had his coat off and his sleeve rolled up. He handed me a needle, one of those tiny butterfly needles. He asked me to shoot it into his vein."

"Did you know this was going to happen?"

"No! I told him I wasn't going to shoot him with anything. I thought we were meeting to drive to dinner. Well," she looked at the altar again, "he said he found out only two weeks ago that he had an incurable cancer. A very rare one, behind his eye. It was in-operable and the pain would be considerable. He'd be blind and immobile. I cried. I couldn't help it."

"He knew you were a true friend. And he loved you." Marion's voice was consoling.

"I asked him wasn't there some way he could go to hospice? Hospice of the Piedmont is really good down where he lives, but he said no. If he did, he would live maybe two or three more months.

He'd be drugged useless, or if he refused, in hideous pain. He said he wanted to leave this world while he still felt, strange to say, alive."

"Did he tell you how he discovered his cancer?"

"Yes." Jean took a deep breath. "He kept breaking blood vessels in his right eye. His vision blurred but it would clear up, sort of. But he knew the eye wasn't really getting better because the blurring came more frequently. So he went to his eye doctor, Dr. DiGirolomo, who told him to go to a specialist. He gave Harry three names and told him all were terrific. He said the one at Virginia Commonwealth Hospital had operated on a friend of his and did a fantastic job. But he said the doctors at UVA were also outstanding. So Harry made an appointment with the Virginia Commonwealth doctor. In fact, Dr. DiGirolomo called from his office so Harry would be seen the next day. That's how Harry knew something was very wrong."

"He drove to Richmond alone?"

Jean nodded. "He could drive although that wasn't going to last long. The doctor ran tons of tests. He asked Harry if he could return tomorrow."

"Poor Harry. He had to know something was up."

"Well, thanks to Dr. DiGirolomo being close to this fellow, they rushed the results to him and when Harry came to the office the doctor told him he had an extremely rare form of cancer. It was advanced, which wasn't uncommon because it doesn't affect a person until the end. He couldn't operate. It's right behind the eye. There's not a way it can be done. And, as you know, the brain is right there, too."

"Did he tell you the expert's name?"

"Dr. Isaac Fuqua. I wanted to dial that man right from my cell-phone but I knew Harry was telling me the truth."

"Yes."

"According to Dr. Fuqua, Harry, at best, would live another two months and it would be awful. So he turned to me with that crooked smile of his and said he wanted to go out now. He could feel this thing taking hold of him but pretty much he felt good. He drove up here, after all.

"I didn't have to think about it, Marion. I mean, I didn't want to get caught but if this was his last wish, he trusted me with it."

"He trusted you period. You gave him the shot?"

"First we got out of the car. He held out his arm and told me not to worry because these little butterfly needles don't leave a mark. Closes over immediately. He said he would in essence have a heart attack, which he would feel, but that it would be quick. So I gave him the shot. He put on his coat and walked over to the steps.

"I asked him what he was doing. He said if he climbed the steps it would bump up his heart rate. He thought he would die faster. He also said he wanted to die outside. His happiest times in life had been outside. He started up the steps and then he groaned and dropped."

Another long silence followed this.

"You did the right thing. And he was right. Nothing showed. Do you know what was in the needle?"

"Potassium."

Another silence followed this. "I knew something was nagging at you."

"Marion, I killed a man."

"No you didn't. You released a dear friend. You granted a last wish and it's a wish I'm sure other people pray could be granted to them. You did the right thing."

Tears ran down Jean's cheeks. "Thank you."

"Neither of us will ever have this discussion again. But you did the right thing. My one question is, what was he doing with the Erté ring?"

"I showed it to him, took it out of the case. He put it on, said he'd give it back after my meeting. I think he slipped it in his pocket and then he forgot about it. Harry would never steal a ring or anything. I totally forgot about it."

"You both were distracted."

"Funny, Marion, Harry was clear. In total possession of his mind and emotions." She paused. "When he died I knew I couldn't move him. This would have been easier in his car. He would have been found the next morning, but he was adamant about his last moments being outside, inhaling the cold air, feeling the cold tingle on his face, and when he fell, he cracked his head. I had to leave. If I'd stayed there or called 911 I might have been caught. I was distraught. I didn't trust myself. So I left, and you know the rest."

They rose, the dogs, too, walked back outside, two old friends bound by many things, now this.

Marion spoke at last. "Dignity. It's really about dignity."

They walked the rest of the way in silence.

CHAPTER 29

March 28, 2019   Thursday

A thin silver blanket lay over the meadows at Fairies Bottom. One could imagine fairies playing underneath it. The temperature at forty-eight degrees Fahrenheit, low clouds slowly dispersing, promised good conditions for scent sticking.

A least that's what Sister hoped as she climbed onto the mounting block. As she swung her leg over Lafayette, his ears flicked forward and back. She settled into her saddle, breathed in. The cool air invigorated her. Returning to this old fixture felt wonderful. Every master knows a hunt can never have enough fixtures. Population pressures, divorce, death, odd events can erase fixtures, and once a development builds on that land that's the end of it, often for wildlife as well. Although foxes have a way of finding what humans throw out.

Fairies Bottom and Pitchfork, once a vibrant part of Jefferson Hunt, were lost thanks to an unfortunate struggle over furniture. It wasn't that the Ticknors, young then, pulled their land from the hunt, but what master would take the chance of following a fox onto adjoining land, creating a mess.

Smiling, Sister looked around.

"Good to have you back." Phipps came up, offering his hand.

She reached down to take it. "Good to be here, and the day promises a few bracing runs."

The last trailer pulled in. Sister hoped it was the last trailer. She wanted to get hounds off while the ground fog hung over the land. Hunt staff had arrived early, setting up, which helped members, especially those who had never hunted Fairies Bottom, know they were at the right place. Most of the members had never hunted back here.

Betty, Gray, Sam, and the Bancrofts remembered the old days. For everyone else this was a new day and people looked around from their perch atop their horses, marveling at the place. The ridge behind the house divided this land from Crawford's. Fences, sturdy, needed paint in some sections but the farm nestled into the land. It belonged there. Nothing fancy, a clapboard farmhouse with an addition built onto it, so it was an L shape. The stables, no longer used, had been maintained, as had a garage and a twenty-by-forty equipment shed. Painted light blue with white trim, a bit unique in these parts. Fairies Bottom cast an inviting glow.

Drew had walked alongside Sam Lorillard.

"How is that horse coming along?"

"Good. Crawford wants to hunt Trocadero next season with his hounds." Sam thought a moment. "He's a good boy but young. Good to be back here."

"I look forward to it. I bet a fox will run over to Pitchfork."

"You never know." Sam smiled. "Isn't it a relief to hack to a hunt?"

"Sure is." Drew smiled then walked over to Alida and Kasmir, striking up a conversation. His stable girl, Wanda, was already at the back of First Flight, as she was riding as a groom.

"I had no idea this was back here," Alida commented.

"You'd be surprised what's hidden on some of these back roads or up on ridges," Cindy Chandler, waiting with Kasmir and Alida, said. "You can't go wrong in central Virginia. Pick a spot, it will be lovely."

They chatted about topography, the old homes, and the new ones.

Sister, speaking to Weevil, Betty, and Tootie, suggested drawing first up the drive toward Pitchfork Farm, but off the road. This way, if a fox crossed they could follow without too much difficulty, the zigzag fencing would be easy to clear.

"If by chance a fox goes all the way across the flat pastures there, goes through that woods, and on, we will actually wind up at Mousehold Heath, as you know, since we all checked the topo maps."

"And if a fox heads to the right?" Weevil asked.

"Straight up. But don't go down on the other side, as I said when we read the maps. Beasley Hall has Crawford's stock out in the pastures; St. Swithin's, his small chapel; plus Marty's gardens ready to awaken. We've finally reached agreement on hunting Old Paradise if a fox goes there. If we go down into Beasley Hall, that will be the end of that."

"What about the whips?" Weevil worried.

"Skiff will be in her truck at the bottom on his side of the ridge. I talked to Crawford last night and I talked to Skiff when she was over with Shaker. The whips have permission to ride down, but he prefers we try everything else first."

"Not much you can try if hounds are on a fox." Tootie rewound her thong.

"No one ever said Crawford understood hunting." Betty tried not to sound sarcastic.

"We will all do our best. Well, let's hope for a good hunt, a memorable one for our return. Ready?"

"Yes, Madam." Weevil looked down at an obedient but ready, very ready, pack of American foxhounds.

"All right."

Pansy looked up at her huntsman. *"Finally."*

The clatter of hooves followed the hounds as they drew alongside the tertiary road, which soon turned into a stone road. The state displayed an odd set of qualifications for what roads deserved their attention and what ones did not. However, the Ticknors and the Taylors took up the slack.

Thirty-two people rode out filled with the usual excitement of revisiting a former fixture. Tinged with melancholy, for only one hunt remained, heads up, heels down, they were ready.

Two hundred yards, more or less, behind the unused stable, Dreamboat veered toward the stable. As he was a reliable hound neither Weevil nor the whippers-in moved to stop him nor to deter the three couples who now followed. Weevil stopped a moment. Soon the whole pack filtered behind Dreamboat, noses down. Circling the stable, a pause, then feathering.

Hunt staff moved closer while Sister scanned the area she and

Betty had only peered at from an open car window on that colder day. She could make out the vestiges of the trail she had seen from the car.

"Dog fox." Dreamboat inhaled, then walked briskly up toward the beginning of the steep rise, the ridge.

"Let's go." His sister opened.

Hounds, ducking under brush, charged up the ridge.

Weevil stuck with his hounds by finding a narrow deer trail. Betty, remembering the territory, had already headed up toward the top. If hounds hit the ridge she'd be the only impediment until they got to the bottom, where she prayed Skiff was sitting with Shaker in the car. Shaker knew the ground on this side of the ridge and Skiff knew Crawford's territory.

Sister followed Weevil. The field followed her, but one by one. Two people could not have ridden side by side.

Hounds stopped midway, hooked hard left, now all speaking. Sister could hear the bush branches swishing as they ran. Years ago a middle trail followed the ridgeline. Still there.

Weevil found it first, of course, and he flew behind his hounds, all wide open. Odd pine trunks, woodpecker holes much in evidence, crossed the trail in spots, but even Second Flight could get over.

Hounds continued on, then another quick check. They turned down. Going down was harder than going up. Again, Weevil, good eye, found the deer trail.

Sister paused a moment.

Drew called out from behind the Bancrofts, Alida, and Kasmir. "Master, allow me."

"Please." She squeezed to the side as he rode up.

"There's a good trail up ahead. We won't lose much time and more importantly we won't lose any people."

She let him go first as Lafayette snorted. That his beloved master would allow a Warmblood, no less, to go in front of him was an insult. However, he did as he was asked and followed the good-looking bay, Binny, although the Thoroughbred thought Drew's horse clunky.

Halfway to the bottom, Sister could see her pack stream out of the undergrowth and the woods on the ridge. Drew trotted down then stopped, as a large tree, an old, really old hickory, blocked the path. Given the wicked winds this winter, the old tree finally had fallen over, having lived an exceptionally long life.

Looking around, for there was no way to clear the crown of such a massive tree, Drew quickly dismounted to pull aside brush from behind the hickory. Low-hanging branches from other trees created another problem.

Sister, too, dismounted, leading Lafayette behind Drew, who pushed forward, holding back branches for his master. They were losing time and the pack was on full accelerator.

Looking down, Sister saw a figure walking toward the house.

"Damn. I told him to stay inside," Drew cursed while pulling back a thick vine.

Finally clear, Sister chose not to mount up on such a steep angle. She and Drew continued down on foot, as did the entire field behind them. The second she hit solid, flat ground she was up. Some people struggled, some did not, but everyone got up.

By now the pack was crossing the dormant hayfield to the Fairies Bottom side of the farm, the fence line between the two properties visible from the distance.

No need to cluck. Lafayette knew his task and that long fluid stride, that beautiful Thoroughbred movement, paid off.

Within minutes she could see her tail hounds. Betty, to the right, was up near the front of the pack, as was Tootie on the left on the other side of the fence.

Tootie had cleared the fence. She didn't bother to look for a jump. Sister sent up a prayer of thanks that she had such terrific riders whipping-in.

On and on they ran. The footing though soft wasn't bad. It was forgiving. A plus.

After ten minutes of this, a longer time than one realizes when mounted, hounds disappeared into a thick wood then they slowed. Weevil did likewise, and Sister, seeing his scarlet coat ahead, also slowed to a walk. One doesn't run into one's huntsman.

By the time she reached him he was moving off at an extended trot. She could stay behind, keep him in sight. Then he stopped.

The field, some on a decent path, a few off to the side to try and see what was happening, stood still.

"Get 'em up. Get 'em up," Weevil encouraged.

Hounds fanned out in a large half circle. Betty didn't move as hounds came back to where they had lost scent. Tootie, now visible, also stood still.

"He can't have gone into his den. We were close enough we'd find it." Diana spoke with certitude.

Dreamboat looked around. Hounds could easily run in this wood. There wasn't as much undergrowth, but the soil wasn't as good as that in the pastures.

He put his nose down, walking to the side, thirty yards from where they had lost the line. Dasher, another "D" hound, mirrored his brother on the south side. Now hounds moved off from where scent disappeared.

Zorro walked over to a fallen tree, a thick trunk. He leapt up, putting his nose down.

"He used this," the sleek tricolor called out.

That fast the whole pack reached him, some now on the trunk with him, others on both sides of the uprooted tree.

"Got him!" Aero called out in triumph.

They started in the direction from which they'd come. The fox was heading back. He didn't double exactly on his tracks, for hounds had gotten too close, but he was returning to safety, most likely his den. Sister prudently turned back on the path. If the fox headed north she'd figure it out somehow but if he was going to where they had found his scent or a den somewhere, this was a better bet.

The pack, running hard, shot out onto the pasture again, running along the fence line then turning, but this time toward Drew's four-stall barn. They checked before reaching the barn then headed off to the back, down over a small swale into one of those Virginia ravines cut by a blade. A human could walk down there but only one at a time and the grade punished horses.

Weevil started to head down then thought better of it. Sister also sat on the edge. Hounds milled about downed trees next to a large thick brush pile of branches, vines, some tree limbs.

"Not a fox." Trinity was intrigued.

Thimble pawed at the large entangled pile; then Dreamboat, who also smelled the alluring non-fox odor, kept pushing past it.

"He's gone back up." Dreamboat began the climb to the rim, as he found fox scent again.

Diana, wise, ran next to her brother. *"He knew that would slow us down. Mask his own scent."*

Dreamboat didn't reply but kept running, the entire pack now behind the two lead hounds. Weevil turned as they shot out of the ravine, then waited for the whole pack to come up. So did Sister.

Hounds ran behind the stable, around the stable back out toward the house, then behind the house. This time they paused at the base of the ravine, moved around, then found scent again. Up they ran.

The fox reached the top of the ravine. Skiff and Shaker had been trying to listen, to no avail, but now the whole pack ran along the top of the ridge, dipped a bit toward them, then crossed back over, heading down toward Pitchfork Farm.

By the time staff and Sister reached the top, horses were breathing heavily. So were the people. Sister stopped. Hounds appeared back up on the ridge then charged down again. She swiveled in her saddle to look behind.

"Better not," she said to herself as she carefully walked down the trail, even though hounds were screaming.

When she reached the bottom, they had stopped behind the stable, a yip here, a yap there.

Weevil waited, as did his two whippers-in. Everyone needed a breather, which the fox had thoughtfully provided them.

Sister waved her hand to Kasmir, who rode up. "Hold them, will you? I'll be right back."

"Of course."

She rode to Betty perhaps a half a football field away. "Hounds are where we saw the puddle of blood."

Betty squinted. "It can't be there now."

"No, but whether it soaked in or was washed away, they'll pick up a hint of it. Our fox must have come back this way. There's no reason for hounds to stray to the back of the stable."

"It is strange." Betty dropped her reins, rubbed her hands, then picked them up again. "Hell of a run."

"Good to be back. Wondered if you'd noticed."

"Actually, I did not. I'm trying to catch my breath and to see where the pack goes next. I swear we'll wind up at Mousehold Heath yet."

"I expect only staff horses could make it, given this season. At least we kept everyone in work no matter what. Look around. Maybe something or someone will pop up. You know, someone red." She smiled and rode back to the field, happily waiting.

Horses and people needed the break. Passing flasks around helped the humans. Sister could not drink, as staff is not to drink alcohol while hunting. This is often ignored in the breach, but not by Sister, a real stickler.

"What do you think?" Zane asked his brother Zorro.

"He mingled scent. But if we walk with this scent, faded, we might get his line again and it will be hot."

Zorro proved prescient as Dasher, moving away from the group, slowly walked toward the distant woods. *"Something."*

Dreamboat hurried over, nose touching the flattened grass. Shoots had not yet appeared. With a little luck they'd break upward in a week or two. It couldn't stay winter forever. He, too, walked with deliberation.

Zane, Zorro, and Dreamboat headed away from the stable. Weevil did not chide them. He trusted his hounds. They weren't skirting.

"Diana, help," Dreamboat called out as she was circling the stable to make sure the fox didn't have an entrance dug into it.

Joining the three hounds she, too, was puzzled. *"He's walked this old scent line. Old but strong enough to give him time."*

Zane, younger than the "D" hounds, said, *"It's human, isn't it? Old but human."*

"Yes. He's really smart, this fellow. He almost lost us by the brush pile. Stronger there." Diana broke into a lope.

The other hounds saw her, as did Weevil, who called to them. Within minutes the pack, together, followed this line, although no one was opening. It was confusing; two scents had definitely been mixed. But when?

Near the edge of the woods, Zorro called out. *"It's him!"*

Indeed it was. Back through the woods they flew, he turned again. So did the pack. The humans, back on a decent trail, regrouped, but feeling how long they'd been running stayed as close to their field master as possible. Her eyes never left Weevil's scarlet coat.

A mile into the woods, a check.

Then Tinsel, who'd been a little bit behind, turned toward the stable, which wasn't visible. She had the line and she sang out.

Everyone headed back, and once out in the pasture again the entire pack shot down the narrow ravine. This time Weevil dismounted to go with them.

Given the length of the run, the long time of the run, the fact that the hunted fox returned to that brush pile made Weevil think either he had a den there or one close by. Why he chose not to use it before, the huntsman had no idea. Foxes could be peculiar. That they were smarter than all of the other creatures was never in doubt.

He grabbed some overhanging branches as he slid down. Tootie and Betty stayed at the edge. If he needed them he'd yell.

Hounds surrounded the large, dense pile but they didn't dig. They waited for their huntsman.

He reached them, knelt down, peering in. He couldn't see much but he did see a baseball cap. Nothing reached his own nose, but he was a country boy. Something or someone was in there. The nights had light frosts. Whatever was there he couldn't smell but hounds could. He stood up. He trusted his hounds and he knew human noses needed a strong scent to register.

Climbing back up he walked to Sister. "Something is in that mess of a brush pile. Not our fox."

"Alive? You know, a skunk or something like that?"

"No. I think something is dead in there, and I saw a baseball cap."

"Weevil, say nothing. Let's go back to the trailers. I'll call Ben Sidell. If he'd been out today he'd have a better idea than any of us how to proceed."

Back at the trailers, hunt members set up a tailgate. Drew declined because he said he was so mistrustful of Morris. Even if he was locked in his room he could scream and pound on the doors.

Sister did not wish to trouble the Ticknors. Those cardboard tables set up in a minute, tailgates dropped, and Walter, with Kasmir's help, lifted down the Yeti cooler filled with drinks.

As all this transpired, the Ticknors were the first people handed drinks. Sister called Ben from the cab of her truck.

"Sister, how was the hunt?"

"Terrific. We picked up a sporting fox. This may be me worrying too much, but hounds twice ran into a narrow ravine. There's a huge brush pile there, fallen trees. You can't get down on horseback but the second time hounds ran back, Weevil dismounted and managed to get down. He believes something is in that brush pile. He says he can't see anything or smell anything but hounds could. He did see a baseball cap. I'm probably making too much of it."

"You've given me a chance to get outside. No need to wait for me. I know the way."

"Ben, either Weevil or I will wait, because you don't know where the ravine is," she politely reminded him.

"You're right. See you soon."

The hunt breakfast, convivial, had members slouched in their director's chairs, others sitting on the back of those dropped tailgates that didn't have food. As the runs had woken everyone up, brisk and challenging, all were in a good mood.

Usually singling Freddie out, Drew seemed a bit distracted.

Sister sat down next to Betty, Weevil, and Tootie, who put out a chair for her. Gray and Sam fussed over Aunt Daniella and Yvonne. Aunt Dan was giving a highly personalized history of Fairies Bottom.

"Red, don't you think?" Sister asked her huntsman.

"I do. Wish we could have gotten a view." Weevil knocked back his ginger ale with a twist of lemon.

"Do we have two more chairs?" Sister stood as she glimpsed Skiff's truck rolling down the lane.

Betty turned her head. "I'll find some. You sit down."

Skiff parked and Shaker, Southern gentleman that he was, walked around to open the door for her.

Being a Yankee girl, this used to disturb her but she'd adjusted, especially after his injury. Being able to perform small services for the lady he was learning to love made him feel strong again.

Also Sister, Betty, Aunt Daniella had set her down one cold night in Aunt Dan's living room to give her the rules of being a Southern lady, which boiled down to: be gracious, allow men to do for you, and don't fear they won't listen to you, they will. Speak in warm terms.

Poor Skiff struggled but eventually she began to remember the little details, like let him open the door, let him walk on the outside of the sidewalk. Basic stuff.

So many people hurried to greet Shaker. Perked him right up.

Drew came over. "I've got Blanton's." He named a special bourbon, which he brought from his house after riding to his stable with Wanda. She took care of the horses. "I know you're a Woodford Reserve man, but let me fetch you a drink after I bring one to this lovely lady."

"I thank you in advance." Skiff had learned.

Freddie also walked over. "What could you hear?"

That was all the two huntsmen needed. Freddie and Drew guided them to the chairs Kasmir pulled from his trailer. They talked excitedly walking, sat down still talking.

"Before Crawford bought the land, most of that was a pumpkin patch, which we could hunt." Shaker was warming up. "Pumpkins, squash, but the real draw turned out to be two acres of Muscadine grapes. Oh my God, do foxes love grapes."

Weevil, on the edge of his chair, emboldened Shaker to more memories. "You must have had great runs."

"One fall day, cubbing, we hit a line where the house now

stands over there and we ran and ran and ran. We wound up at Mousehold Heath and then we ran north. We damn near reached the kennels."

"Too bad Crawford didn't name Beasley Hall Grape Expectations." Freddie laughed.

They all laughed with her as Ben drove up. Sister leaned toward Weevil, he nodded. They rose, as did Betty and Tootie.

"Why don't we get in the squad car?" Betty volunteered. "Tootie, climb in the back. This way we don't have to unhitch a truck from the trailer. The hounds will be fine. We won't be long."

Sister and Weevil asked Yvonne would she drive them back to Pitchfork Farm, which she was delighted to do. Then Sam hopped into her car. Aunt Daniella barely noticed, since she had a crew of people sitting around her in a semicircle.

Drew noticed them piling into vehicles. "Need a hand?"

Sister replied, "No thank you. We're going to check out something at your farm."

"I'll follow." He smiled. "I don't want you all getting lost on Pitchfork Farm, although I'd put out a cooler loaded with food for you to find." He motioned for Wanda, who had already put his two horses in stalls, thinking to come back quickly to the tailgate.

Sister and Weevil laughed then closed the doors to Yvonne's big SUV. "Dammit."

Yvonne drove behind Ben. "What's the matter?"

"I don't know but I have an uneasy feeling about this."

"You can't stop a man from going to his home," Weevil sensibly said.

"I know but . . ." She shook her head. "I should have paid more attention to the hounds."

"We were on a fox." Weevil picked up her growing unease.

Yvonne followed Ben, directed by Betty. They crossed the pasture, soil firm enough for an SUV.

Drew followed in his SUV, since he hadn't needed a truck that morning, having hacked to the meet. Once the horses were up, he got in her car.

Ben stopped at the woods' edge. Betty and Tootie disembarked. Sister, Weevil, and Yvonne got out as Drew parked and joined them.

"Follow me," Weevil said. "Betty and Tootie, why don't you go to where you were when we were down here. You don't have to go as far, but Ben might want to know where we all were."

"Steep," Drew warned them then turned to look back at the house. He could see the back door closing. "Excuse me. Something's up at the house. I hope Morris didn't get out."

"We do, too," Betty reassured him.

Weevil first, sideways for better footing given the steep grade, began the descent. The others followed. He reached the huge pile as Betty and Tootie took their positions on the right, on the left.

"Ben, hounds came here twice, as did our fox. But they were baffled a bit then found the line, encouraged by Weevil."

Weevil added to Sister's recall. "The second time I got down on my hands and knees." He did that and Ben did also.

"A lot of debris."

"See the cap?" Weevil pointed.

After a minute or two Ben said, "Yeah. This stuff is so thick we won't know what's in there without light. I've got an LED flash in the car."

"I'll climb back up with you," Betty offered.

The two, using low branches to pull themselves, managed to get up in time to see the SUV pull out of the drive, hit sixty, and go. Then the truck followed.

"What the hell?" Ben commented.

"Pray it isn't Morris." Betty put her hand over her eyes.

Ben sat in the driver's seat, called the dispatcher, gave him a precise description, and ordered him to get people on the two vehicles immediately. People didn't just fly out of their farms without reason.

"Come on, Betty. We need to find what's in that pile."

Down they went, neither one talking.

Ben knelt down, hit the light. "No wonder they're running."

Sister, Betty, Weevil, and Tootie knelt down to peer into the morass as Ben shined the light.

"Morris." Betty gasped.

"He didn't die a natural death, I can tell you that."

Ben hurried as best he could, the others behind him. Back to his squad car. He gave orders, clear and concise.

"Weevil . . . actually all of you can go. I'll get statements soon enough."

"Would you like one of us to stay with you?" Sister offered.

"No thank you. The team knows what to do. If you can send the people home from the hunt breakfast, that would be a help. We don't need an audience."

Drew raced east and Bainbridge raced south on back roads. Roadblocks had been set up.

Back at the tailgate people had seen the SUV then the truck speed by. No one knew what was happening.

Drew managed to get to Black Cat Road east of Keswick. Hearing sirens, knowing they were closing in, he parked the SUV, got out, ran into a woods there. Thanks to his business he knew central Virginia inside and out. Shedding his scarlet coat, he slowly worked his way toward old Route 22. If he could reach it he felt certain he could elude the sheriff's department and anyone else. Taylor Insurance covered a lot of properties in this area, many of them had outbuildings or old log cabins filled with equipment, or in some cases used as guesthouses. He had places to hide.

Bainbridge, on the other hand, flew on back roads in the truck, hit a pothole at high speed, and flipped over. The driver's door, crushed, held him in. Alive but unconscious, he was taken to the hospital by ambulance.

Drew kept out of sight for the day and night. Ben put small teams on Route 22, Route 20, alerted the Orange and Louisa sheriffs' departments. The TV station covered the car chase, told people a man was on the run, then identified him.

An alert landowner spotted a man in britches, boots, and a white shirt, skirting the back of his farm on the east side of Route 15 in the Green Springs area of Louisa.

By the time the law enforcement officers reached the old, well-tended farm, Drew had disappeared, but not for long.

Two miles over soft rolling hills from where the first man saw Drew, a couple saw him dip down into a streambed. So did their dog, who followed him briefly before returning to his owners.

The Louisa County Sheriff's Office finally cornered him on the back of a farm he had circled, one he insured, Eastern View.

Drew refused to surrender, pulling out his handgun. This

turned into a standoff, and as is the way with such situations, within an hour there must have been twenty squad cars there. Overkill.

And when Drew finally shot, it was overkill. The cops hid behind their cars, weapons drawn as Drew, in a small wooden shed, could watch all of them. No one could approach him without him knowing.

After three hours of this, one of the cops had the bright idea to smoke him out. To their credit they didn't set fire to the small structure, but they threw in tear gas.

They heard one shot. Drew didn't come out and no one could go in without a tear-gas mask, which a supporting officer from Louisa County happened to have.

Once inside the building, he found Drew sprawled, dead. He'd shot himself in the head.

His nephew at UVA hospital lay in a guarded room, hooked up to an array of monitoring equipment, blood dripping into his arm with a painkiller pump inserted.

Sister, keeping track as best she could, called Wanda, who kept the stable. The young woman had no idea what was happening but she promised to feed Binny and Ugh until further notice.

Sister, Gray, the staff, and club members, glued to their TVs and cellphones, tried to get the news.

It wasn't until Friday afternoon that they found out that Drew had shot himself. Bainbridge's accident, overturned truck, also made the news. Drew's fate was broadcast much later.

Sister, Gray, Weevil, and Tootie sat in the library.

"If Bainbridge regains consciousness, maybe we'll know." Sister rested her hand on Rooster's head, Golly behind her on the sofa back.

"Has to be about Morris. They both knew he was dead or they wouldn't have run." Gray was right.

"But why kill him?" Tootie wondered. "If he was violent, they could have put him in a home with a medical staff. He'd be on drugs, but to kill him?"

Weevil, next to her, said, "People have their reasons. We'll find out in time."

"What keeps crossing my mind is Harry Dunbar slips to his death, Drew kills himself. Two men tied by a past disagreement and now two men dead within a short span of time," Sister thought out loud. "I don't think Drew killed Harry. I doubt there was a connection except in other regards. Life plays tricks on you."

Gray agreed. "So it will always be. I'm glad Drew was a bad shot."

"Until the end," Tootie quietly said.

C H A P T E R 3 0

March 30, 2019   Saturday

A refreshing breeze swept over Roughneck Farm. Daffodils opened although the temperature remained cool. Longer sunlight gave the yellow plants hope and up they popped. Sister, Gray, Betty, Weevil, and Tootie marveled at how quickly a landscape can transform. No, it wasn't spring announced by trumpets, but perhaps a few woodwinds.

Hounds, full, flopped on their raised beds. Others walked out to their huge runs to crawl into the condos or even sprawl a bit on the decks surrounding the condos.

Inky, gregarious once hounds were in the kennels, walked to the girls' outdoor run.

Diana, head hanging over the deck, which she found comfortable even though it looked the reverse, opened one eye.

"Good day?" the black fox asked.

"Okay. You heard some of it," Diana replied.

"You all left here and rushed over the wildflower field. What I heard

was a bit of shouting and then everyone was over the hog's back jump. Aunt Netty?"

"No, a visiting fox. I thought perhaps he'd come for you." Diana sat upright.

"Not me."

"Season's over." Diana sighed. "I hate that. Then again, I think I'd hate running in August."

"I never seem to shed enough. I'd be willing to be the first bald fox." Inky laughed.

Diana laughed, too. "Humans shave house dogs. I've seen it. Well, the best thing to do is dig a nice dirt bed under a tree and lay down in it. The earth is cool. Keeps the bugs off."

"Ever find out about the dead human you all smelled?"

"Well . . ." Diana leapt off her deck, walked to the fence so she and Inky could talk face-to-face. "Listening to talk in the kennels we knew they found him. Sister, Betty, Tootie, and Weevil took the sheriff to the big pile. They couldn't smell a thing. Terrible, terrible noses. It's a wonder they can live. Oh, I'm babbling on here and you know a hound isn't supposed to babble." She laughed at herself.

Inky smiled. "Diana, you never babble. You are imparting news."

"When we first flanked the brush pile we knew, of course, a dead animal was in there, most likely human. Distinctive, alive or dead." Inky nodded in agreement, so Diana continued. "Anyway, the fox scent, pretty hot, kept us on track but then we went back. He used it, of course, but Weevil called us to him and that was the way. I mean, staff saw us rummaging around."

"How long do you think? Dead, I mean?"

"Cold nights, cool days. No flies yet. I'd say two days, maybe three. Nothing could get to the corpse. We could pick up the sweet smell but not *humans. Now, they can smell a dead body in a day in high heat. So I figure two days, maybe three. I couldn't smell blood. I smelled human hair though. Mostly I smelled the woods, the faded fox scent. Whoever put the body in that brush pile had to work hard at it."*

"Hmm. People kill one another. It's natural but they declare it isn't. We rarely kill one another, if you think about it. They make a habit of it."

"Inky, I think that depends on the human and the circumstances. But they do kill more than we do. I mean, if we kill it's to eat. They kill for strange reasons. Things we can't imagine."

"True."

The crunch of tires on the crusher-run road diverted Diana. *"Ben Sidel. He wasn't out today."*

"He rides Nonni?" Inky liked Ben's mare.

"Poor fellow. If a human does wrong he has to find them. Can you imagine tracking down other foxes?"

Inky considered this. *"No, but if a fox stole one of my toys or some food, say when I was out of my den, I'd try to find out who it was and then take it back."*

"Bite their sorry butt," Diana teased as she watched Ben walking into the tack room, close the door.

Bridles hanging from tack hooks filled the space, everyone cleaning their own bridle today. Part of the lingering was a way to make the hunt last longer. They looked up as Ben, in uniform, came through the door.

"Ben, sit down. Can I get you anything?" Sister asked.

He dropped into a chair. "No thank you. Bainbridge was finally able to talk. That will be on the news tonight, I expect, or tomorrow. The short version is he killed his father. Drew was an accessory. Both dragged the body down into that tight ravine."

"Good Lord." Betty stopped wiping down reins.

"Was he too much trouble?" Weevil wondered.

"That's an extreme way to end it," Betty replied.

"Sit down, you all. Those bridles are about done. You found him although you didn't know what was under there. I'll start from the beginning, as Bainbridge was willing to confess first time around."

"Concussion?"

"Concussion, broken pelvis, smashed ribs. Enough to hurt for a long time." Ben settled into the chair. "He started with stealing the silver, which he now admits he took."

"The silver was his, was it not?" Gray remembered.

"Half. He was loaded, on drugs. We've all seen worse in the department, but let's say when he was picked up with the bag in the car he was not an impressive sight. But he deliberately took it."

"Which means Drew had become an obstacle of sorts," Sister posited.

"The silver is what brought uncle and nephew to an agreement, oddly enough. Drew offering to pay any of Bainbridge's bills, to put him in rehab, set off no warning lights for me. I didn't know the Taylors as you did, but a family member, even one fighting with the addicted member, sometimes does step forward." Ben put his feet up on the coffee table when Sister motioned for him to do so. Ben had been wiggling in his chair, a little uncomfortable.

"Drew and Bainbridge never fought as much as Morris and Bainbridge. Which makes sense," Betty added. "Fathers and sons."

"Bainbridge watched his uncle buy new cars, a new three-horse trailer, take trips to Paris, to Belize, to Hong Kong, to Patagonia, all over. He'd been watching this for two years. Finally he realized Taylor Insurance wasn't paying for all this. He had a good idea of Drew's abilities plus his laziness. He realized his father was paying for it. He wanted his share."

"What do you mean?" Tootie asked.

"Drew received all of Morris's pension checks, as he was now in charge of his brother, had power of attorney. Well, he was blowing every penny. Granted, he didn't mistreat Morris, didn't starve him or lock him up, although I suspect the latter would have happened soon. So Bainbridge made a deal with his uncle."

"And that's why he moved into the cottage?" Betty was figuring all this out.

"Yes. Bainbridge totted up how much his uncle had spent of his father's pension funds. He demanded the receipts. Well, Drew really had no choice but to show him. So Bainbridge said he would look after his father along with the now part-time male nurse. In exchange, Drew would, over time, pay back half of the money he stole."

"Why half?" Sister asked.

"To keep Drew on the team. Half per month would come to about five thousand dollars. Remember, Morris was a nuclear physicist, worked for big projects. He'd made money. So Bainbridge forgave half so long as Drew recognized that he was his father's sole heir. Which is in Morris's will."

"Ah. And Bainbridge won't say if he sweetened the pot. After all, if they killed Morris, how did he know his uncle wouldn't kill him?" Sister folded her hands together.

"So they killed him for the money?" Tootie was horrified.

"Ultimately, yes," Ben said. "But Morris was going down fast. Even if Drew and Bainbridge had locked him in his room, that couldn't have lasted too long. He was tearing things to hell. Eventually he would need to go into assisted living. Then the pension funds would be under their control. That's usually how they work those things. If there isn't enough money to pay the monthly bills, they sell the dementia patient's property. Given Drew's funds, there was no need."

"Money." Betty pressed her lips together.

"Love or money. Usually what murder is about. Morris had become violent. In their minds he was better off. People can justify anything, as you know." Ben spoke without rancor. "Drew could justify using Morris's money for all his trips, the trailer, the vehicles, because in his mind he earned it by keeping Morris at Pitchfork Farm."

"How did they do it? Would he tell you?" Sister asked.

"He'll tell us anything to get his sentence reduced. He'll sing for us, for the judge, for the jury. He's scared. They took him outside for a walk and shot him in the head with a .38 pistol. The gun is in the house. We picked it up right where Bainbridge said it would be."

"I thought I saw Morris. When Sister and I drove over to check the fixture." Betty wondered.

"No. That must have been Bainbridge," Ben responded. "Morris was dead by then. They thought they could keep the fiction of Morris being still alive going, maybe for a year or two. We'd all seen the deterioration. So it would be no surprise if Morris were locked up."

Sister hung up her bridle, as it was swinging near her face, then turned around. "They resembled each other from a distance. Who would know?"

"That was their plan, so no one would know Morris was dead.

From time to time someone would see Bainbridge from a distance, thinking it was Morris."

Weevil leaned forward. "Drew and Bainbridge needed people to think Morris was alive. Otherwise the milk train wouldn't stop there anymore."

"You're right about that." Sister frowned. "Those monthly checks had to be wonderful. Free money, although I'm sure, as you said, Ben, Drew deluded himself into thinking he'd earned it."

"What about Wanda? She was there five days a week." Betty liked the stable girl.

"Don't think they thought that far ahead but they could tell her Morris was violent and in his bedroom. Let her go if she questioned too much. We questioned her, of course. She had no idea. She's worried about Binny and Ugh. Doesn't want anything to happen to the horses."

"Tell her not to worry. We'll take them. There are people in the hunt club who could use two good, made hunters," Sister offered.

Gray nodded. "We can pick them up tomorrow."

"Now what?" Betty asked.

"Nothing to do except listen to everyone respond, give their ideas. The usual swirl of gossip and bullshit." Ben put his hand to his mouth. "Sorry."

Gray smiled. "Human nature."

"Does Bainbridge know Drew shot himself?" Sister asked.

"He does. He doesn't seem the least bit concerned. Even if he gets, say, twenty years, when he gets out he'll be in his early fifties and he'll have a lot of money. We can't touch the money. Morris's investment accounts, Pitchfork Farm, all go to Bainbridge."

"For murder?" Tootie was incredulous.

Ben smiled at the earnest young woman. "His father did attack him. Others had seen Morris violent. In the supermarket, for one. It's his first big felony. You'd think he'd have more of a drug record but Drew paid off everyone handsomely and I suspect when Morris was competent he did, too, even though he loathed Bainbridge. Keep the family name clean, that sort of thing. It's easier to do than we'd like to know. Yes, the crime is a big one but it still shows up as a first offense. His uncle was the thief. Bainbridge didn't catch on until late in the game. He perhaps got the benefit of one month's pension funds. A good lawyer, and Bainbridge has the money for the best, will argue convincingly that no one is in danger from Bainbridge. Why keep a young man in jail for the bulk of his life? Morris's murder happened under extenuating circumstances. Tootie, I see this, as does every other law enforcement officer, all the time. We bring them in, a lawyer gets them off."

"Come on up and have some supper," Sister offered the sheriff. "We'll talk about more pleasant things."

"Thanks. I should get back but I wanted you to know the real story before the media has a field day with it. Nothing more to say except I was sorry to miss the last hunt of this rainy season."

After he left the five sat there not saying much.

Betty put her hands on the chair arms. "Well, we were all fooled. Drew rode well, helpful in the hunt field, easy to be with. Who would have thought him capable of this?"

"As you know, I deal with senators, cabinet officials, you name it," Gray said. "Our firm was the one you called if you suspected trouble. What I learned is that the successful crooks are likable.

Bernie Madoff. Or at a more dramatic level, say a Baby Face Nelson. Stealing usually takes more cunning than shooting someone. So the thief pleases people. You never suspect them until something trips them up or they get cocky. They steal from you and over time you figure it out. A Ponzi scheme."

"Alcibiades." Sister named the gorgeous, dazzling man from fifth century BC Athens, who betrayed his city-state and still people couldn't help but be swept away by his presence.

"I often wonder about us. A dog will steal another dog's bone. If that dog is bigger, older, the younger dog submits. Among primitive peoples I expect it's the same dynamics. Maybe under a dictatorship as well," Weevil, a thoughtful young man, posited. "But theft by stealth, you know, Cary Grant in *To Catch a Thief*, we glorify it. Something like this, stealing from the incompetent, we don't much notice. And I fear we don't much care."

"Aren't these the kinds of crimes usually committed within families?" Tootie wondered.

"Families or friends. A house, assisted living, for such people, even a halfway house, comes under scrutiny. If the patients aren't being properly fed, their money taken, cheaper food substituted, sooner or later it will be found out."

"Not if they pay off the inspector," Gray said.

"There is that, but a state employee who drives a new Mercedes will attract attention, or one who goes on a long cruise, one of those Alaska cruises," Betty noted.

"Will any of us ever look the same way at someone with Alzheimer's or senile dementia?" Sister sighed.

"We surely will never look the same way at the home they are in or their family," Tootie replied.

"Let's hope we never have to deal with this again." Weevil meant that.

"Oh, I think one such case is enough for Jefferson Hunt but I expect others will face this in their private lives. We do the best we can, and if you think about it, what kind of life would we lead if we suspected the worst from everyone? Maybe it's better to be fooled some of the time than be suspicious." Gray stood up.

"Better to mistake a sinner for a saint than a saint for a sinner." Sister rose also.

"And where does that leave you?" Betty tweaked her master's elbow.

"You're asking?"

A FEW FACTS

Cases of elder abuse are likely underreported, according to the National Center on Elder Abuse.

The cost of same are estimated to range between $2.9 billion and $36 billion annually.

No one knows because this is hidden within families and caregivers, hence the above large spread.

Unfortunately, banks are part of the problem. Banks reported 24,454 cases of elder abuse, financial, to the Treasury Department in 2018. Up twelve percent from 2017 and double that reported for 2013. Where the banks fit into this is that a banker may have given bad advice to a client, not realizing the client was beginning to suffer from dementia or Alzheimer's. There have also been intentional acts of financial advisers who have given advice favorable to the bank but unfavorable to the investor.

There's enough blame to go around.

Given that this primarily occurs within families and friends of the afflicted, it is highly unlikely that the fraud can be truly diminished, no matter what laws are passed.

Greed will ever remain one of the Seven Deadly Sins.

ACKNOWLEDGMENTS

Mark Catron, vice president of Wells Fargo Bank in Charlottesville, Virginia, outlined protocols concerning clients suffering from dementia. Banks are bound by a plethora of rules, but if a client is in denial there's not but so much they can do.

April Fletcher, a foxhunter and lawyer, gave me blue chip advice, but then she always does, plus she makes me laugh.

Kathleen King, another lawyer and a former civil servant, also contributed to this novel with advice and facts, most of them dismal.

Mr. Michael G. Tillson III, MFH of Radnor Hunt, west of Philadelphia, gave me the phrase "Scarlet Fever," along with a Tillson definition.

The "Divas" at Horse Country tolerated my questions, plus I threw them in this book. I assume they will still be talking to me. My thanks to: Marion Maggiolo, Roni Ellis, Suzann Strong, Jenny Young, Martha Kelley, Jean Roberts, and Courtney Nashwinter.

In one form or another, I fear, Reader, you will observe or care for someone suffering from senile dementia or Alzheimer's disease. Try to remember the afflicted person in their prime.

PHOTO: © MARY MOTLEY KALERGIS

RITA MAE BROWN is the bestselling author of the Sneaky Pie Brown mysteries; the Sister Jane series; the Runnymede novels, including *Six of One* and *Cakewalk; A Nose for Justice* and *Murder Unleashed; Rubyfruit Jungle;* and *In Her Day;* as well as many other books. An Emmy-nominated screenwriter and a poet, Brown lives in Afton, Virginia, and is a Master of Foxhounds and the huntsman.

ritamaebrownbooks.com

To inquire about booking Rita Mae Brown for a speaking engagement, please contact the Penguin Random House Speakers Bureau at speakers@penguinrandom house.com.

ABOUT THE TYPE

This book was set in Baskerville, a typeface designed by John Baskerville (1706–75), an amateur printer and typefounder, and cut for him by John Handy in 1750. The type became popular again when the Lanston Monotype Corporation of London revived the classic roman face in 1923. The Mergenthaler Linotype Company in England and the United States cut a version of Baskerville in 1931, making it one of the most widely used typefaces today.